THE VAULT

Chief Inspector Wexford has retired, and with his wife, Dora, spends his time between Kingsmarkham and their daughter's coach-house in Hampstead. A relaxed lifestyle, yet he misses being the law. However, a chance meeting in a London street changes everything. Detective Superintendent Tom Ede, a young police constable when Wexford knew him, now wants the retired Chief Inspector to be an adviser on a difficult case. Four bodies have been discovered in the old coal hole of a house in St John's Wood. None carries identification. But one dead man's pockets contain pearls, diamonds and sapphires — jewellery valued in the region of £40,000 . . . Wexford accepts — not anticipating he will face extreme physical danger.

Books by Ruth Rendell
Published by The House of Ulverscroft:

RUTH RENDELL

THE VAULT

Complete and Unabridged

CHARNWOOD
Leicester

First published in Great Britain in 2011 by
Hutchinson, London

First Charnwood Edition
published 2012
by arrangement with
Hutchinson
The Random House Group Limited, London

British Library CIP Data

Rendell, Ruth, *1930 –*
   The vault.
   1. Wexford, Inspector (Fictitious character)- -
   Fiction. 2 Kingsmarkham (England : Imaginary
   place)- -Fiction. 3. Police- -England- -Fiction.
   4. Detective and mystery stories.
   5. Large type books.
   I. Title
   823.9'14–dc23

   ISBN 978–1–4448–1124–7

Published by
F. A. Thorpe (Publishing)
Anstey, Leicestershire

Set by Words & Graphics Ltd.
Anstey, Leicestershire
Printed and bound in Great Britain by
T. J. International Ltd., Padstow, Cornwall

This book is printed on acid-free paper

To Paul and Marianne with love

1

'A curious world we live in,' said Franklin Merton, 'where one can afford a house but not a picture of a house. That must tell us some profound truth. But what, I wonder?'

The picture he was talking about was Simon Alpheton's *Marc and Harriet in Orcadia Place*, later bought by Tate Britain — simply 'the Tate' in those days — and the house the one in the picture, Orcadia Cottage. His remark about the curious world was addressed to the Harriet of the picture, for whom he had bought it and whom he intended to marry when his divorce came through. Later on, when passion had cooled and they were husband and wife, 'I didn't want to get married,' he said. 'I married you because I'm a man of honour and you were my mistress. Some would say my views are out of date but I dispute that. The apparent change is only superficial. I reasoned that no one would want my leavings, so for your sake the decent thing was to make an honest woman of you.'

His first wife was Anthea. When he deserted her he was also obliged to desert their dog O'Hara and to him that was the most painful thing about it.

'You don't keep a bitch and bark yourself,' he said to Harriet when she protested at having to do all the housework.

'Pity I'm not an Irish setter,' she said and had

1

the satisfaction of seeing him wince.

They lived together for five years and were married for twenty-three, the whole time in that house, Orcadia Cottage or Number 7a Orcadia Place, London NW8. Owing to Franklin's sharp tongue, verbal cruelty and indifference, and to Harriet's propensity for sleeping with young tradesmen in the afternoons, it was not a happy marriage. They took separate holidays, Franklin going away ostensibly on his own but in fact with his first wife, and he came back from the last one only to tell Harriet he was leaving. He returned to Anthea and her present Irish setter De Valera, intending to divorce Harriet as soon as feasible. Anthea, a generous woman, urged him to do his best to search for her, for she couldn't be found at Orcadia Cottage. The largest suitcase, most of her clothes and the best of the jewellery he had bought her were missing, and it was Franklin's belief that she had gone off with her latest young man.

'She'll be in touch as soon as she's in need,' said Franklin to Anthea, 'and that won't be long delayed.'

But Harriet never got in touch. Franklin went back to Orcadia Cottage to look for some clue as to where she might have gone but found only that the place was exceptionally neat, tidy and clean.

'One odd thing,' he said. 'I lived there for all those years and never went into the cellar. There was no reason to do so. Just the same, I could have sworn there was a staircase going down to it with a door just by the kitchen door. But there isn't.'

Anthea was a much cleverer woman than Harriet. 'When you say you could have sworn, darling, do you mean you would go into court, face a jury and say, 'I swear there was a staircase in that house going down to the cellar'?'

After thinking about it, Franklin said, 'I don't think so. Well, no, I wouldn't.'

He put it on the market and bought a house for Anthea and himself in South Kensington. In their advertisements the estate agents described Orcadia Cottage as 'the Georgian home immortalised in the internationally acclaimed artwork of Simon Alpheton'. The purchasers, an American insurance broker and his wife, wanted to move in quickly and when Franklin offered them the report his own surveyors had made thirty years before, they were happy to do without a survey. After all, the house had been there for two hundred years and wasn't likely to fall down now.

* * *

Clay and Devora Silverman bought the house from Franklin Merton in 1998 and lived there until 2002, before returning to the house they had rented out in Hartford, Connecticut. The first autumn they spent at Orcadia Cottage the leaves on the Virginia creeper, which covered the entire front and much of the back of the house, turned from green to copper and copper to red and then started to fall off. Clay Silverman watched them settle on the front garden and the paving stones in the back. He was appalled by

3

the red sticky sodden mass of leaves on which he and Devora slipped and slid and Devora sprained her ankle. Knowing nothing about natural history and still less about gardening, he was well-informed about art and was familiar with the Alpheton painting. It was one of his reasons for buying Orcadia Cottage. But he had assumed that the green leaves covering the house which formed the background to the lovers' embrace remained green always and remained on the plant. After all of them had fallen he had the creeper cut down.

Orcadia Cottage emerged as built of bricks in a pretty pale red colour. Clay had shutters put on the windows and the front door painted a pale greenish-grey. In the paved yard at the back of the house was what he saw as an unsightly drain cover with a crumbling stone pot on top of it. He had a local nursery fill a tub with senecios, heathers and cotoneaster to replace the pot. But four years later he and Devora moved out and returned home. Clay Silverman had given £800,000 for the house and sold it for £1,500,000 to Martin and Anne Rokeby.

The Rokebys had a son and daughter; there were only two bedrooms in Orcadia Cottage but one was large enough to be divided and this was done. For the first time in nearly half a century the house was home to children. Again there was no survey on the house, for Martin and Anne paid cash and needed no mortgage. They moved into Orcadia Cottage in 2002 and had been living there for four years, their children teenagers by this time, when Martin raised the possibility with his wife of building underground. Excavations to construct an extra room or two — a wine cellar, say, or a 'family room', a study or all of those things — were becoming fashionable. You couldn't build on to your historic house or add an extra storey, but the planning authority might let you build subterraneanly. A similar thing had been done in Hall Road which was near Orcadia Place and Martin had watched the builders at work with interest.

A big room under Orcadia Cottage would be just the place for their children to have a large-screen television, their computers, their ever-more sophisticated arrangements for making music, and maybe an exercise room, too, for Anne, who was something of a work-out fanatic. In the late summer of 2006 he began by consulting the builders who had divided the large bedroom but they had gone out of business. A company whose board outside the Hall Road house gave their name, phone number and an email address were next. But the men who came round to have a look said it wouldn't be feasible. A different firm was recommended to him by a neighbour. One who came said he thought it could be done. Another said it was possible if Martin didn't mind losing all the mature trees in the front garden. Nevertheless, he applied to the planning authority for permission to build underneath the house.

Martin and Anne and the children all went to Australia for a month. The house was too old, prospective builders said, it would be unwise to disturb the foundations. Others said it could be done, but at a cost twice that which Martin had estimated. They said all this on the phone without even looking at it. The project was put an end to when planning permission was refused, having had a string of protests from all the Rokebys' neighbours except the one who had recommended the builder.

All this took about a year. In the autumn of 2007 the Rokebys' son, who had been the principal family member in favour of the underground room, went off to university. Time went on and the plan was all but forgotten. The house seemed bigger now their daughter was away at boarding school. In the early spring of 2009 Martin and Anne went on holiday to Florence. There, in a shop on the Arno, Anne fell in love with a large amphora displayed in its window. Apparently dredged up from the waters of the Mediterranean, it bore a frieze round its rim of nymphs and satyrs dancing and wreathing each other with flowers.

'I must have that,' said Anne. 'Imagine that replacing that hideous old pot.'

'You have it,' Martin said. 'Why not? So long as you don't try getting it on the flight.'

The shop sent it, carefully packed in a huge crate, and it finally arrived in St John's Wood in May 2009 by some circuitous route not involving aircraft. A local nursery agreed to plant it with agapanthus and sedum spectabile, but before this was done Martin emptied the plants and soil out of the wooden tub, placed the remains of the tub into a black plastic bag and put it out into the mews for the rubbish collection.

'I've often wondered what's under that lid thing but never bothered to have a look.'

'Now's your chance,' said Anne, uninterested.

'It's probably too heavy to lift.'

But it wasn't too heavy. Martin lifted the manhole cover to disclose a large dark cavity. He could see nothing much beyond what appeared to be a plastic bag or sheet of plastic lying in the depths. Better get a torch, he thought, and he did, thus wrecking his life for a long time to come.

An exaggeration? Perhaps. But not much of one. By shining that torch down into the dark cavity, he gained a place for his wife and himself and his home on the front page of every daily newspaper, put an end to his and his family's peace for months, attracting mobs of sightseers to the street and the mews, reducing the selling price of his house by about a million pounds and making Orcadia Place as notorious as Christie's home in Notting Hill and the Wests' in Gloucester.

2

Chief Inspector Wexford, who was no longer a chief inspector or a policeman or a permanent resident of Kingsmarkham in the county of Sussex, sat in the living room of his second home in Hampstead reading the Booker Prize winner. He was no longer any of those other things, but he was still a reader. And now he had all the time in the world for books.

Of course, he had many interests besides. He loved music: Bach, Handel, lots of opera. Walking he found a bore when he always walked the same route in Kingsmarkham, but London was different; London walks were a never-ending source of interest and excitement. Galleries he visited, usually with his wife Dora. It was a mild winter and he went on the river with her, took the canal trip with her from Paddington Basin to Camden Lock and back. They went to Kew Gardens and Hampton Court. For all that, for all this richness, he missed what had been his life. He missed being a policeman.

So the chance encounter with Tom Ede as he was walking down the Finchley Road changed things. They had first met years ago when Tom had been a very young police constable and Wexford staying with his nephew Chief Superintendent Howard Fortune in Chelsea. Wexford had taken an interest in one of Howard's cases and Tom had come to his attention as exceptionally bright and persevering. That had been more than thirty years ago, but he had recognised Tom at once. He looked older, of course, but it was the same face if overlaid with lines, the same hairline if grey now instead of brown. Must be because he hasn't gained weight, Wexford had thought at the time, rueful about his own increased girth.

He'd looked at Tom, hesitated, then said, 'It's Thomas Ede, isn't it? You won't know me.'

But Tom did — just — when he had taken a long look. He was Detective Superintendent Ede now, based at the new Metropolitan Police head-quarters in Cricklewood. They had exchanged phone numbers. Wexford had gone on his way with an extra spring in his step and now he was hoping Tom would phone. For what? To arrange to meet on some social occasion? No, don't deceive yourself, he thought. You want the improbable: that he'll ask for help. He went back to last year's Booker winner, enjoying it but with maybe a small fraction of his mind thinking about the phone and how Tom had said he would ring 'around lunchtime'.

It was six months now since he had retired and been presented with the pretty carriage clock which, on the coach-house (how appropri-ate!) living room mantelpiece, told him that the time was well into what he called lunchtime. He had eaten the lunch Dora had left him, the meat and ciabatta and ignoring most of the salad. Still, even now, his mind went back to what might have happened, *would* have happened, if Sheila hadn't offered them this place.

'Of course, we don't want rent, Pop. You and Mother will be doing us a favour, taking on the coachhouse.'

The real meaning of retirement had come to him the first day. When it didn't matter what time he got up he could stay in bed all day. He didn't, of course. Those first days all his interests seemed petty, not worth doing. It seemed to him that he had read all the books he wanted to read, heard all the music he wanted to hear. He thought of closing his eyes and turning his face to the wall. That was on the first days and he put on a show of enjoying having nothing to do for Dora's sake. He even said he was relishing this slack and idle time. She saw through that; she knew him too well. After about a week of it he said how much he wished they could live in London. Not all the time, he loved their Kingsmarkham house, neither of them would want to give that up.

'You mean have somewhere in London as well?'

'I suppose that's what I do mean.'

'Could we afford it?'

'I don't know.'

A studio flat, he had thought. That was an elegant term for a bedsitter with one corner cut off for a kitchen and a cupboard turned into a shower room. Gradually learning how to use the Internet, he found estate agents online and looked at what they had to offer. Dora asked her question again.

'Could we afford it?'

An unqualified 'no' this time.

They said nothing about it to either of their daughters. Saying you can't afford something to a rich child is tantamount to asking for financial aid. Their elder, Sylvia, was comfortable but not rich. Sheila, the successful actress on stage and TV, had an equally successful husband. Their large Victorian house on the edge of Hampstead Heath, if it were up for sale, would be one of those that estate agents' websites offered as 'in excess of eight million'. So they said nothing to Sheila, even pretended how happily their lives had been transformed by his retirement. But Sheila knew him almost as well as his wife did.

'Have the coachhouse for a second home, Pop.'

That was what it was called, a kind of garage for a brougham when people possessed such transport, with a stable for the horse and a flat over the top for the coachman. Carefully converted, it was now a small house with two bedrooms and — unheard-of luxury — two bathrooms.

'I still can't really believe it,' Dora said on their first evening.

'I can,' said Wexford. 'Don't forget, I've lived in a world where the improbable happens all the time. What would you rather do tomorrow, go by train to Kew Gardens or have a boat up the river to the Thames Barrier?'

'Couldn't we do both?'

During those months they had twice been back to Kingsmarkham for a week at a time and that, too, had been enjoyable, like coming home from a holiday while still wanting to resume that holiday later. But it was a mixed pleasure; this

11

was his manor, this was where he had been the law incarnate for so long. It brought home to him how much he missed being that law.

He walked such a lot in London that he was losing weight and was beginning to know his way around without the satnav of the London *Guide*. He had his car with him and he drove it, but not often. Driving and being driven he didn't miss. Being a policeman was what he missed. Would he always?

He picked up the Booker winner once more and as he opened it at the marked place, the phone rang. Pleasantries were exchanged, the 'how are yous' that no one really wanted an answer to, but seem to be requisite at every meeting. In spite of his fantasy, Wexford couldn't quite believe it when, after replying that he was very well, Tom said it was help he wanted.

'In what capacity?'

'Well, I was thinking. I mean, you may not want to do this at all. You may not want anything to do with it. You've retired and no doubt thanking your stars you have but . . . If you did, if you'd just think about it, you could be an adviser. Expert advisers are very popular these days, not to say trendy. And I do see you as an expert. Maybe I'm kidding myself but years and years ago I think you spotted some sort of aptitude for police work in me and now — well, I'm remembering a real talent for it in you. If you were my adviser you could come anywhere with me, have access to anything — well, almost anything. I expect you're busy now, but if not . . . '

'I'm not at all busy,' said Wexford.

'It's the Orcadia Place case I'm talking about and if . . .'

'Are you at your new HQ in Cricklewood?'

'That's it. Mapesbury Road. Strike while the iron is hot then.' Tom paused, said with slight embarrassment, 'There wouldn't be any — er, emolument, I'm afraid. We have to tighten our belts in these hard times.'

Wexford wasn't surprised.

He meant to walk all the way, but it was longer than he thought and carefully buying a ticket from a machine, he got on a bus. It was a beautiful day, June as it should be but seldom was, the sky a cloudless blue, the sun hot but cool in the shade of the trees. To think that before he came here, in spite of numerous visits, he had believed there were no gardens in London or if there were a few they would be arid plots of dry grass and dusty bushes. The flowers amazed him. Roses were everywhere, bush roses, standards, climbers and ramblers dripping blossom over ancient moss-grown brick walls.

Even Shoot-up Hill had its share of flowers. The bus stopped near the end of Mapesbury Road where the new Met headquarters was a huge glass ziggurat in a street of big Victorian villas, and he felt glad he would be visiting and not working there. That word 'working' stimulated a rush of adrenalin and he speeded up his pace.

Automatic doors, of course, and a huge foyer that seemed to be mostly windows and marble floor. It might have been a hospital or the offices

13

of some large company. The house-plants standing about in black ceramic tubs were the kind you can't tell are real or artificial unless you actually touch their leaves.

A young woman sat behind the long boomerang-shaped counter, engrossed by the screens of three desktop computers. He was so used to presenting his warrant card that he was feeling in his pocket for it before he remembered that he no longer had it, that he was no longer *entitled* to have it. He gave his name, said Detective Superintendent Ede was expecting him.

'Take the lift,' she said, scarcely looking up. 'Third floor, turn left and it's the third door on the right.'

While he waited for the lift to come he was transported back in time to when, in very different surroundings, he had started his first day as Detective Constable Wexford with the Brighton Police. Years, decades, had gone by, yet he thought he felt much the same, apprehensive, excited, wondering what the coming weeks would bring.

3

'You'll have read about it or seen it on TV. God knows it's had enough media coverage. It's one of those cases where people start asking if they've found any more bodies.'

'Except that these were all in the same place,' said Wexford.

'That's true. We don't even know if they were murdered — well, one was. Probably.'

'Only probably?'

'Three of them have been there so long we can't tell how long they've been dead, let alone what they died of.'

Detective Superintendent Thomas Ede was sitting in his chair behind his desk in his glass-walled box of an office, the glass being the kind you can see out of but no one can see in. Laminated wood floor with a faux fur rug, the fur looking like the skin of a hybrid tiger and giraffe. Ede was a tall, thin man with a small head and tense, sharp features. He wore a dark grey suit and a white shirt, but no tie, a style of dressing Wexford thought looked fine on women, less 'right' on men, though it was becoming universally popular. Wexford sat opposite him in the clients' seat, the interviewee's place. This was something new to him, something he had to get resigned to. And he was getting there, it was all right, it was inevitable.

'I've read about it,' he said, 'but you tell me.

15

That way I'll get it right.'

'Well, as you know, this all started a month ago. We were first called at the beginning of May. The location is a street in St John's Wood called Orcadia Place, but that detail wasn't in the papers, was it? You're looking as if something's struck you.'

'I'll tell you later,' Wexford said. 'Go on.'

'The house itself is called Orcadia Cottage. It's not a cottage as we know it but a sizeable detached house, very pretty if you like that sort of thing. Front garden's full of flowers and trees, the back is a kind of courtyard or patio. Orcadia Place is one of those streets in St John's Wood that are more like country lanes, hedges, big trees, cobbled roadway, that kind of thing. Orcadia Cottage belongs to a man called Martin Rokeby. He bought it about seven years ago for one and a half million. It would fetch four now — or would have before what was found in the coal hole. By the way, we call it the 'patio-tomb'. Got to call it something, haven't you?

'The set-up is peculiar to say the least. On the face of it, the area, paved in York stone, is quite large and plain with a border round its edges. The way into the patio from the house is by a door from the kitchen and a pair of French windows. A door in the back wall opens into the mews. More or less in the middle of this patio is the manhole cover, circular, which when closed — and it always was closed — lies flush with the paving. A tub stood on it and entirely covered it up.

'Now Rokeby had never lifted up this manhole

16

cover. Or so he says. He had no survey done when he bought the house as he had no mortgage and distrusted surveys on old houses, reasoning that they were bound to be full of faults but never fell down. It's a point of view. You can spend a fortune on surveys and most of the time needlessly. Anyway, Rokeby says he didn't even know the manhole cover was there. The tub which stood on it was a half-barrel of wood bound in iron, not particularly attractive, and Mrs Rokeby said she'd like a new one. She's the gardener. Well, the two of them were on holiday in Italy — they went on a lot of expensive holidays, Australia at the time he was planning the underground room — and in a shop in Florence she saw this, I quote, 'amazingly beautiful amphora', whatever that is, that some boat dredged up from out of the Mediterranean. I don't know about these things. Maybe you do. Anyway, she had to have it — they're not short of a penny or two, as you'll have guessed — couldn't, needless to say, take it home with them on a flight, so she asked to have it sent. Heaven knows what that cost but it doesn't matter.'

Wexford noted that 'heaven' where another man would have said 'God'. He wondered what it meant, if anything, vaguely remembering that Tom Ede, when young, had a connection with some nonconformist church or cult.

'Much to their surprise,' Ede went on, 'when they emptied the soil out of the half-barrel and took the thing away, what did they find underneath but this manhole cover. Now

17

Rokeby, quite reasonably, supposed this to be covering a drain or a fuel store that was no longer in use, and at first he intended to leave things as they were and just stick the amphora thing on the top with some lilies planted in it.'

'Why didn't he?' said Wexford.

'Curiosity, he says. The manhole cover wasn't heavy. He lifted it off and instead of the drain or drainpipe he expected, leading away into the mews, he found himself looking down into a black hole. At the bottom was something he couldn't properly see apart from a kind of shininess that seemed to be a sheet of plastic. That was covering a multitude of sins, but he didn't know it then.

'Now before he did anything more, he went into the house and fetched his wife. The two of them looked down into the darkness and at that shiny thing and what looked — he said they could just about see it — like a woman's shoe. If the way into this hole was by the manhole, where was the way out? Was there a way out? Rokeby actually asked his wife if they had a cellar that he didn't know was there. She told him that of course they hadn't. There would be a door down to it in the house, there would be a staircase.

'Well, Rokeby went indoors and fetched a torch. A big powerful halogen thing, apparently. In the circumstances it might have been better for them if it had been a feeble little job with a failing battery. He shone it down the hole and there he saw a large plastic bag full of what he called 'something horrible', as well as two skulls, the bones of a skeleton and a badly decomposed

18

corpse. Anne Rokeby also saw it and she fainted. He took her indoors and called us after he'd been sick.'

Wexford nodded. 'You believe neither of them knew anything about it beforehand? I mean, that the existence of the hole was a surprise to them?'

'Well, you know, Reg, I'm inclined to believe it. But I'm open to having my mind changed.'

'What was it? A coal hole?'

'In the days when people had coal fires and coke boilers, coal was delivered by way of the mews and the sacks emptied down the hole.'

'And the occupants of Orcadia Cottage would fetch up the coal by going down the steps to the cellar and thence to the coal hole.'

'Ah, so you might assume,' said Tom Ede, 'but they couldn't have because, though there's a cellar that communicates with the coal hole, there's no way into it from the house.'

'No stairs down?'

'Stairs down, but no door to them. I can take you up there. We can go and look.'

'Tomorrow?' Wexford asked.

'Tomorrow, certainly. Two minds with but a single thought. But before we make arrangements. I went down to Orcadia Place with my sergeant that you'll meet. By the time we got there they'd got a ladder down into the coal hole but not, of course, touched anything. I went down. I was the first. There was no smell, just a sort of stuffiness, though of course a lot of air had been getting in there by that time.

'It was — well, a grim sight. You know the kind of things we have to see in the course of our work, but I think I can say I've never seen anything to come up to this. Or perhaps I should say come down to this. The thing sealed up in a big plastic bag was a man's body badly decomposed, as was the body of the older woman. I don't know why but I expect the forensics people do. The young man was a skeleton, the skull almost detached. The younger woman was in the best condition but decomposing. She, of course, had been there much less longer than the others. The pathologist determined that with no trouble. All the bodies were fully clothed, but with only a single clue to their identities and that not much of a one. None of them were carrying identification. The women's clothes looked as if they had been dressed for indoors, so hadn't had handbags with them and women don't put stuff in pockets, do they? The young man had some coins in his jeans pocket and a piece of paper with 'Francine' written on it and under that 'La Punaise' and a four-digit number — and, wait for it, a lot of valuable jewellery. Not only in his jeans pocket but in the pockets of the jacket that was still on the body: strings of pearls, a diamond and sapphire necklace, a gold collar thing, bracelets, rings and other stuff, you name it. The lot has been valued at worth something in the region of forty thousand pounds.

'The bodies were photographed where they were. The pathologist came and looked at them where they were, and after all that stuff was gone through they were taken away. It was then and only then that I and DS Blanch had a good look round the coal hole and the cellar. The door from the coal hole to the cellar had been closed, but we opened it — of course we did — in case there were more bodies on the other side, but there weren't. There was nothing, not even any coal or wood or the kind of junk people put in cellars. Nothing at all. Except, of course, the stairs. The stairs went up from the cellar floor to a blank wall.'

'The bodies?' Wexford asked. 'There's been nothing in the papers about that, there wouldn't be. Only that they were there. DNA?'

'I think I'll keep that for tomorrow, Reg. I'll come and pick you up, shall I? Bright and early — nine a.m. too early for you?'

'Nine is fine. The address is The Coachhouse, 2 Vale of Health Lane, Hampstead.'

He felt rather diffident giving Tom Ede this classy address. Tom, he knew, lived in a flat in Finchley, and Wexford was already learning the niceties and fine shades of where in London it is de rigueur to live and where not quite so posh. He had learnt how it is quite OK to live in West Two and North-west Eight, top drawer to live in West One, North-west Three or South-west Three, less so in North Eleven or South-west Twelve. It was better to have a phone number preceded by a seven than by an eight. Much as he despised this postcode and number snobbery, he found it fascinating. Still, it was difficult when he had to give someone like Tom an address in the best part of Hampstead — not that it was his except on loan, not that he had any right to what belonged to his daughter. When the time came he was going to have to explain to Tom how he and Dora came to be staying there. He hadn't yet made himself say 'living there'.

'Open confession is good for the soul,' said Tom, 'and I'll tell you frankly, I've asked for your help because so far we're getting nowhere fast.'

★　★　★

Home — it was sort of half-home now — on the bus. On two buses, the second one up Haverstock Hill because he didn't know a less complex route. He used his newly acquired Freedom Pass in its purple case. The beauties of Hampstead still drew his eyes, the church where Constable's tomb was, Holly Mount and the Everyman Cinema, but his mind was still with Tom Ede in Orcadia Place. It must be the same, he thought. Did Tom know? Did it matter whether he knew? One of the most famous of modern paintings it must be, still unknown to many. He got off the bus and walked down into the Vale of Health.

The kitchen and living area were on the ground floor where a Victorian family's brougham had been once housed and the horse stabled. Stairs went up to the two bedrooms and two bathrooms. It was all very light with white paint and big windows but not stark, nothing like being the shubunkin in a fish tank. He found Dora with Anoushka on her knee, reading *The Tale of Samuel Whiskers*.

'It's just me today, Grandad. Are you pleased?'

Wexford gave her a kiss, then kissed Dora. 'If I

say I'm pleased you'll tell Amy and she'll think I like you better than her.'

'You do like me better,' said Anoushka.

'I like you both the same, but for different reasons. Where is she anyway?'

'Gone to her dancing class. I hate dancing.'

'So do I,' said Wexford, 'but don't tell Amy.' He addressed his wife. 'All those books and papers we brought here from home' — Kingsmarkham was still really home — 'what happened to them?'

'You stuffed them into that big cupboard in the spare bedroom. You said you'd tidy them up, put them in the bookcases, but they're still waiting.'

Wexford pulled a hangdog face which made Anoushka laugh. 'There's something I want to look for.'

'Can I come?'

'Of course you can. You can help.'

This provoked sardonic laughter from Dora. Wexford and Anoushka went upstairs to the spare bedroom and Wexford opened the double doors of the cupboard. The books were stacked at the bottom, a mass of papers, which threatened to fall off but didn't, occupied the top two shelves. Better remove the lot. He brought down two armfuls of magazines, papers, sheets of paper, forms, catalogues, and spread them about the floor.

'What are we looking for, Grandad?'

'A picture of a house. You know what a calendar is?'

'A thing you hang up on the wall that's got

23

pictures and numbers on it.'

'Exactly.'

'I'll look!'

He let her look, knowing that when a child wants to help you must patiently let her, perhaps encouraging her but never never intervening because you know you will do it faster yourself. Anoushka found two calendars but not the one he wanted. His eye caught that one, lying half under an old copy of the *New Statesman*, but nothing would have made him reach for it while she was in the room. She was bored now and after graciously accepting his extravagant thanks, said she was going back to Grandma for more adventures of two rats and a family of kittens. Once he heard the reading start again, he picked up the calendar and leafed through it, passing the Waterhouse for January, the Laura Knight for February, the Sargent for March — and there it was for April: a reproduction of the painting whose name had alerted him when Tom Ede named a street in St John's Wood.

It was of a man and a girl standing in front of a house, she in a dress the same red as her hair, he in a dark blue suit. The expressions on their faces were of passionate love for each other. Behind them was a living wall of green leaves and under the picture was the legend: *Marc and Harriet in Orcadia Place* by Simon Alpheton, 1973. The red dress, he remembered reading somewhere, was by the great Venetian designer Mariano Fortuny, and reading somewhere else that the painting had been the Royal Academy's Picture of the Year. Since then it had been on

24

postcards, calendars, posters, advertisements.

It had been painted thirty-six years before. Marc Syre had been a pop star and celebrity or 'sleb', as they called them today, Harriet simply his girlfriend. She was very likely still alive, but Marc Syre was dead. Wexford remembered hearing or reading that he had died from taking LSD and jumping off Beachy Head. But once he had been the owner or tenant of Orcadia Cottage. Before his cellar became a charnel house, a repository of the remains of two men and two women unknown to him or not yet born.

I shall not call it a charnel house, he decided, or a patio-tomb. I shall call it 'the vault'. He took the calendar into the kitchen where he had left his briefcase and put it inside the case so that Anoushka wouldn't see and went into the living room, carrying the two others she had found as if they were of immense value to him.

4

So that was what he was, Detective Superintendent Ede's expert adviser. It made him laugh
every time he repeated it to himself. He laughed
now as he picked up his briefcase, kissed Dora
and went off outside to await the arrival of Tom's
car in the Vale of Health. Wexford knew he would
be absolutely on time and he was. Tom came in
an unmarked car — as an unmarked policeman,
of course he did — driven by a young woman he
introduced as his sergeant, DS Lucy Blanch.
Lucy, as she wanted Wexford to call her, was a
slim black woman with a pretty face and ebony
hair. He would have liked to ask her if she
plaited those corn rows herself or did a
hairdresser do it, but he was always conscious of
anything that might be construed as racist. Tom
had been sitting next to her but when Wexford
got into the back he came and sat beside him.

'So that we can talk a bit more about the case.'
Tom didn't comment on Sheila's stately
house or the wide garden or the little gabled
coachhouse at its gates. By this time Wexford had
learnt to categorise visitors as likeable or not by
whether they said he'd done all right for himself,
hadn't he, that must be costing him a packet, or
noticed his second home with no more envious
deference than if it had been a one-bedroom flat
in Tooting. It was a test that Mike Burden had
passed with honours, but then Mike had worked

for him and with him since Sheila had been a young girl and knew all the circumstances.

Lucy drove along Fitzjohn's Avenue, getting caught up in a traffic jam halfway down. Roadworks again. Wexford was daily amazed by the cones and barriers spread out everywhere while holes were dug, pipes exposed and apparently essential work carried out if London were not to break down and come to a standstill. Here temporary lights had been put up, staying red much longer than for a normal traffic-light span.

'Before we start,' Wexford said, 'I've got something to show you.' He opened his briefcase and took out the calendar. '*Marc and Harriet in Orcadia Place*. But perhaps you know about it.'

Tom Ede took it in both hands. 'I've heard about this, but not seen it. The painter was Simon Alpheton, was it?'

Wexford was pleased. 'You can see the date is 1973. Has it changed a lot?'

'A previous owner called Clay Silverman had the Virginia creeper cut down. Who are or were Marc and Harriet?'

'Marc was Marc Syre, a rock musician in a group called Come Hither. The woman in the red dress was his girlfriend. I think her name was Harriet Oxenholme. He died — Marc Syre. I mean, killed himself after taking LSD. I don't know what happened to her.'

Tom was silent for a moment, considering. The temporary light turned green and Lucy moved along in the queue of cars and vans and a bus. 'This Syre must have rented it. A John

Walton owned it until 1974 when he sold it to a man called Franklin Merton, who had a survey carried out. That's important, as you can imagine.' Tom paused to look at a sheaf of notes he had with him. 'Merton sold the house in 1998 to Americans called Clay and Devora Silverman. They dispensed with a survey and relied on the surveyor's report Merton had had done. Apparently the place was very much in demand and in 2002, as Silverman was suddenly sent back to the United States, he wanted a quick sale. The Rokebys also didn't bother with a survey, paid cash and moved in within five weeks.'

Wexford thought about it. 'This means that three of the bodies, the two men and the older woman were probably put in the vault' — his first use of the word — 'during Merton's occupancy. Is it known how long they've been there?'

'The trouble is,' said Tom, 'that however long ago it is, it's a long time. Between ten and fifteen years is the estimate, later narrowed down to between eleven and thirteen — we'll say twelve years. That would very likely be at the end of Merton's occupancy, as you say. But Merton is dead. He was in his seventies when he sold the house and he died last year.'

'And the younger woman?'

'That's difficult. She's been dead between two and two-and-a-half years. Say two to three. We assume she's been in the tomb that same length of time but it may have been only two years.'

'I suppose it depends,' said Wexford, 'on

28

whether her killer had the vault in mind before he killed her or only thought of it as a possible burial place later on.'

They were nearly there. Lucy was a good driver, precise and dashing, squeezing through spaces between a bus and a lorry with a skill Wexford was sure he couldn't have mustered. She directed his attention to the Beatles' Abbey Road Studios as she pulled up to allow three teenagers to stand in the middle of the pedestrian crossing and have their photographs taken.

'It's a funny thing, sir,' she said, 'that none of the drivers who have to stop for this sort of thing ever sound their horns or shout or anything even if whole droves of kids cross and do that. It's a tribute to the Beatles, don't you think?'

Wexford laughed. 'I expect you're right.'

She drove on down Grove End Road, turned right into Melina Place and then into Orcadia Place. A country lane it might have been, but one where all the trees had had the attention of a tree surgeon, every weed had been removed and each wild flower had been replaced by a pansy or a tuft of primulas. A high wall concealed all but the upper floor and almost flat roof of Orcadia Cottage, but there was a wrought iron gate in this wall, set between pillars on which stood two falcons in terra cotta. As he got out of the car Wexford could see through the bars and curlicues roses of many shapes and colours, but no scent as far as he could tell. Tom paused to put on a red and blue striped tie, somewhat the worse for rough handling.

A small crowd of perhaps six people had gathered by the gate, in hopes perhaps of some such event as their arrival. The very large young woman with a plump child strapped into a buggy stepped back reluctantly for Lucy to open the gate and let Tom and Wexford through. The man in sunglasses and a lounge suit looked as if he were going to come up to them and ask for an autograph, but he quickly put his notebook away as if he feared he might be doing something illegal.

Shallow steps mounted to the pale grey front door and on these steps stood stone pots of bay trees and others planted with purple pansies and pink petunias. A trailing plant with dappled leaves, green and white, dripped from the rims of urns and vases. But the Virginia creeper of the picture had gone, as Tom had said, and in its absence all the pale brickwork was revealed with the medallion that was a copy of one by Della Robbia. Under the eaves a frieze of green and blue tiles ran round the house. A cottage it might be called, but in Wexford's eyes it seemed a sizeable house and one which, from its garden, no other house could be seen. All was screened by shrubs and conifers and hedgerows and roses of many colours. And the place was very quiet. Only if you strained your ears to listen could you hear a distant hum from St John's Wood Road and Hamilton Terrace.

Lucy took a key from her jacket pocket and opened the front door. The interior was a disappointment, department-store furnishings and window drapings in conventional creams and browns. No books. A picture, framed in heavily ornate gilt occupied the centre of each wall. The whole place looked lifeless and smelt stuffy.

'The Rokebys no longer live here then?'

'Anne Rokeby couldn't stand it. They're renting a flat in Maida Vale. No doubt they'll come back when the investigation's done with. When we've found the answer, whenever that will be.'

Tom led the way down a passage which led to the kitchen. The door was closed. Alongside it, to the left, was an area of wall on which a picture hung, a reproduction of Manet's *Bar at the Folies-Bergère*.

'The cellar and the stairs to it are just under here,' Tom said. 'The flight of stairs — there are twelve of them — come up here and reach to just where our feet are. There ought to be a door but there isn't. That wall is where there once was a door, it has to be. Let's go outside.'

They went by way of the backdoor which opened from the kitchen. Outside was a kind of backyard, too large to be called a patio, paved in York stone, with narrow borders on three sides, planted with lavender and heathers, not yet in bloom. In the high rear wall was a solid wooden door, painted black, which Lucy told Wexford led out into the mews. Tom opened the gate and Wexford saw garages with flats over them and a block of flats. Lucy told him they were flats, though they looked like a terrace of houses, two storeys high with balconies on top and bay windows on the ground floor.

31

In the middle of the paved courtyard, slightly to the left, was a gaping hole, rectangular and uncovered. Incised on its metal cover which lay on the stones beside it were the words: *Paulson and Grieve, Ironsmiths of Stoke*. The sun was shining and when Wexford knelt down to look into the hole, the flat, slightly irregular paving felt warm to his touch. There was nothing to be seen down there and nothing, any longer, to be smelt. He could just make out the brickwork of the walls and the shape of the door into the cellar.

'That is where they all were,' Lucy said. 'Sort of piled on top of each other.'

They returned to the house, standing in the hallway outside the kitchen door. Wexford looked once more at the blank wall and put out one hand to touch it, as if it might give way and fold inwards to reveal the staircase.

Tom said, 'You can understand someone removing a door and bricking up the doorway if it serves no useful purpose, but this door — and there must have been a door — did serve a purpose. It was there solely to lead to the steps down into the cellar.'

'This is conjecture,' Wexford put in, 'but it looks to me as if whoever put the bodies of the two men and the older woman into the hole also bricked up the doorway. This would leave only one means of access into the hole, that is by the opening in the patio.'

'Does that mean he was a builder? A skilled handyman? I couldn't do it. Could you?'

'No, Tom. I couldn't. The idea of me doing it

32

is a joke. But that leads me back to the opening in the patio. If he's skilled enough to remove a door and brick up and plaster over a doorway, why didn't he brick up or pave over the manhole opening?'

'Maybe he meant to,' said Lucy, 'but he was interrupted or even couldn't get hold of the materials.'

'If he could get hold of bricks and plaster, he could get paving stones. If it was an interruption it must have been a very significant one, because once he had sealed up that opening he would have been safe, not for just eleven or twelve years, but for ever. Those bodies would have been enclosed in an impregnable tomb.'

'And no one could have gone there two years ago and added a fourth body. It was two years ago, wasn't it?'

'It was two years ago that she died. We can't be certain that she was put there immediately after death but someone put her there,' said Tom. 'No doubt about it.' They moved into the kitchen and sat down on stools. 'It wasn't Rokeby. He'd have to be a very dark horse indeed. If he put that fourth body down there the last thing he'd do is call us to tell us what he'd found in the hole.'

'You mentioned something about DNA,' Wexford said.

'Right. I did. The samples that were taken showed that the older man and the young man were related. Not father and son or uncle and nephew but maybe cousins. The women had no connection with them or with each other. The — well, baffling thing is that none of them

33

correspond to the descriptions of any persons reported missing around twelve years ago. And that in itself is very strange. Not so much in respect of the men. Men are less likely to be reported missing than women. These two may have been loners. There is no reason to suppose they lived together.

'How did they die? We don't know. There is nothing on the bodies to show how they died. With the women it's a different matter. Both had severe skull fractures. According to pathology each was capable of causing death.' Tom looked at his watch. 'All right. I've an appointment to see Mrs Anthea Gardner at eleven-thirty in Bolton Mews. She's been seen before, but not by me. She's the one person we know of connected to Orcadia Cottage in the Mertons' time. So if you'll drive us to Boltons Grove, Lucy, we'll leave now.'

'Who's Anthea Gardner?' Wexford asked when they were in the car.

'The sort of widow of Franklin Merton, who owned Orcadia Cottage from sometime in the Seventies until 1998.'

'Ah, including the relevant period. What does 'sort of' mean?'

'He was married to her before he married someone called Harriet and who seems to have been the Harriet of the picture. For some reason he never divorced Harriet, but went back to live with Anthea from 1998 until he died last year.'

As Lucy pulled away, Wexford looked back at Orcadia Cottage. There was something serene about it, a stillness and a quiet as if nothing had ever disturbed its peacefulness. No breeze swayed the branches or ruffled the leaves. He told himself he was being fanciful in imagining that the house smiled calmly, and that if it could speak would say, 'I have been here for two hundred years and seen many foolish human beings come and go, but I shall be here for another two hundred years when those corpses in my foundations are forgotten.'

The car turned into Grove End Road and started on its journey, through congestion and roadworks and capricious traffic lights to South Kensington.

5

He would never become accustomed to London's Georgian houses. Not that they were truly Georgian but mid-Victorian, and not just that they were beautiful; they had a diversity about them which amazed him, a multiplicity of bow windows and columns and arches and balconies. He hadn't seen many yet, but enough to decide they were all different, each one a surprise, ivory stucco all of them, as if carved from vanilla ice cream, their slate tops shallow, no-longer-used multiple chimneys forming crests across their roofs. It seemed to him as they passed into the Old Brompton Road that here they clustered in greater numbers than anywhere else but for Bayswater, and in the Boltons assembled in gleaming ranks, their creamy facades interrupted only by black-painted balcony rails, intricate as lacework.

Anthea Gardner lived in such a one, a small house pretty enough to hold its own with the stately palaces between which it stood. The front door was the same pearly green-grey as that on Orcadia Cottage and Wexford decided that when he next had to have his Kingsmarkham house painted he would choose that colour. Tom fished a rather shabby tie, with red and blue stripes, out of his pocket and put it on. Wexford rang the door-bell and from inside came a steady and placid barking.

'Oh, please,' said Tom. 'Not a beastly dog.'

Wexford noticed that 'beastly' just as he had noticed the 'heaven' of the day before. Another man would have said 'bloody' or worse. It interested him and while he was speculating the door opened and there was the now silent dog with its owner, who grasped it by the collar round its chestnut-coloured neck. Not quite chestnut perhaps, but a rich near-crimson. The incongruous thought came to him that it was exactly the same shade as Harriet Oxenholme's hair in the picture.

'Do come in,' said Anthea Gardner. 'This is Kildare, by the way. He's OK, he won't bite.'

Instead of red, her hair was grey, the elderly woman's wiry cap, short and trim. She was thickset but not fat, dressed in a pleated skirt and blouse, her face pleasant and intelligent, the kind that has never been good-looking, but which may have been very pleasing to confront across the breakfast table each morning. The house was as beautiful inside as out, furnished with pretty antiques and small charming paintings, including a still life of fruit and Stilton. A mouse in the corner looked daringly and wistfully at the cheese.

Wexford, rather embarrassingly introduced as Tom's adviser, remarked on it and asked if it was an Alpheton.

'Yes, it is,' she said. 'My late partner brought it here from *that* house.' There was no doubt which house she meant. She wrinkled her nose. 'Well, he brought most of this furniture from there. Oh, and the mirror. He was very fond of that mirror.'

37

So that was how she got over the difficulty of referring to the man who had been her husband. Her late partner.

'That was rather a strange business, Mrs Gardner,' Wexford said. 'What do you think became of your — er, partner's wife, Mrs Harriet Merton, that is.'

Her right hand resting on the setter's smooth crimson head, Anthea Gardner hesitated and said, 'I never met her, you know. Franklin went off with her and we were divorced. Well, eventually we were. I made him wait five years. By that time I'd met Roger Gardner, so Franklin and I were divorced and I married Roger. I was with him till he died and then Franklin and I ran into each other by chance in St James's Park. Then we got together again, but I never met Harriet. There was no reason why I should.'

'Mr Merton tried to find her, I believe you told us?'

'Well, yes and no. Frankly, he thought she'd turn up and try to find *him*. He went to Orcadia Cottage and found that she'd taken most of her clothes and jewellery. Some neighbour told him she'd gone off with a chap called Keith Hill.'

'But you didn't go to Orcadia Cottage with him?' Wexford asked at a nod from Tom.

'No, I never did. I've never been near the place. All I know about it is what I've seen on the TV and in the newspapers. There's one funny thing, though, you may be interested in. Franklin came back from there and said to me he could have sworn there was a staircase going down from behind a doorway in the hall into the cellar,

38

only there wasn't. I said to him, 'What do you mean by 'could have sworn', would you take your oath on it in court?' and he had to say he wouldn't.'

'Surely he must have known whether there was a staircase or not. He lived in the house for thirty years.'

'I'm only telling you what he said,' said Anthea Gardner.

Wexford's thoughts went back to the DNA tests. 'Did you ever hear of any relatives of Harriet's? Brothers, sisters, even cousins?'

'Her parents are both dead,' said Tom. 'Well, that's not unlikely. Harriet would be sixty or more if she were alive.'

'I don't think so. I mean, I never heard of anyone. I don't think she had any family, but they wouldn't come near me if she had, would they?'

Wexford took a last look at the mirror Franklin Merton had been so fond of. Its frame was a delicate medley of inlaid woods, grey, gold, blond, a pale greenish blue. Its glass reflected his admiring gaze. Anthea Gardner shut the dog in the living room and came to let them out. Outside, Lucy was waiting for them in the car. When he was sitting in the back Wexford said, 'The skeleton — I suppose — of the older woman, was there any hair on it or near it?' A bracelet of bright hair about the bone . . .

There was, but bright it hadn't been. Tom said, 'There was some hair, red hair but originally grey and dyed that colour. Which doesn't tell us much.'

39

Women who have had red hair dye it red when it goes grey, Wexford thought. Come to that, grey-haired women dye their head red even if it was once blonde or dark. 'How about the neighbours in Orcadia Place? Some of them must have known her.'

'This is London,' Tom said. 'People don't know their neighbours. You can live next door to someone for years in London and not know their name. Besides, we have to go back twelve years. Among the neighbours, there aren't many who were there then, and those who were say they knew Harriet by sight only. There's one woman in a flat in the mews who seems to have known her. She's divorced now and she's in South Africa. I don't mean she lives there, but she goes there on extended visits. I've talked to her on the phone and she's given me more information about Harriet than anyone else, but that isn't much. She's coming home in about a week and I hope to talk to her more — well, in depth.'

'What's her name?'

'Mildred Jones. You noticed Anthea Gardner mentioned Keith Hill as the man Harriet may have gone off with? Well, Mildred Jones told me she'd met this Keith Hill and it was her told Franklin Merton. A young chap, she said, who drove some sort of vintage car, a big American thing called an Edsel. She saw him park it in the mews once or twice. Twelve or thirteen years ago, she thinks it was.'

'You said 'a young chap'. How old would that be?'

'Mildred Jones said 'about twenty'. Oh, I know

what you're thinking, that on the whole men of twenty don't elope with women of fifty. I really need to talk to Mildred face to face.'

Tom wrenched off his tie and sent for coffee. They sat in his glass office. A few men and women in uniform or plain-clothes passed by. There was something uncanny about seeing them, yet knowing they couldn't see in.

Tom said suddenly, 'Are you anywhere near West Hampstead Cemetery?' Wexford said he didn't think so. 'There's a tomb in there to the Grand Duke Michael of Russia. He was some relation of the last Tsar, but he was exiled after he married a commoner. She was a countess but that wasn't good enough for the Imperial family, so he had to leave Russia. A piece of luck or good judgement or you could say that God moves in mysterious ways his wonders to perform. Michael would have met the same fate as the rest of them when the Revolution came. Instead he lived a peaceful life in Hampstead with the wife he was wise enough to marry and died of natural causes.'

'I'll go and have a look at his grave,' said Wexford. He was to learn that Tom sometimes digressed in this way. Quite abruptly Wexford said, 'Teeth!'

'Yes, well, of course. Teeth were almost the first means of identification we thought of. But you know something? Teeth — or I suppose I should say dentition — aren't the infallible clue to who someone is they used to be. We've such a large immigrant community. We have asylum seekers. Trafficked women, too, I'm sorry to say.

41

A lot of these people who come here from Asia or even Eastern Europe have never been to a dentist. Or if they have the dentist may never be found. And with NHS dentists difficult to find, thousands of people who haven't money to spare economise by not looking after their teeth.'

'And this applies to the four in the coal hole?'

'The patio-tomb is what I call it,' said Tom.

The vault, Wexford thought to himself. He repeated his question.

'It would seem to apply to three of them. The older man's teeth were what you might call in ruins. He'd lost a few and the remaining ones must have given him a lot of pain, but it appears he'd never been to a dentist. He'd had no treatment at all. Ever. The younger man also had had no attention to his teeth, but he was young and apart from one molar which needed a filling, his were all right. The younger woman had fairly bad teeth which must have pained her, but she'd had no dental treatment, while the reverse is true of the older woman. She had had a number of implants, crowns and bridges — very expensive dental work, but so far we've been unable to trace where this was done. It may even have been in America and we'll find out, but it takes time.'

'This again points to her being Harriet Merton.'

Tom nodded abstractedly. He looked at his watch, said, 'Well, I'm needed at this conference in half an hour's time, but we'll be in touch. I'll ring you. Meanwhile, Lucy will drive you home.'

Wexford told himself not to feel he had been peremptorily dismissed. If Tom had a conference

42

to go to — and Wexford knew only too well how many conferences, seminars, symposia, launches, lectures, meetings and exchange-of-views groups now filled policemen's lives — so well and good. He couldn't complain. They had discussed everything that needed to be discussed. Tom would call him. But he refused the offer of a lift home. He would take a bus and walk the nicest part.

Up Pattison Road to the West Heath in the sunshine. Someone had told him that the ex-King of Greece lived up here and he looked with a sightseer's interest at the house he thought must be the one. But there was no sign of royalty and Wexford felt a certain disappointment as he had never seen a king. He paused to sniff at a branch of white blossom, but was disappointed. Still, the tree on which it grew was so elegant that for it to have a scent as well was evidently too much to expect.

* * *

In the early evening, the sun still high in the sky and dusk a long way off, he went back to Orcadia Place, this time with Dora. She refused to walk, telling him that he was getting 'one of your obsessions' about going everywhere on foot. She had spent an hour and a half in the gym she had joined and that was enough exercise for one day. Wexford looked at his new figure in the mirror and realised that he was acquiring something worse than a straightforward exercise obsession: he was worrying that he would immediately put on pounds if he took a bus or a taxi. They took a taxi.

A small crowd remained outside the gate. It wasn't quite the same crowd. The young woman with the child had gone, but the man in the big sunglasses was still there or, more likely, had come back. His companion, also wearing sunglasses, was probably his wife. The gum-chewing boy in a hood was also a newcomer. Perhaps the sunglasses man kept an eye on the house each time he passed it on his way to work and his way back. Wexford and Dora walked round the corner into the mews. There, no one was about.

'I find it hard to believe,' Wexford said, glancing at the block of flats called Orcadia Court, 'that no one in those flats or the houses in the streets round here has any information to give us — I mean, give the Met — about Harriet Merton.' When he had been a policeman he had been careful to keep his work apart from his family, but it was different now. He had described the events of the morning to Dora. 'Tom says neighbours in London don't know each other. That may be true up to a point, but they're people like people anywhere else. They must be gregarious, they must enjoy gossip.'

She nodded. 'They may do, but all this is supposed to have happened twelve years ago and I expect you'll find that those flats have changed hands a few times.'

'I wish I could go in and talk to them. Like one of those amateur detectives in fiction.'

She said nothing, but she lightly squeezed the

hand she was holding.

'You don't have so many of them nowadays,' said Wexford, suddenly aware that 'nowadays' was an obsolete word. 'These days, I mean. Every detective story writer had an amateur detective who was cleverer than the police. Sherlock Holmes, of course. Poirot. Lord Peter Wimsey . . . '

'Albert Campion.'

'Roderick Alleyn.'

'Alan Grant.'

'Who on earth was he?'

'Josephine Tey's detective. But no, Reg, I forgot. He was a bona fide policeman.'

'The point I'm making is that all these people were enormously respected by the police. They went everywhere with police officers, questioned suspects, were privy to secrets, read forensic reports and ultimately were the first to come up with answers. And they were celebrities. Everyone had not only heard of them but they were famous.'

'I don't suppose it was really like that.'

'Probably not. The thing is I'm an amateur detective now, but I haven't got Lord Peter's right of entry into a suspect's home or a right to question him or her.'

She looked at him, but he was smiling and sounded cheerful. He went up to a door in the high brick wall and turned the handle. To his surprise the door opened. 'We were here this morning,' he said, 'and when we went someone left the door unlocked. Not my responsibility, though, and that's rather a good feeling.'

There was nothing to see. The cover was back on the manhole. *Paulson and Grieve, Ironsmiths of Stoke.* The fronds of the lavender swayed a little in the evening breeze. A black-bird was singing its going-to-roost song in one of the gardens. Wexford thought of Auden's poem, the one called 'Musée des Beaux Arts', about life going quietly on regardless of terrible happenings. 'The torturer's horse,' he remembered, 'scratches its innocent behind on a tree.'

'The bodies were in there?' Dora pointed to Paulson and Grieve's iron lid. 'In a hole under that?'

'In a hole under that,' Wexford echoed. 'And an ill-assorted bunch they were. Two men, two women. Two young, two older. Let's go. There's nothing to see.'

They walked up to West Hampstead. It was Wednesday and Tom would call him tomorrow. He had the coachhouse landline number and Wexford's mobile number. Tom had asked him to be his adviser and he would call him tomorrow. A taxi came and they got into it. He was constantly surprised by the amount taxis cost and had learnt that they were more expensive after eight in the evening. Ten pounds to go from one side of Hampstead to the other even before eight . . .

It was starting to get dark. Sheila's cat, a British Blue called Bettina, was sitting on their doorstep when they got back. 'Back' not 'home'. He hadn't reached that stage yet and perhaps he never would. The cat let out a loud piercing mew and ran inside when Dora unlocked the front door.

46

'Shall I give her a saucer of milk?'

Dora looked shocked. 'Oh, no, you mustn't. Milk's very bad for cats, apparently. They can't digest it.'

Wexford did some digesting himself, then said, 'Are you telling me that for centuries man has been giving cats milk in life and in literature? Every book or story with a cat in it has it drinking milk. Milk is what cats drink, live on, like, enjoy. If you were doing one of those tests where you're given a word and have to say the first other word that comes into your head, if you were given 'cat' you'd probably say 'milk'. And now you tell me milk is *bad for cats.*'

'I can't help all that, Reg. That's what Sheila said. Her vet told her.'

'The next thing will be bones are bad for dogs.'

'Well, as a matter of fact, a lot of people say they are. Bones can splinter, you see.'

The cat appeared contented with nothing but their company. She sat with them until Wexford switched on the *News at Ten* and then, apparently having an aversion to television, took her departure, a slender slinky shape under her thick blue coat, streaking up through the dusk to the big house.

★ ★ ★

He wasn't going to stay in on Thursday and wait for Tom's call, but he took his mobile out with him. He walked by way of the Heath to Kenwood, intending to make it to Highgate, but

47

that would have meant finding some sort of transport to bring him back. It was too far to walk both ways. Highgate could be saved for another day. St Michael's Church where Coleridge had a memorial tablet could wait till next week and so could Highgate Hill where Dick Whittington and his cat turned to look down on London and its gold-paved streets. 'I would bet you anything you like,' Wexford said to no one in particular, 'that he gave milk to his cat.'

Tom didn't call. Nor was there a message from him on the landline when he got back. Never mind. He and Dora went to the cinema to see *Slumdog Millionaire* and next morning, in the absence of any phone call or message, he said to Dora, 'Let's go home for the weekend.'

'We are at home.'

'No we're not. Not really. If we go before three we'll avoid the get-away-from-London rush.'

6

It was the first time he had sat in the bar of the Olive and Dove as an ordinary member of the public and not as a policeman. 'Why don't we go into the snug?' he said to Mike Burden.

'The snug's gone. It's been converted into a ladies-only bar.'

Wexford stared. 'Can they do that? Isn't it what we now have to call gender discrimination?'

'Probably. There's a big fight on about it. It's been the lead story in the *Courier* for the past week. Red wine?'

'That hasn't changed.'

Wexford and Dora had reached home in the late afternoon of the day before. As it had been last time, it was a little like returning from a fortnight's holiday, but knowing you could go back to that holiday as soon as you liked. Dora had phoned Sylvia within an hour and was with her now in her rambling house in the countryside. It rather gratified Wexford to see that both his daughters had bigger houses than he, though of course he now had two. He had joined the ranks of the second-homers. He had become one of those who battle through the nightmare of traffic congestion to reach a country house they will find cold and comfortless. Not in the spring, though, and now with windows open a little way, the stuffiness was past and the air breathable. It was very warm and he was sitting by one of those windows, looking at the lawn — you could almost see the grass growing longer and longer — when he phoned Burden. He had small hope of the new Detective Superintendent being free on a Saturday night, but Burden had said a quick yes, he'd love to meet.

As Burden walked back to their table carrying the two glasses of wine, Wexford found himself studying him. It was as if he expected his old friend and one-time subordinate to be changed in appearance, to be taller or heavier or more dignified. Absurd, of course. Only a few months had gone by. Burden was still slender, still perfectly dressed for whatever the occasion happened to be. A Saturday evening drink in a hotel bar? Burden wore grey flannel trousers with a grey nail-head tweed jacket over an open-necked dark green shirt. His hair, once caramel-colour, was now the grey of his jacket. But that, too, was unchanged from their last meeting.

Inevitably, he asked Wexford what he had been doing. The faint note of concern in his voice was slightly irritating. Wexford told him about Tom Ede, his unorthodox appointment as Ede's adviser and about the contents of the vault. The four bodies, one of them half-inside a plastic bag of the sort used to cover a bicycle or motorbike. The jewellery. Most of this part had been in the newspapers, had for a week back in May dominated the national dailies. For a moment Wexford had hesitated, but none of this was secret, certainly not from a detective superintendent.

'It's an intriguing case.' Even in no more than four words, Burden sounded relieved. What had he expected? That Wexford would be bored with his new life, frustrated, harking back to time past? 'I suppose there's no possibility of this Rokeby being the perpetrator?'

'Ede thinks not. And it's hard to imagine a man applying to the planning authority for an underground room when this would mean excavating the very place he least wanted to be discovered. He did apply and the reason his application was rejected appears to have been the neighbours objecting. And you have to remember that it was he who removed the manhole cover. Why would he do that? And if he did, knowing what was underneath, why tell the police?'

'Where was he twelve years ago? You did say twelve years?'

'He and his wife and their children had a house in West Hampstead. They sold it eight years ago and it fetched one and a half million, just enough to buy Orcadia Cottage. It's hard to see how he could possibly have put three bodies into an underground tomb in a house he very likely didn't know existed twelve years before.'

'So are you saying,' said Burden, 'that whoever did the deed would have had to be living in the house?'

'Not quite, Mike. The manhole is in a paved area or patio with access to a mews by means of a door in the wall. Now that door can be locked and bolted too, but my guess is that it was often left unlocked and unbolted. For instance, it was

51

unlocked when Tom Ede and his sergeant and I went to have a look at the place. It's quite possible that someone could have brought those bodies there in a car and there has been mention from a neighbour of a man being seen in a big old American car called an Edsel at about the right time.'

Burden, who liked cars, looked close to nostalgic. He gazed dreamily into the middle distance like one seeing visions. 'An Edsel Corsair,' he said. 'Well, think of that. Fords made it. Dates from the late Fifties. Lovely, but it was never popular and it didn't sell well.'

'How do you come to know all that?'

'My dad was mad about cars. He told me the Edsel was promoted on E-Day, September 4th, 1957. I've never forgotten it.'

'Evidently,' said Wexford in a dry voice.

Burden took no notice. 'I wonder if it was a two-door or a four-door hard-top? Potential buyers are very stupid about this sort of thing. They didn't like its grid, a pursed mouth instead of a wide grin, if you can believe it. And then the onset of the recession of 1957 was one of the external forces working against . . .'

'All right, Mike, all right. I don't want to buy one.'

'It came in red, of course, and blue and rather a nice discreet sort of pale greenish yellow, and other colours too . . .'

Back to his old form, Wexford almost growled. 'Pale yellow, I think. What does it matter? It was big enough to carry bodies in. And whoever he was, he parked it in the mews, sometimes overnight. It must have been a spectacularly recognisable car, which makes me wonder why whoever used it did use it. Why not hire a van if hiding bodies was his purpose?'

'If it was. Let's say it was. Using the Edsel as his means of transporting bodies must be because that's all he could use. Was it his or had he borrowed it? So why not hire something else? Because he was poor, he couldn't afford it. Can you think of a better reason?'

'No, but I can easily think that a man in the mews in an Edsel around twelve years ago had nothing whatsoever to do with the bodies in the underground tomb — I call it the vault, by the way. And how about the fourth body?'

'Ah. The young woman. Now you say she's been there only two years.'

'About that, they think. She was only about twenty or less. She had quite bad teeth but had no dental treatment. Now, though that's not rare in old people it is quite rare in the young. But if you look at those photographs in the papers of crowds in Asia or even Eastern Europe you'll see that quite a lot of even young women have discoloured teeth or prominent teeth or gaps between their teeth. I'm wondering if she could have come from one of those places and have been an asylum seeker or an illegal immigrant. But I mustn't jump to conclusions.'

'Whoever put her in the — er, vault, maybe your Edsel owner, must have known about the vault in advance. I'm thinking he came there with the three bodies twelve years before, and when he killed again thought of it as the ideal

53

place to hide another body.'

'He would have had to count on the door to the mews being unlocked.'

'For all we know, Reg, it was always unlocked. Has anyone asked Rokeby?'

Wexford shook his head, but he didn't really know. He thought of what a lot he didn't really know and that finding out might be closed off from him. He couldn't go to Rokeby and ask him. He couldn't even phone him and ask him. He wasn't Lord Peter Wimsey or Poirot, he wasn't even a policeman any longer. What he could do, he thought, was find an Edsel dealer or some dealership (as Americans called it) where they had sold Edsels in the past. They must have been rare even twelve years ago. Remembering that Burden had said they dated from the Fifties, he began to lose heart. But no, this must have been a real vintage car in the Nineties, it wouldn't have been forgotten . . .

Burden said as they parted, 'It's good to see you.'

* * *

While still in Kingsmarkham he searched the London phone books he had for car sales, but all he could find were car body repairs, car accessory manufacturers and car hire. Then he tried 'Edsel' but nothing was listed. Most people these days, he thought, would investigate the Internet or go online, as they called it. Dora was better at this than he was. She told him she would Google Edsel and she did so with

54

remarkable speed. He was surprised to find so many Edsels from 1958 to 1960 for sale. There were pictures, too, and for the first time he set eyes on one of these large — and in his eyes monstrous — vehicles, red ones, green ones, as well as a photograph of a chocolate brown leather interior. They were all for sale privately or from someone who apparently specialised in Edsels and offered them at prices ranging from $2,500 to $25,000. Prices were all in dollars and since those advertised gave their owners' locations, the cars came from Tennessee, Georgia, Indiana and Virginia.

None of this was any use to him. None of this could help him find the identity of an Edsel owner twelve years ago. But he studied the pictures, the descriptions and the prices. These cars, for all their failure to corner the market back in the late Fifties and early Sixties, seemed to be cherished by those who owned them. One advertisement said 'one owner, never in an accident, only 70,000 miles' and another 'garage kept, in perfect condition'. Unfortunately for him, you could only find out more by email. No phone numbers were given and really that was as well, considering he didn't want to pay for God knows how many calls to the United States, and he would have to pay. He was no longer in a position to claim the cost of such calls.

But these pages of advertisements had taught him something. Edsels were valued, they had vintage standing. Back in the late Nineties the Edsel he was interested in would already have been about forty years old. Through those years someone had treasured it, kept it in a garage, nursed it, replaced spare parts and accessories. It seemed unlikely in these circumstances, very nearly impossible, that it would have ended up on a dump somewhere, to be crushed into a block of metal and disposed of. If the owner was poor, as Burton had himself suggested, he might try to sell it, he might have succeeded in selling it. It could even be one of those pictured on the site — but no, they were all in Canada and the United States. So was it still in this country? Was it still around, cherished and kept in a garage by some new owner?

After a good deal of fumbling around, losing the email page and then losing the Internet altogether, he told himself to take it slowly and be patient. Eventually he succeeded in enquiring about Edsel dealerships in the United Kingdom and asking for the name of some English expert who could help him, and when that was done, in sending his first ever email. Or he thought he had until one arrived to tell him that someone called the postmaster wanted him to know that delivery had failed. How to find out what had gone wrong? He clicked on 'sent' and the failed one appeared. No wonder it hadn't gone to Jonathan Green of Minneapolis, master, apparently, of fifteen Edsels. Wexford had typed Jonathangrene@greenco.com. He tried again and this time it went.

No reply to his request could be expected, he told himself. What would this American Jonathan Green know about Edsel dealerships, if any, in England? What would he know about some

English person Wexford could talk to personally rather than by encounters in cyberspace?

★ ★ ★

Sunday passed as Sundays do, quietly and emptily. Though with no commitment to churchgoing, Wexford and Dora were both affected by Sunday's apathetic yet restless dormancy. You may phone your friends on Saturday, you won't think twice about it, but phoning them on Sunday is an intrusion. Calling on neighbours without prior notice is an affront. Maybe even the sending of emails on a Sunday was 'not done'. When Monday is to be all rush and activity because you have a job and a responsible one, Sunday can be appreciated as a day of rest. But what if Monday is likely to be much the same as Sunday? What then?

It might have been different, he thought, if Tom Ede had phoned. But there had been no word from him and now Wexford, who had never been in such a position before, was beginning to think it would be better for all concerned if he were to give Tom a call himself at midweek, and tell him that being his adviser wasn't going to work out and thanks, but no thanks. During the day he looked twice at his inbox but there was nothing from Jonathan Green and he wasn't surprised. Why would the man answer when there was no sale in it for him?

Sylvia came round in the late afternoon and brought Mary with her. Both Wexford's grandsons were still in education, the elder away at

57

university, the younger at school. Mary told him excitedly about her new rabbit and the hutch called a Morant hutch it lived in, one which gave it a small lawn of its own to nibble.

'Mummy said I could name him, so I've called him Reginald after you, Grandad.'

'Thank you very much,' said Wexford. 'Does he ever get called Reg for short?'

Mary was shocked. 'No, never.'

Dora went to look at his inbox just before they went to bed. 'Two for you, Reg.'

'You'll have to call me Reginald now. After the rabbit.'

The first email was from Tom Ede, saying he hoped to see him on Tuesday. He had forgotten he had given Tom his email address, but of course he had, tentatively, along with his phone number. When Wexford saw the name 'Jonathan Green' he realised something. Minneapolis time would be six hours behind British Summer Time, which meant that when he sent his request it had been four o'clock in the morning there. Green had replied at nine-thirty his time. And what he said was that the only Edsel dealership he had ever heard of in Great Britain was Miracle Motors of Balham, London, but so far as he knew they had sold their last one in 2001. Wexford could try them. They might well know the location of all the Edsels in the United Kingdom.

He slept soundly that night and they set off back to London at nine next morning.

7

Miracle Motors were in the phone book. But he wouldn't call them; he'd go there on Monday afternoon. He had paid visits to south London in the past but they had been rare. The Tube and the Northern Line were the obvious transport choice, for he had rejected the idea of driving through the traffic congestion. Miracle Motors was in the High Street, not far from Balham tube station.

By this time he had learnt quite a lot about Edsels from Wikipedia, because he had at first intended to present himself as an Edsel enthusiast. But he now saw the flaw in this, for such an expert might be expected to know more about the whereabouts of this Ford model than any salesman at the showroom. Instead, finding a girl of about twenty (something of a surprise, this) seated in a small glass-walled reception area, he simply told her the truth or half of it, that he was trying to trace an Edsel last seen in St John's Wood about twelve years ago. Neither she nor the manager she fetched showed the least interest in what might prompt this investigation, though the manager appeared to think he was some sort of inquiry agent. In a way he was.

'I've only been manager here for two years, but I can tell you we haven't sold an Edsel for — oh, I'd say it'd be eight or nine years.

Collectors buy and sell them online. This is one particular one you're looking for, is it?'

'It was a pale yellow colour or greenish-yellow. 1958 or 1959 — I'm guessing there. I don't know if it was two-door or four-door. The owner or driver in 1998 seems to have been a very young man.'

The manager thought about it. 'Your best bet may be to ask Mick.'

Wexford looked at him inquiringly.

'Mick worked here for years. Mick Bestwood. He retired three years ago. But he knows all about Edsels. He's even got a couple of them. He's only just round the corner in Crowswood Road or I can give you a phone number. I'm sure he won't mind.'

He would have found Mick Bestwood's house without any directions. What had once been a front garden had been concreted over and become the parking place for an enormous car Wexford recognised from the Wikipedia pictures as an Edsel Citation convertible, probably of 1958. It was sky-blue, not a pale greenish-yellow and so large and long as to dwarf the already small house behind it and the garage joined on to it.

The front door was opened by a young woman in a pink tracksuit he took to be Bestwood's daughter, but she turned out to be his wife. Bestwood was a small spry man, maybe sixty-five but because of his still dark hair looking much younger. The marriage appeared to be quite recent to judge by the way the woman he addressed as Cassandra kept flashing her wedding and engagement rings. Wexford wondered if marriage had assumed a special status it hadn't had for thirty or forty years now that so many couples lived together without benefit of registrar.

Mick Bestwood showed not the least surprise that someone had come to inquire about Edsels. The first thing he asked was if Wexford had noticed his own in the front garden. Wexford didn't say he could hardly help noticing it and that a more appropriate question would be had he noticed the house, but simply answered that it was a nice car and in perfect condition.

'It is,' said Bestwood, 'and only ten years younger than me. Wish I looked as good.'

'Oh, Mick,' said Cassandra. 'You look lovely, you know you do.'

Bestwood took hold of her ring-flashing hand and smiled. 'I've got another one in the garage — not mine. I'm looking after it for a customer.' He said like a doctor, 'So how can I help you?'

Wexford repeated what he had said to the Miracle Motors man. The hand was dropped and Bestwood got up.

'Come with me,' he said. 'I've got something to show you.' They went outside the way Wexford had come. 'The chap was called Gray or Greig, can't remember which but something like that. He had this Edsel, used to bring it to us for service and repairs. He worshipped that car. We heard he'd left it behind with his nephew and gone to live in Liphook, but when I say we heard it that was from the nephew, there was never a word out of Gray.'

Bestwood lifted up the up-and-over door on the garage. Inside, filling it, so that the first thing that struck Wexford was what skilful driving it must have taken to wedge it in there unscathed, was an enormous greenish-yellow car, streamlined and finned and spotlessly clean.

'Where are the number plates?'

'Are you asking me? Someone had nicked them before I ever set eyes on it.' Bestwood gave the car a little pat as he might a beloved pet which had suffered some small injury. 'Miracle Motors know very well it's here, but that new manager's got a head like a sieve,' he said. 'What happened was this. The nephew tried to sell it to us but we weren't having that, not without the owner there or at least notification from him, not without the registration document. It was me told him to get his uncle to come in himself, but he never did and we never heard another word from him. Then one day — it would have been '97 or '98 and winter or autumn — I was in Notting Hill, passing through, I mean, on my way from Shepherds Bush, when I spotted this vehicle parked on a yellow line and plastered all over the front with parking tickets and without its number plates. I couldn't stop then, but I went back later and had a good look. I talked to the then manager. We didn't have an address for the nephew and all we had for Mr Gray or Greig was Liphook. It was what you might call a dilemma. We decided in the end to fetch the car. Oh, we hadn't got the keys, but there are ways as I daresay you know. We brought it back to Miracle Motors, paid the fine incidentally and set about trying to contact Mr Gray. Or Greig.'

'You did all this for someone else's car?'

Bestwood looked at Wexford the way one might look at a man who has just taken an ice cream from a child or kicked a dog. 'I'm talking about *this car*. This is an amazing car, a dream of a car. Right?'

'If you say so.'

'Well, me and Mr Mackenzie — he was the manager then — we talked about it, thought what to do. I don't know if you know Liphook? It's a small place. We didn't know where to start, though. We'd no contact details for the young guy. All he'd said was his relation had gone to Liphook. The young guy up in St John's Wood — what did he look like?'

'I don't know.' Wexford thought of the young man's body in the tomb. He hadn't seen it, but he could imagine. But he had no reason, no reason at all, to connect that young man with one seen driving the Edsel. All he knew about the one in the tomb was that he had never been to a dentist and was in need of having one of his teeth filled, had been dressed in jeans and a jacket, whose pockets were full of jewellery worth £40,000 and a piece of paper with 'Francine' written on it and 'La Punaise'. Oh, and a number, a four-figure number. None of that need be told to Bestwood. 'What were you going to say about Liphook?'

'Only that the young guy called him his 'relation'. Funny that, wasn't it? No one talks about his 'relations'.'

'You don't remember the name?'

'Only that it was the same name. Gray or Greig.'

'It wasn't Keith Hill?'

'I told you. Gray or Greig. I tell you what, Wally Mackenzie might know. He knew all about it, said we should hang on to the vehicle, but he didn't know where, there not being that much room at Miracle Motors, so I said let me hang on to it and he said why not. It was all above board. And I've had it ever since, taken good care of it, it's been kept in perfect condition for Mr Gray or Greig if he ever comes back for it. Not likely now, though, is it?'

'Do you know where Mr Mackenzie can be found?'

'I know where he lives or used to live. Somewhere in Streatham.'

'The registration document would help,' Wexford said.

'Sure it would, but where is it? I've never seen it.' Bestwood went back to the open front door and called, 'Cassandra, would you be a duck and fetch me the phone book, darling?'

Cassandra quickly became a duck and fetched it. 'Here we are,' said Bestwood. 'W. P. H. Mackenzie, 27 Villiers Road, Streatham. It's got to be the right one. No one else'd have three initials.'

Wexford said, 'D'you mind if I have a look inside the boot?'

'Be my guest. But you'll find nothing in there. It's all clean as a whistle.'

Wexford lifted the boot lid. The boot was empty. Of course. It was clean and odourless.

'What are you looking for? Dead bodies?'
Bestwood laughed at his own joke.

★ ★ ★

Walter Mackenzie still lived at the Streatham
address. He had left Miracle Motors two years
before and gone into partnership with a friend
starting a dealership in vintage cars in Norbury,
a business which he told Wexford, when he was
scarcely in the door, was feeling the recession's
bite. He was a small thin man, much younger
than Bestwood, a sharp-voiced man whose tone
held a hint of bitterness. The homely, even cosy,
atmosphere *chez* Bestwood was lacking here. The
place was furnished with the bare essentials, but
cluttered with stacks of paper, magazines and
what looked like bills and invoices in need of
filing.

'I remember him,' he began. 'He'd pinched
that car from his uncle. Not a doubt about it.
Wanted to sell it to us but I could see through
that. I wasn't born yesterday.'

'They were uncle and nephew? You're sure of
that?'

'How can you be sure of something like that?
He *said* he was his uncle. Why would he if he
wasn't?'

'All right. What made you think he'd stolen
the car?'

'I knew the uncle. What was the name? Bray, I
think. Or maybe Breck, something like that. His
first name was Kenneth. Ken Gray. That guy
loved that car, an Edsel Corsair it was. Wouldn't

65

even have let anyone have a lend of it or drive it round the block, let alone sell it.'

'The uncle's first name was Kenneth?' But it couldn't have been his uncle ... 'It wasn't Kenneth or Keith Hill, was it?'

'No, he wasn't called Hill. He may have been Keith, not Ken. The nephew may have been called Hill, for all I know. I saw through that boy, whoever he was.'

'No doubt you told the police?'

'I what? You must be joking. It was a family affair, wasn't it? The kid had nicked it while his uncle was away or whatever. Gone to Liphook, he said. On holiday, I reckon, and while the cat's away the mice will play. That's all it was, a try-on. I said to him, if he wants to sell his car, you get Ken or Keith to come in here and see me. Of course he never did.'

'If you can't be sure of the name,' said Wexford, 'have you got any idea where the young man lived or his uncle?'

'Now that I can't tell you.' Mackenzie spoke as if he had already given Wexford valuable information. 'I can make an intelligent guess.' Wexford composed his face, to conceal the fact that he strongly doubted this boast. 'I'd guess it was north London or north-west London. He didn't seem to know his way round south of the river.'

★   ★   ★

Using the Internet to trace a Keith or Kenneth Hill didn't occur to Wexford. It had occurred to

66

Tom Ede. He set their DC Garrison on to electoral registers in those areas of London and then widened his search when no one was found of suitable age.

'There's a Keith Hill who's a well-known Labour MP,' said Tom. He and Wexford were sitting in his office. 'I've heard of him, so he must be well known. There was a footballer, but he's dead. There's someone who makes musical instruments. There are hundreds of Keith Hills and Kenneth Hills. It's a common combination of names.'

'Our one,' said Wexford, 'if he's the one, would be missing. Not dead but missing.'

'Sure, but there was no register of misspers twelve years ago. The older man and the young man, were they both called Keith Hill or, come to that, Kenneth Hill? Was one Keith and the other one Kenneth?'

'I don't know, Tom. We don't even know if the young man who gave Mildred Jones the name Keith Hill gave it because it was his own name or because it was his uncle's name. He may have thought it up on the spur of the moment. And although we know that the young man who gave his name as Keith Hill was driving a car which we know belonged to a man called Ken or Keith something, who now lives in Liphook or did live there, we don't know if this was the young man who tried to sell the car to Miracle Motors. He may have bought it from that man. He may have stolen it.'

Electoral registers are no good, Wexford thought, or they are only any good if these two men are alive and therefore not our two men. They are good only for elimination.

★ ★ ★

If a trace of bitterness had shown itself in Walter Mackenzie's words, it was nothing to Martin Rokeby's. He was plainly a man who saw his whole life as ruined by one small and innocent action he had taken two months before. Or, thought Wexford, he was a consummate actor, one who knew that pretending to a ruined existence, a family break-up and financial disaster as a result of one small move, would do a great deal to free him from suspicion.

No sooner had he sat down in Tom Ede's state-of-the-art office, all laminate floor, tubular steel and black glass, than he began on his woes.

'Maybe I shouldn't say this to a policeman, but you don't know how many times I've wished I'd never lifted that manhole cover or put it back once I'd seen what was down there. What harm would that have done, I'd like to know? Nothing to the harm that's been done to me. I've lost my home, I'm paying an exorbitant rent for a crummy flat more or less under the flyover, it'll soon be their holidays but my children won't come home — even supposing there was anywhere for them to come — they're staying with friends. I ask you, could anybody have let himself in for more grief just by lifting up a manhole cover and looking inside?'

'Well, Mr Rokeby,' said Ede, 'do you think you'd have slept comfortably in Orcadia

Cottage, do you think you'd have had a moment's peace, if you'd lifted it and just put it back? You could have kept what was underneath to yourself for years? I don't think so.'

'I didn't and that's all that matters now. What have you got me here for?'

It was said with the maximum ungraciousness, but if the man was innocent Wexford could easily understand his resentment. Ede introduced Wexford as his 'violent crimes adviser', which Rokeby acknowledged with a minuscule nod. Tall and straight, he was a good-looking man, with regular features and greyish-blond hair, but to Wexford his thinness seemed new as if he had lost weight in those two months. The small dewlap under his chin looked as if he had once had a thicker neck. But all this meant nothing relative to the man's innocence or guilt.

It was virtually impossible that Rokeby could be responsible for placing the bodies of the older man and woman and the young man in the tomb, but the presence there of the young woman was a different matter altogether. Nothing would be easier than for the occupant of the house — say he had inadvertently killed this girl — to lift the manhole and cover and drop her body down to join the others. This meant that he knew the others were there, but he might easily have done so. He might have examined the contents of that underground space in exactly the way he said he wished he had done. Why then had he disclosed the contents to the police a few years later?

Ede took his time answering Rokeby's enquiry.

'I'd like you to make a statement, Mr Rokeby. Nothing to be alarmed about. It won't be about you or your family at all. I'd like you to list everyone you can remember coming to the backyard of Orcadia Cottage, that is the paved patio area, in the past, say, four years. This will be specially relevant to the people who came — surveyors, contractors, maybe people from the planning authority — who looked at the place in connection with your application to build an underground room.'

'I can do that,' Rokeby said, 'providing you allow that I can't remember every name.'

'Just do your best.'

Wexford caught Ede's eye and Ede gave an infinitesimal nod. 'Are you aware, Mr Rokeby, that there's a staircase in the cellar part of the underground area?'

Rokeby shrugged. 'I've never seen it. I've been told there is.'

'There is. And because these stairs mount upwards towards the ground floor, there must have been a door at the top. This door would have been at the end of the hallway, probably next to the kitchen door. It's not there now. The doorway has been filled in, bricked up and plastered over. Do you know anything about this?'

'There was no door there when I bought the place.'

Rokeby compressed his lips and looked away, plainly indicating his intention to say no more about the staircase or the missing door. But he promised to list the people who had surveyed the place or simply looked at it four years before. There was also the building firm which had converted the largest bedroom into two smaller bedrooms eight years before.

Once the door closed after him, Ede heaved a sigh and said, 'Liphook is going to be a hard nut to crack.'

'The Internet?' Wexford was on shaky ground here. He never quite knew what the Internet or a search engine could or could not do.

'We have the name Keith or Kenneth Hill. Whatever the nephew called himself we're pretty sure the owner of the Edsel was called Ken or Kenneth, possibly Hill, possibly Gray. If this uncle character had the Edsel with him it would help. According to the young man who tried to sell the Edsel, his Uncle Ken or Kenneth went to live in Liphook twelve years ago. We don't have the name of a street in Liphook, we don't even have the man's name, only probabilities. You've not found the car, I suppose?'

Wexford told him. 'The Edsel is in Balham, in a garage, being looked after by an Edsel fanatic called Mick Bestwood. It's been so thoroughly cleaned and polished you could eat your dinner off the bonnet.'

The laugh which greeted this was typical of Tom who (as he put it himself) always gave honour where honour was due. 'Excellent. Well done. We'll have Forensics go over it just the same. You know they say it's impossible to eradicate all that sort of evidence. There'll be something. We've started inquiring at service stations in Liphook, at car parks and at motor repair shops. There aren't too many of those — Liphook's not very big. But all that's pointless now.' He repeated, 'You've done well, Reg.'

'Still, he may be living in Liphook.' Tom had evidently forgotten Wexford's home was in Kingsmarkham, not many miles from Liphook. 'It's not much more than a big village.'

'The woman who wrote *Lark Rise to Candleford* used to live there,' Tom said. 'Flora Thompson. I saw about it on television when they did the serial.' He went off into one of his digressions, speculating as to whether Candleford was Liphook and ending with a mini-biography of the author.

Wexford waited patiently before asking if the inquiries in Liphook had had any results.

Tom shrugged. 'Maybe Kenneth Hill used to live there, but if he did he didn't make much of a mark. Lucy Blanch and DC Garrison have talked to a good many of the residents and no one remembers Hill.'

'Medical centres?' Wexford queried. 'What we used to call doctors' surgeries? Hotels? Pubs.'

'Lucy's tried all those and there's nothing. The fact that he's not there is no evidence for us, it's another negative. I'm inclined to believe he never lived there. It looks to me as if it's just something the young man said to your Miracle Motors people because he thought that would be an excuse for the uncle not coming in with the Edsel himself. Liphook was probably the first name that came into his head. He knew someone there or he'd seen the name written down.'

'I'm afraid you're right.'

'Mildred Jones is home from South Africa,' said Tom. 'We'll go and see her. She's our only source for the name Keith Hill. Let's hope she has total recall for a conversation she says she had with him twelve years ago.'

8

She lived in one of the garden flats in the block
in Orcadia Mews. Her front door was directly
opposite the door in the rear wall of the Orcadia
Cottage paved yard. Three of the front doors
were painted black but Mildred Jones's was
fuchsia pink. A Virginia creeper, now in new leaf,
rambled over the brickwork of the flats, completely concealing some of it, and Wexford thought
of the same climber which had figured in Simon
Alpheton's painting and had been cut down by
Rokeby. For some reason, he wondered if the
climber had any significance in this case, but he
was at a loss to think what it could possibly have.

Tom had forgotten to put his tie on or had
deliberately left it off, but fished it out of his
pocket and was putting it on as the front door
was opened by a short but rather heavy woman
in a green trouser suit. She gave Tom and his tie
a glance of distaste. She was one of those people
whose heads seem too big for their bodies, their
features handsome enough but almost overpow-
ering. The heavy gold jewellery she wore seemed
to weigh down her neck. Her hair was grey,
styled to look like as if sculpted from metal or
stone, her face thickly made-up, the eyebrows
shaped with excessive care.

The room she led them into was small, stuffed
with chintz-covered furniture, the French window hung with over-ornate brocade curtains,

braided, pleated, fringed, its pelmet adorned at its sides with bunches of tassels. But the garden visible outside was like a rectangle cut out of a hayfield.

'I told you on the phone that we spoke to him,' Mildred Jones said. 'He said his name was Keith Hill. I told you that too.'

Wexford said, 'He didn't mention his address?'

'No. Why would he? You don't say to someone you've just met, 'My name's Keith Hill and I live at number something or other, do you?''

Neither policeman answered her. 'What did he look like?'

'Young, about twenty. Very good-looking if you like the sulky type. Tall, dark. He was obviously one of Harriet's.'

'One of Harriet's what?' Tom asked.

'Boyfriends, bits on the side. Oh, I knew all about it. She had a lot of young fellows visit her, plumbers, electricians, blokes she'd send for to do jobs for her while Franklin was out. They did the jobs all right.'

Tom's face set into lines of disapproval and he curled up his mouth in distaste. He reminded Wexford of a portrait he had once seen of John Knox at his most censorious. Suppressing the signs of amusement, he said, 'You said *we* spoke to him, this Keith Hill. Who were 'we'?'

'Oh, me and my then husband. Didn't I say?'

Wexford hardly liked to ask if the man had died. He had no need to.

'We split up a couple of years ago and got divorced.' Mildred Jones uttered a sound halfway between a chuckle and a snort. 'It was just after that girl Vlad burnt his shirt. Not that it was because of that or the girl. He had an eye for the girls but he never fancied those skinny blondes.'

'Vlad?'

'The cleaner. Her name was Vladlena, only I called her Vlad the Impaler. 'Burner' would have been more like.'

Tom was anxious to get her back to the subject.

'Would you tell us everything you remember about Keith Hill? Exactly what he said when you and your ex-husband talked to him?'

'Well, the first time I just said good evening or hello or something and he just said good evening. I was out for a walk with my little dog. I had a dog then but he died. The second time I was in my friend's car and I saw him and I waved but he didn't wave back. The next time I was coming back in the car with Colin — my ex, I mean — and this Keith Hill was in the mews but without his car that time and I thought he looked shifty — well, as if he'd been up to no good. I said, 'You again' or 'We meet again' or something, and he said, 'Yes' or 'Right'. He said his car was in for a service. Those leaves were lying all over the place and getting wet and I said to him how someone I knew had slipped on them and broken her leg. I thought I'd let him know I knew what he was up to with a woman three times his age and I asked him how Harriet was. He said she was fine and I said, tell her Mildred said hello or give her my love or something.

'We went indoors after that and watched him

76

from my front window. I don't know what he was doing. I went out again then, carrying my rubbish bag for the council to collect in the morning. After I was back in the house again I saw him go through the door in the wall into the backyard of Harriet's house. I said to Colin, he knew it like he lived there, like he owned the place.'

'Thank you, Mrs Jones. That's very helpful. Can you remember how he was dressed?'

'Like they all do. The young, I mean. One of those zipper jackets, jeans of course, a black T-shirt, I think. He had that car, but he wasn't very confident driving it. I thought he was going to scrape it against the wall out there. He was nervous and not just about the car.'

'And he went through the door in the wall into the backyard of Orcadia Cottage?'

'I've told you he did.'

'Mrs Jones,' Wexford said, 'does the name Francine mean anything to you? And what is La Punaise?'

He expected an answer of sorts to his first question, only perhaps to say that she had heard the name but couldn't remember where. What he didn't anticipate was a full and highly informative answer to his second inquiry.

'I can tell you what La Punaise is.' She began to laugh reminiscently. 'Harriet told me. Well, she showed me. It was a way of remembering her pin number. Seemingly, *la punaise* is French for a pin. She'd got a lot of restaurants written down in her address book. Her and Franklin, they ate out all the time. So she wrote La Punaise in the book like it was a restaurant and wrote a phone number underneath, only it wasn't a phone number, it was a London exchange followed by the four digits of her pin. Oh, she thought herself very clever, I can tell you.'

So the boy, Keith Hill or whatever he was called, had had access to Harriet Merton's address book and had also been clever enough to decipher her purpose in storing her pin number by this means. He had been in the house, must have had intimate knowledge of the house. Her pin number he would have wanted for illicit purposes, to say the least. Why had he written it down on that paper under the name Francine? Because Francine was French and could translate the name for him?

'Thank you very much, Mrs Jones,' he said.

Tom asked, 'Did you ever go into — er, Harriet's house? Orcadia Cottage, that is?'

'Of course I did,' said Mildred Jones. 'How d'you think I got to see her address book? She was bored stiff, nothing to do if one of her young chaps hadn't come round. Sometimes she'd ask me in for a drink. It'd be lunchtime and I'd go, but I'm not much of a drinker especially at midday.'

Wexford asked her, 'What was the house like inside?'

'You mean the furniture, pictures, that sort of thing? Oh, it was lovely. Beautiful stuff they had. Of course, it was all Franklin's. He was a connoisseur.'

'Mrs Jones, I'd like you to think very carefully. Imagine yourself in the hallway, looking towards

78

the kitchen. Can you do that?'

'OK. I'm doing it.'

'Can you see the kitchen door?'

'Of course I can.'

'Now look to the left of it and tell me, is there another door there or a blank wall?'

'What is all this?' Mildred Jones was indignant. 'Haven't you been inside the place? Of course there's a door. It leads down the stairs to the cellar where all those horrors were found. It makes me shudder to think of it.'

'There is no door there now, Mrs Jones,' Tom said.

She stared. 'But I saw it. The first time I was there the door was open. Harriet had been down there to fetch something up — bottled gas or something. She had to do all that for herself. Franklin never lifted a finger. I looked down the stairs just to get a sight of the cellar, but there was nothing down there, only an empty space and a couple more of those gas bottles. You want to go down there yourselves and take a look.'

'We'd like you to come in there with us and take a look,' said Tom.

Mildred Jones was reluctant to accompany them. Tom explained to her that the bodies in the vault were long gone. The house itself contained nothing of Harriet's, nothing of Franklin Merton's. Two sets of owners had lived there since the Mertons, as she must know.

'It's the idea of those dead bodies lying in there, under the ground, for all those years . . . You've got to admit, it's enough to give you the shivers.'

'It would be a great help to us if you would come in there with us for just a few minutes.'

'I don't see how it could be, but OK, if it's really a help.'

They walked out of the mews, Mildred Jones's high-heeled green shoes having some difficulty with the cobbles, round the corner on to the smooth stone pavement. 'I noticed you've got a Virginia creeper on your flat,' Wexford said while Tom unlocked the front door of Orcadia Cottage. 'Is it the same variety as was on this house until it was cut down?'

'As far as I know. I don't know anything about gardening, plants, that sort of thing.'

'When the leaves fall it makes a lot of mess?'

'Oh, yes, dreadful. My cleaner has to sweep it up and she makes a big fuss. I don't mean that Vlad, she's gone long ago. And the one after her too. Of course I don't keep them on when I'm away in South Africa and they don't like that.'

Mildred Jones stepped in fearfully over the threshold, but when she had advanced a few steps her nervousness left her and she stared at the blank wall facing them on the left-hand side of the kitchen door.

'Someone's made a wall there!'

'Yes.'

'Maybe one of Harriet's boys. They were all builders of some sort or another.'

The young man who might or might not have been called Keith Hill came into their minds, but it wasn't until Mildred was back home and the two policemen were back in the car that Tom spoke of it. He wrenched off his tie. 'We've no

80

reason to think he was a builder or a friend of Harriet Merton's or that he built that wall, have we?'

'Except that we both have a feeling that all those things are true,' said Wexford. 'That's all. Assumptions.'

For ever afterwards, for the rest of his life, Wexford would remember that it was here, on the corner, where Abbey Road comes into West End Lane, that the phone call from Dora came. 'Assumptions' was the last word spoken and then his phone rang. As their driver rounded the corner where Quex Road turns off to the left he heard Dora's voice, a trembling shaken voice, and Dora's news.

'I'll be back in five minutes — well, ten,' he said. 'As soon as I can. And then we'll go home. Straightaway.'

The driver said, 'What is it?'

He told her. 'My daughter — my daughter Sylvia . . .'

'It'll be five minutes,' she said. 'Not ten. Sooner if I can make it.'

9

The sun was setting and all the lights were on. They sat at Sylvia's bedside. 'Only five minutes at the most,' said the intensive-care sister. She came back after four minutes and shepherded them to the relatives' room, a carpeted place with armchairs and a television set. Who, in their situation, would want to watch television? Dora, who had been dry-eyed at the bedside, now began crying quietly. When the door was shut Wexford took her in his arms and held her, not speaking.

Sylvia's ex-husband Neil Fairfax was sitting there, though he had not been allowed to see her. Nor had Mike Burden, who had met them at their house when they arrived and driven Wexford and Dora to the hospital. Everything goes when your child is at death's door, Wexford thought, every other preoccupation, worry, hope, fear. She is all. You don't even notice if the sun is shining or rain falling. Nothing else matters and, humiliatingly, you pray. You pray to a god you don't believe in and have never believed in. It's a mystery how you know what to do, what to say, how to frame a prayer.

He gently released Dora, sat beside her, holding her hand. Burden said, 'Any change?'

Wexford shrugged. 'Just the same. They say she's stable. They're worried about her blood pressure. Well, I think they are — it's hard to know.'

It was Burden who had told them, he who made that phone call. Sylvia had been fetching her little daughter Mary home from a pre-school for four year olds. The house, an old rectory, absurdly large for one woman, one child and two young men who were most of the time away at school or university. Sylvia had parked the car on the long winding drive, half overgrown with shrubs and trees in full leaf, had pushed open the passenger door for Mary to get out, got out herself and before she could take a step been stabbed by a man who had stepped out from the hawthorn thicket and plunged a knife into her chest. The knife had missed her heart but grazed a lung.

While Neil was producing coffee for everyone from the machine, Burden told the story all over again. 'Mary was a marvel,' he said, smiling at Mary's father as he took his coffee. 'She got herself to Mary Beaumont's. You know who I mean?'

Wexford nodded. He had nodded the first time. He knew this was just Burden's well-meant effort at distraction. 'Sylvia's friend. Mary's named after her.'

'Mary Beaumont says she doesn't really know what had happened — Mary couldn't tell her, just said there'd been a man and a lot of shouting. Mary ran back with little Mary and there was Sylvia — well, you can imagine the rest. The car was gone, but he didn't take her handbag or apparently any money or credit cards. Thank God, whoever he was, he didn't touch the child.'

For a car, for nothing but a car. If he'd come to me, Wexford thought irrationally, I'd have given him a car and anything else he wanted not to touch my daughter. Only life isn't like that and people don't behave like that.

Dora asked, 'Where is Mary now?'

'With Mary Beaumont,' Neil said. 'She knows her, she loves her and Mary was happy to have her.' Neil was the little girl's father, though she had been born long after her parents' divorce. 'I shall take the day off work tomorrow so that she can be with me, but after that — well, I don't know. We'll arrange something.'

Suddenly Dora looked better, more hopeful, less distraught than she had since the news came. 'Let us take her, Neil. She can stay here with us or we can take her back to London to Sheila.' Her lip trembled. 'I would love to do that,' she said shakily. 'Mary is happiest of all when she can be with Amy and Anny. Do let us.'

'Not yet,' said Wexford, more gruffly than he intended. 'I'm staying here, in this hospital until we know.'

* * *

But the Princess Diana Memorial Hospital refused to let them stay. If there was a change they would be phoned, but they couldn't be allowed to remain overnight in the relatives' room or elsewhere.

'You let mothers stay with their sick children,' said Dora, 'and I'm a mother and Sylvia is my child.'

84

'Yes but she's grown-up,' said the intensive care sister. 'I'm sorry but we have to stick to our policy.'

They went home and sat up, drinking whisky. Even Dora had a small glass and made a face at the taste. They tried putting on *News at Ten* but for all that sunk in they might as well have done without it. Wexford was thinking about what he had been told, that the knife had been thrust into Sylvia's chest millimetres from her aorta. A second blow had grazed a lung, and surgery — carried out within an hour of her entering the hospital — had saved it.

'Mr Messaoud is one of the finest surgeons in the country, the top man,' said one of the intensive-care nurses.

Everyone you ever heard of who had an operation, Wexford thought, always described their surgeon like that, as being Britain's finest, the top man. It made you wonder what the second-class surgeons did, whom they operated on. Maybe they stood about and watched. He put the whisky bottle back in the cupboard. It was no good swigging scotch, it dulled but it didn't help, it never did. Dora had fallen asleep, stretched out on the sofa. She woke up when the phone rang, sat up, made a little inarticulate cry. But it was only Robin, their elder grandson, at home in his mother's house, waiting for his brother to arrive from school. Robin's university was up for the long vacation but Ben, whose school term continued for another three weeks, would come home for a few days.

'I've not seen Mum yet. I thought I'd wait for

85

Ben. We'll go together in the morning.'

'She's just the same, Rob,' Wexford said. 'There's no change.'

Robin asked no questions. If Wexford had been asked how his grandson sounded he would have said 'sick at heart'. When the receiver had been put down he started thinking about the man who had attacked Sylvia. For him to have been waiting there, hiding in the bushes, he must have known Sylvia's movements, perhaps that she lived alone with a child, that she worked only in the mornings and returned home, bringing Mary from pre-school, at 12.45 p.m. Great Thatto Old Rectory was in a remote place, deep countryside. The nearest village, Myland, was small enough, but Great Thatto had only sixty-five inhabitants and Wexford had often wondered how tiny a Little Thatto would be if this one was great. How had Sylvia's assailant got there? By car surely. That was impossible. He couldn't have driven both his car and Sylvia's four-by-four at once, and no car had been found in the wilderness grounds.

A bus from Stowerton stopped in Myland. Walking two or three miles hardly fitted the image of a thug who would attack a woman with a child. He wondered about his granddaughter Mary. Had this man tried to stop her as she ran away? If so, why hadn't he succeeded? Wexford would have liked to know if she screamed all the way to Mary Beaumont's, but nobody could know that except Mary herself. The picture he had of the terrified little girl running and screaming down the road to the one person who could give her sanctuary, sickened him and made him grow cold.

He tried to think of something else. Orcadia Cottage. Mildred Jones. The bodies in the vault . . . The young man *might* be Keith Hill; the older man might be related to him; the older woman was very likely Harriet Merton, but all that was still mainly conjecture. He had been wondering if the woman with the exotic name who had worked for Mildred Jones and had burned a shirt might be the fourth body, the one that had been in there for only two or three years. But why had he even considered that? He had no grounds for supposing it.

His thoughts drifted away at this point, flowed back to Sylvia. It was no good. Whatever else he succeeded in thinking of, it would last for no more than a very few minutes. He could see her lying there with all those tubes — lines, they called them — attached to her, her dark hair spread across the pillow, her face and neck still and pale as a marble bust. She may die, a voice inside his head said to him. She is at death's door, that door still closed but trembling a little as a hand tried to open it from the inside. Don't think like that. But how else could he think? She might be dead already and no one phoning them until the morning. It was ten minutes to one.

Our children should not die before us. If they do, if one of them does, that must be life's greatest tragedy. He asked himself what he would do if Sylvia died. How could he handle it? How would he live? How would Dora live? When you first met them and started talking, people asked you if you had children and you would no longer be able to say you had two. You had just the one. Perhaps you would also have to say that you had two but one died . . . There was a line in *King John*, a woman mourning her small dead son. 'Grief fills the room up of my absent child, lies in his bed, walks up and down with me . . . ' That was how it would be. He would never see her again. Never. He got up, telling himself to shut up, to stop it.

Perhaps Dora had been asleep or just pretending to be. She sat up. He sat beside her on the bed and held her. She rested her face on his shoulder and they clung to each other. After a minute or two she said, 'What shall we do?'

'God knows. Wait.'

'How early can we phone the hospital?'

'Probably any time we like. She's in intensive care. She won't be left alone, so they'll know if there's any change.'

'It gets light very early now.'

'We'll wait till it gets light, Dora.'

She asked him if it would be better to go downstairs, but he said no, let's stay where we are. Well, he'd go down and make them both a cup of tea. But he'd bring it back up here and wait for the dawn, for sunrise. Waiting for the kettle to boil, he thought how he had been in this kitchen with Sylvia a couple of weeks ago. Was that the last time he would ever see her? Her white face on the pillow in intensive care didn't count. He remembered her as a child, as a teenager, her marriage when she was only eighteen, then divorce and Dora's distress.

Dora's horror when she said she was going to be a surrogate mother, to have a child for her ex-husband and his girlfriend. That was Mary, who in the event had never been given up to them . . .

He made the tea, waited for it to 'draw' as they used to say in the days before teabags. Not at the time but later, he had speculated that Sylvia's willingness to have a child for those two people had been less altruism than pride that she could bear children with ease, while poor Naomi was, in her own harsh, outdated term, 'barren'. Sylvia — a mix of the wildly generous and the relentless. Like her mother, perhaps. He poured two cups of tea, carried them upstairs. Dora was lying flat on her back with her eyes shut. He opened the curtains to let in the dawn, a pale grey glow behind the roofs and treetops.

They drank the tea, but they didn't speak. There was nothing left to say. The strange thing was that they both slept a little — so much for the effects of caffeine. The bedside phone woke them, its blast amplified to screams. Wexford surfaced, reached out and picked up the receiver.

10

She was awake, she had spoken, she was breathing without assistance. Wexford said a quiet thank you to Robin, who had phoned. He looked at the clock and saw it was ten past nine.

'Oh, my God, and I was asleep!' Dora sat up, struggled to get up. 'My daughter might have been dying and I slept. What kind of a mother does that make me?'

Wexford said irritably, 'Don't be so daft. I'm the emotional one, you're the calm one — remember? Come here.' He hugged her, said, 'We'll get up, have showers, eat an enormous breakfast and then we'll go and see her. Let her be with her kids first. On second thoughts, I shall have a bath. I hate showers, always have. Showers are for speed, baths are for celebration.'

It was eleven before they reached the hospital. As they walked up the steps and into reception Dora said, 'You never told me you hated showers.'

'No point. You couldn't change things. It's one of my laws: half the people in the world prefer showers and the other half baths.'

Sylvia was sitting up. Or lying down, propped up on pillows. Dora looked at her almost fearfully, seeming afraid to approach her, but Wexford kissed her cheek and Sylvia put up an unsteady hand to touch his face.

'You see, I'm alive,' she said.

Then Dora did kiss her. Sylvia closed her eyes. Her breathing was regular, too steady for a wakeful state, and Wexford thought she had fallen asleep. She looked very young, almost as she had when she was a teenager. At the same time he noticed that there were strands of grey in the dark hair she wore long and which was now spread across the pillow. After a moment or two she opened her eyes and smiled.

'Your lot will want to talk to me,' she said.

'My lot?'

'The police.'

'Not my lot any longer, but I expect they will.'

A nurse came over, said that was enough for now and sent them off to the relatives' room. Robin and Ben were both there, having had their time with their mother an hour earlier. And with them was Detective Superintendent Burden.

'I'm practically a relative,' he said to Wexford. 'One of the family for now.'

'For always, Mike,' said Dora and burst into tears.

⋆ ⋆ ⋆

For more than two days Wexford had thought of nothing but Sylvia. He thought of that cliché he hated, 'putting it on the back burner', along with 'level playing field' and 'kicking whatever it was into the long grass' — all often used by Tom Ede — but for him, now, the metaphor had been apt. He had put Orcadia Cottage on to the back burner along with the forensic aspects of the attack on Sylvia. That wasn't allowed to continue. He had barely spoken to Burden when his phone rang, followed by the double note indicating that a message had been left. It was Tom. As soon as they left he would call Tom and explain. Meanwhile, here was Mike . . .

'I'm going to talk to her myself,' he said, 'as soon as they'll let me. I think she'd rather talk to me personally than to Hannah or Barry.'

'I'm sure she would.'

Robin said, sounding years older than his age, 'Are you going to talk to my sister?'

'Your sister?' Ben sounded years younger than his age. 'She's my sister too.'

'Yes, right, OK. But are you?'

'I don't think so,' Burden said. 'Not directly at any rate. I'd like to talk to your mother first and depending on what she says — well, it might be best if Mary's grandmother talked to her about what happened when the attack was made on her mum.'

'Me?'

'I don't think anything you might say to her would frighten her, but I'll speak to Sylvia first.'

A nurse put her head round the door and said Sylvia was asking to see her sons again. 'Five minutes,' said the nurse, 'and then you can all go home and come back later.'

* * *

As soon as he was at home Wexford called Tom Ede.

He hadn't explained about Sylvia but now he did, keeping it short because he knew that few people care to hear much about others' troubles. But Tom was sympathetic, asking questions, apparently delighted to hear that Wexford's daughter was going to be all right, angry and quite aggressive about the violence that had been done to her. He said and said it devoutly, 'Thank God.'

Wexford remembered how he had said 'heaven' rather than done what they called 'taking the name of the Lord in vain'. He was almost shocked when Tom said, 'I said a prayer for her — well, several prayers actually.'

A rather awkward 'Thanks' was all Wexford could respond to that.

'I don't suppose you want to know about the bit of progress we've made. You've got enough on your plate.'

Another cliché, but Wexford didn't care. He felt quite affectionate towards Tom and the hackneyed phrase was endearing. 'I'd very much like to hear,' he said.

'Well, we've identified the older woman as Harriet Merton. Her dental records showed up in California, a very prestigious and expensive dentist. Apparently, she had all those implants, crowns and bridges done there. Must have cost old Franklin a packet.'

'Yes, indeed.' Wexford thought briefly of the red-headed girl in the red dress against the background of bright green leaves in Simon Alpheton's painting, and then he thought of the bundle of grey bones shrunken in designer clothes, its hair dyed crimson. 'Anything more about the two men?'

'We've shown Mildred Jones the clothes the young man's body was dressed in. She was a bit squeamish about them. She should have seen them before we had them cleaned up. The result wasn't exactly conclusive and that's not surprising. She just kept saying that they might have been his, but she couldn't say for sure. A shabby black T-shirt is a shabby black T-shirt. Half the youth in London wears dark blue or black zipper jackets, and jeans are just jeans. His were the kind you'd buy off a street-market stall, brand name Zugu, of which thousands were sold twelve years ago, but to track each one down is obviously impossible. Stallholders don't ask their customers for their names and addresses.'

'So we've got a Kenneth or Keith Gray or Bray,' said Wexford, 'and his young cousin, but not his nephew, possibly called Keith something but possibly Keith Hill.'

'That's about the size of it.'

'OK, if you say so. At least we know for sure that the woman was Harriet Merton. And we know that the young man we have to call Keith Hill for lack of anything else to call him, we know he had been inside the house and had access to Harriet's address book. He wrote down her pin number, disguising it from whoever might see it by labelling it as Harriet herself had labelled it, with a name that sounds to the uninitiated like a restaurant. La Punaise.'

'But why would he do that, Tom? That piece of paper was surely for himself, simply to remind him of the number. He must have had her credit card and have used it or planned to use it to milk her account or even empty it. But why write La Punaise? The only reason I can think of was because he didn't know what it meant and intended to ask for a translation from someone who would know. Francine, whoever she is or was?'

Tom said he would get his team searching online electoral registers for someone with the first name Francine. He sounded far from hopeful. There might be thousands. But he'd leave no stone unturned. 'How old do you reckon she was?'

'If she was his girlfriend, late teens or early twenties. But she might be his French teacher or his French-speaking aunt or the lady next door . . . '

Tom groaned. 'Forensics have been looking over the Edsel, but we've got no answers yet. Let me know when you're coming back to London,' he said. 'I don't mean to chase you up. Hope your daughter gets better soon.'

Wexford thought Tom might say he would carry on praying for Sylvia, but he didn't.

* * *

There was an uneasiness in Burden's manner that Wexford spotted at once. Never effusive, seldom demonstrative, Burden surprised his friend by shaking his hand, something which hadn't happened for more years than he cared to remember. And he kissed Dora, a further departure from the norm.

Another day had gone by, and then another,

95

and the detective superintendent had twice talked to Sylvia, allowed by the ward sister to remain with her only for half an hour at a time. Sylvia was now out of intensive care and her parents had sat with her for most of the afternoon, leaving for home just before Burden arrived at Sylvia's bedside. Now he sat in their living room, nursing with fidgeting hands a small orange juice, having refused all alcohol offers.

Wexford, drinking red wine, said, 'There's something wrong, Mike, what is it? The hospital haven't told you something they're keeping from us?'

'No, no, nothing like that.'

'But you've talked to Sylvia about what happened?' This was Dora, braver than Wexford. 'Are you able to tell us what she told you? If it wouldn't be right . . . '

'No, of course it's right.' Burden set down his glass, picked it up again, apologised for the wet ring it made on the table surface. 'Oh, I'm sorry, I'll get a cloth . . . '

'Mike,' said Wexford, 'what is it?'

'All right. It's just that you're her parents and I just think it would be better if you didn't know, yet I know you have to know.' Burden rubbed at the wet ring with his finger, avoided the parents' eyes. 'But I'm making it worse. I'll tell you straight. It's better that way. The man who stabbed her was known to her. More than that, he'd been — well, her lover. He wasn't hiding in the bushes, he was in the car with her and Mary and they had a row and . . . '

'Mike, begin at the beginning, will you?'

Wexford made a dismissive gesture with his hands, the kind of movement that means, it doesn't matter, just tell us. So long as she's all right, nothing like that matters. 'Just tell us. We can take anything now we know she'll be all right.'

'Well, OK,' Burden's tense shoulders relaxed and he very nearly smiled. 'The story I told you at first I got from Mary Beaumont and she was very discreet but she probably knew little of the true facts. I sat by Sylvia's bed and asked her to tell me exactly what happened when she got home to Great Thatto. She said, 'I'd better start before that, Mike. The guy who stabbed me is called Jason Wardle. He's twenty-one and I've been having a relationship with him.' Then she corrected herself. 'I think a 'fling' might be a better word.'' Burden paused briefly because Dora had made a sound, a wordless whimper of distress. 'I'll go on. She told me he lived in Stringfield. They'd met and had coffee in Kingsmarkham, the purpose of the meeting was to break things off and when she'd done that she was going to pick Mary up from her nursery school. But Wardle wasn't having any. He said he'd kill her first, but of course she didn't believe him. They never do. Oh, God, I'm sorry, Dora. I shouldn't have said that.'

'That's all right, Mike. That's nothing to what you're telling us.'

'Twenty-one, you said?' Wexford found it hard to bring the words out, but he had to know. Young enough to be Sylvia's son. Just.

'So she said. He got into her car and they set

97

off. Mary had apparently met him before and wasn't fazed by his being with them, but Sylvia was anxious that the row shouldn't continue in her presence and refused to answer his accusations but tried to talk only to Mary. He constantly interrupted them and began shouting and when Sylvia was passing Mary Beaumont's house she stopped the car and told Mary to go in there and she would come for her very soon. She watched Mary being let in by Mary and then . . .'

'So all that about Mary running away when her mother was hurt, that wasn't true?'

'Apparently not, Dora. That was the discreet version Mary Beaumont gave me — maybe she believed it herself. Sylvia said to Wardle that she would drive him to Stringfield — where he lives with his parents — but Wardle wasn't having any. She drove up into the Old Rectory drive and stopped the car and they started to argue. Well, Wardle said he loved her and wanted to marry her. Apparently, he said he knew what all this was about. It was because Sylvia wanted him to marry her and she was breaking it off because he hadn't proposed. He was proposing to her now. She started laughing. She said she didn't want to be married and if she did he'd be the last man on earth. She got out of the car and stood there, laughing. He screamed at her and pulled the knife — ironically, it was one of her own kitchen knives.'

'So he had been planning it?' Wexford shrugged. 'I don't suppose he carries a carving knife about with him on the chance he may need to use it?'

'I think they had had a row the evening before

and he took the knife then. Sylvia had the day all this happened off work and he spent the morning with her.' Burden paused, shaking his head. 'There's a lot to come out yet, Reg. A lot we don't know and will have to know. Where is he, for instance? He's not with his parents. They haven't seen him for days. Incidentally, they knew nothing about his relationship with Sylvia.'

'Come to that,' said Wexford, 'nor did we.'

'We've put out a nationwide call for him. And, of course, for Sylvia's car. We've checked on various friends and relatives, but so far there's been nothing. We'll find him, of course, but it'll take time.'

11

Mary, as Dora put it, seemed untouched by her ordeal.

'What ordeal?' Wexford said, his picture of the terrified child negated by the facts. 'She wasn't there when Sylvia was stabbed. She was having a happy time with her godmother. You're imagining things.'

They had been back in London for twenty-four hours. Mary had chattered all the way and was now in Sheila's nursery — Wexford remarked to Dora that he couldn't remember ever previously having encountered the possessor of a nursery — with Sheila's nanny, Amy, Anoushka and Bettina the cat. He had chickened out of Dora's plans to take all the children to a matinee of *The Lion King* and was waiting to be picked up and driven to police headquarters in Cricklewood.

True to her undertaking, Dora had asked Sylvia's permission to take Mary with them to London, and had asked it in her habitual kind and loving tone. It was only Wexford who could hear the underlying note which said, 'Oh, Sylvia, how could you? Are you lost to all morality and decency?' But it was only thought, not said. Would it ever be said?

Naturally, the first remark Tom Ede made to him was to ask about Sylvia, and he seemed delighted when Wexford said she was recovering and would be out of hospital in two days' time. Nothing was said about prayers and Tom quickly reverted to the Orcadia Cottage case.

'I'd like to ask you,' he began, 'how important you think the name 'Francine' is. I mean, do we need to try and trace every Francine in the country? The trouble with that is that so many people who were young twelve years ago have left the country, just as others have come in. If she exists — and we don't know that she does or ever did — she may be anywhere.'

'Perhaps we have to ask ourselves why he would write the name Francine on a piece of paper on which 'La Punaise' and what is almost certainly a pin number were already written. Because this woman with a French-sounding name could translate for him what was obviously a French word? It looks like it. So she must have been someone close to him. You don't ask a casual acquaintance or a person much older than you to translate something which obviously has a criminal connection.'

'He might have just asked her to translate 'La Punaise' and not mentioned the number.'

'True. But wouldn't the meaning suggest a pin number to her? At least wouldn't she question him?'

'I don't know, Reg. Maybe she did question him. Can we construct some sort of scenario out of what we do know?'

'The way I see it, the young man who called himself Keith Hill somehow got into Orcadia Cottage and perhaps even lived there with a French girl called Francine. He found the address book with the pin number and 'La Punaise' made to look like a restaurant, intending to use it to rob Harriet Merton's account.'

'If he was living there, where were Franklin Merton and Harriet? They can't have been there, because it must have been at this time that the pseudonymous Keith Hill removed the door to the cellar, bricked up the doorway and plastered over it. Incidentally, why would he do that?'

'It has to be because he'd killed Harriet and maybe that cousin of his or whoever it was and was sealing them up in a tomb.'

'But he was in there, too,' Tom objected.

'I know there are holes in my scenario. I think we have to see Anthea Gardner again, see if we can find out where Franklin Merton may have been at that time, whenever that time was, and maybe see Mildred Jones first to try and settle this time question. So far all we know is that it was about twelve years ago.'

Mildred Jones was in a better frame of mind than when last seen. Some women are very much affected, Wexford thought, by whether they think they are looking good or are dissatisfied with their appearance or are having, for instance, a 'bad hair day', while men are influenced by the state of their car — he thought of that Edsel — or a bad back or a cold coming on. Mildred Jones's hair had evidently just been done and silver streaks put among the iron grey. The red dress she wore suited her better than the trouser suit, which dwarfed her. Wexford supposed she was aware of these things, a feeling confirmed when she glanced with satisfaction into a mirror on their way to the chintzy living room.

'You want me to tell you when I saw the so-called Mr Hill and his fancy car, do you? I'll have to think.' She was silent for a moment. Then she said. 'When I try to remember when something or other happened I have to try and think of the weather. I mean, if it was summer or winter and raining or whatever.'

Tom was nodding encouragingly.

'It's no good nodding at me like that.' A flash of the old acerbity was showing itself. 'That won't help me. I'm thinking. Ah,' she said. 'I know now. It must have been autumn. The whole place was covered with leaves — no, it wasn't, not covered. That came a week or two later. The leaves from that Virginia creeper were beginning to fall. It must have been October, sometime in October. Does that help?'

'Very much, Mrs Jones.'

'It rained after that and made a thick wet mat of those leaves. I was glad when Clay — Mr Silverman, that is — cut it down. Ours hadn't been planted then. Pity it ever was. That was Colin — he liked the colour.'

She waved to them as they left. Wexford imagined her going back into the house and pausing at the mirror to admire her reflection.

'I don't suppose Anthea Gardner will have silver streaks,' he said.

An unobservant man, Tom looked puzzled. Wexford didn't explain. Anthea Gardner was expecting them at midday and had coffee ready, the real thing made from beans which she had just ground herself. Tom, who had once told Wexford that he only liked the instant kind, sipped his rather gloomily. Mrs Gardner was dressed almost exactly as she had been on their previous visit, only this time instead of grey her skirt was brown and her blouse spotted instead of striped. Kildare had once more to be restrained and eventually shut in the kitchen.

'You want to know where Franklin was in late October 1997?'

'I know it's difficult to remember these things from so far back, Mrs Gardner,' Tom said. 'Think about it. Take your time.'

'I don't have to think. It's not difficult at all. He and I used to go on holiday together long before we started living together again. Harriet and he had been taking separate holidays for years. We were in San Sebastián that year. October it was, the second half of October.'

'Why do you remember so clearly, Mrs Gardner?'

'Oh, that's easy. I remember because it was on that holiday, on my birthday actually, that we decided we'd live together again. Franklin would leave Harriet and come here to me.'

'And when is your birthday?'

'October twenty-fifth,' said Anthea Gardner. 'St Crispin's Day in case you're interested.

'Franklin went back to Orcadia Cottage,' she went on. 'It must have been four or five days after we got back. I told him to. I don't think he'd have bothered if I hadn't made him. When he came back he told me what had happened.

104

The house was empty. He said it was very clean and tidy and Harriet wasn't there. A woman he knew who lived in one of the cottages at the back told him that a man she called Harriet's 'young friend' had been at Orcadia Cottage with her for at least two weeks. This is the kind of thing you want?'

'Exactly the kind of thing we want.'

'It's all coming back to me now,' said Anthea Gardner. 'Franklin said he found a pile of cushions on the living room floor with a scarlet feather boa draped across them. I mean, it was Harriet's feather boa. He recognised it. He said the door in the wall at the back was unlocked and the key was missing. There was a manhole or drain or something in the patio, but the lid was off it . . . '

'Just a minute, Mrs Gardner. You said the manhole was open?'

'Well, I suppose so. I wasn't there. Franklin said the lid was lying near it. The whole place was covered in those leaves which were wet and sort of sticky. He said they were very slippery. He had to walk very carefully not to fall over. Anyway, he managed to lift the cover and put it back on the manhole.'

'Did he ever go back there?'

'Not as far as I remember. He expected to hear from Harriet, asking for money if nothing else, but he never did.' Anthea Gardner was silent for a moment, looking from Ede to Wexford and then down at her own ringless hands. 'He didn't *care*, you see. Women had cost him enough in the past, me included. He simply hoped he'd never hear from her and that perhaps she'd found a man to support her. The feather boa he saw as a defiant gesture, sort of cocking a snook at him, if you know what I mean.'

'Mrs Gardner, do you know if Harriet had much jewellery?'

'She had lots, all bought for her by Franklin, but it was gone, the valuable stuff was gone, he said, when he went to the house. Most of her clothes were gone, the designer stuff, and the best of her jewellery.'

Wexford asked her if she would recognise any of the pieces if they were shown to her, but Anthea Gardner shook her head quite violently. 'I told you, I never met the woman. I know nothing about her jewellery. I know there was a lot of it because Franklin told me he'd spent a fortune on jewellery in the first years of their marriage, but what kind it was and what it looked like I've no idea. And I don't know what was the point of the feather boa.'

'And are you saying he never heard from her again?'

'That's what I'm saying, yes. He never heard from her again.'

As they were driven away out of the white stucco enclaves of The Boltons, Wexford said generously, for the theory had been his alone, 'Can we add to our scenario as a result of what we've heard?'

'We'll have to go back in time a bit. We know how Keith Hill happened to have free access to Orcadia Cottage. Franklin Merton was away on holiday in San Sebastian — where is that anyway?'

106

'Spain.'

'Oh, right. OK. Merton was away on holiday and in his absence Harriet had invited KH to stay. While he was there and maybe she was out somewhere he discovered her pin number, presumably pinched her credit card or one of her credit cards. Suppose, for instance, he had this Francine there and Harriet came back and discovered them together? He kills Harriet . . . '

'Why?' Wexford interrupted. 'Because his elderly girlfriend discovered him with his young girlfriend? Hardly. What could she do? Fornication's not yet a crime in this country.'

'All right,' said Tom, looking rather as if he would approve if it were. 'If you insist. He gets rid of the girl, tries to placate Harriet, but she isn't having any of it. They fight . . . '

'What? Physically?'

'Suppose the door to the cellar was open and she fell down the stairs or he pushed her . . . '

Suppose, Wexford thought. It was all supposition. It might have happened quite differently. He listened to Tom's by now elaborate theory with half an ear, while saying to himself, we have to start again, we have to start from scratch and begin from a different angle. But it's not my case, he thought, it can never be my case. It's Tom's, and what I say doesn't really count. He said it, though, just the same.

'Hardly any attention has been paid to the second woman in the tomb.' How useful, how tactful, the passive voice could be! This version was so much more becoming than if he had said, 'We ought to pay attention to the second woman.'

'Because the tomb must have been opened for her body to be put in?'

'I see it this way. That the people who knew the hole and the cellar were there in the first place are the three whose bodies have been there twelve years. Once they were dead and in there no one knew about it with the possible — no, the probable — exception of Franklin Merton. Once Franklin Merton was dead, had died a natural death, no one knew of it. The big plant pot placed on top of the manhole cover effectively sealed it up. If not for ever, more or less permanently. Until someone discovered it was there and saw it as a potential tomb or, rather, as an existing tomb which was like a vault. It had room for more bodies if bodies there were.'

Tom nodded. 'All right. What next then?'

'Back to Rokeby,' said Wexford. 'He must be the key to identification. It was he who proposed the construction of an underground room. And it has to be that which gave whoever it was ideas. He has yet to list the people who may have come to survey the place — or has he done that?'

'We haven't heard a word from him. No news yet from forensics on the Edsel either. We've still got nothing but conjecture to link the Edsel with the two men's bodies.'

12

'I won't say a word,' said Dora. 'I shall want to, but I won't because it would upset you. Not because it would upset her.'

Wexford smiled. 'That's a very good reason.'

Dora was going back to Kingsmarkham by train, leaving him in London. Her intention was to be in Great Thatto in advance of Sylvia's return from hospital, and she would have Mary with her after the little girl's three days of blissful holiday with her cousins. 'Phone me,' he said.

'Don't I always phone you?'

He laughed. 'Tell me what she says about that miscreant who stabbed her. She wouldn't be daft enough to forgive him, would she?'

'I sincerely hope not.'

He was going to have a long conversation with Martin Rokeby. It was Tom Ede's suggestion that he should see Rokeby alone or perhaps with Anne, his wife. No policeman, only this policeman's aide, as Wexford was beginning to call himself. They would talk. Rokeby would say things to him he might not say to Tom.

A picture of Orcadia Cottage, as it now was or as it had been when Simon Alpheton painted it thirty-six years before, Wexford retained in his head. It was therefore something of a shock to see where the Rokebys now lived. Maida Vale sounds charming and parts of it are, but not St Mary's Grove, its tall shabby late Victorian houses almost pressing against the Westway flyover. Traffic roared across the great arch of the road behind which was Paddington Station and the new glass towers of the canal basin. A flight of steps led up to the front door under a crumbling portico and when the door came open there were more steps, about fifty of them, to the top flat. Rokeby was standing outside his front door.

A smile might have been expected, but Rokeby didn't smile. He had been watching Wexford mount the top few stairs but now he turned his head away, gave that most unwelcoming of greetings, 'You'd better come in.'

Though they had been there for several weeks, the Rokebys had done nothing to make the place more attractive. The rooms were large, apparently retaining their original ornamentation, elaborate and very dusty cornices, shutters at the windows which looked as if they had never been moved, even a couple of fluted columns with Corinthian capitals. A cheap-looking, much-worn carpet covered the floors, wall-to-wall, and the curtains were of thin unlined cretonne. The view from one window was largely of pretty St Mary's, Paddington Green, but from the other all that could be seen was the Westway, dark grey concrete with its sluggishly moving load of traffic. There were no books, no plants or flowers, no cushions and scarcely any ornaments.

Anne Rokeby sat in a cane chair with a seat covered in the same cretonne. She looked worried and worn. She didn't get up when Wexford came in. There was no reason why she should, but no reason either, as far as he could tell, for the momentary shutting of her eyes. He noticed that her hands trembled slightly.

'I would have thought,' said Rokeby, 'that we'd already talked about every possible aspect of this business. What else is there to say? I looked down a hole in my backyard and found those bodies and ruined my life. That's that, isn't it?'

Instead of answering, Wexford said, 'I was hoping for a list from you of the various contractors you consulted about building an underground room at Orcadia Cottage.'

Rokeby shrugged. 'But why? They didn't build it. They said it wasn't feasible and then planning permission was refused. What's to say?'

Policemen don't answer questions. They ask them. But Wexford wasn't a policeman any more. 'Mr Rokeby, three of the bodies you found had been put there or had died there about twelve years ago, but the fourth had been dead only about two years. This means that the coal hole had been opened and another body put in there something over two years ago. What I'd like us to talk about is when you first moved to Orcadia Cottage and you had builders in to convert a large bedroom into two small ones, when you applied for planning permission and when those contractors came to look at the place. I'd like some dates, if possible.'

Anne Rokeby suddenly stood up. 'I don't see why we should tell you. You're not a policeman, are you?'

'I can't suppose you have anything to hide, Mrs Rokeby.'

Her hands had again begun to shake. 'That's not the point, that's not what I . . .'

'Sit down, Annie,' her husband interrupted her. 'It's because we've nothing to hide that we can't have any objection to talking about this.' He turned to Wexford. 'We moved into Orcadia Cottage in the spring of twenty-o-two and we had a builder in called Pinkson. I remember that because it was such a weird name. He was a sort of jack of all trades and we found him because he'd done some work for our predecessors, the Silvermans, cut down the creeper among other things. Then in the spring of twenty-o-six I applied for planning permission to build an underground room and I consulted three or four building firms.'

'Pinkson being one of them?'

'No. He'd gone, moved away or gone out of business.' Something struck Rokeby. 'You're not saying one of those men put a fourth body down there, one of the ones who came to talk about building below ground?'

'I'm not saying anything, Mr Rokeby. I'm hoping you'll say something and give me some useful information.'

'I can't remember the names,' Rokeby said. 'Well, I can remember one. They were called Subearth Structures. I thought it was a stupid name and it stuck in my mind, but as for the others . . .'

Anne Rokeby's tone was cold and curiously dreary. She spoke as if she hated her husband only a little less than she hated Wexford. 'You got the names of the others out of the Yellow Pages.

I said it would be better to act on personal recommendations but you wouldn't.'

'Do you remember the names of the firms you took from the Yellow Pages?'

Martin Rokeby shrugged, then shook his head slowly, but his wife again jumped to her feet. Wexford was making himself ready to restrain her if she did what she seemed about to do, fly at her husband with her hands up like a cat's claws. 'You want to come to the end of all this, don't you?' she shouted. 'You want to solve it or whatever the term is, don't you? I know I can't stand much more of living in this dump. The more you tell him the sooner all this hell will be over . . . '

'But, Annie, I don't know . . . '

'Yes, you do! You marked those firms in the Yellow Pages. I remember. You put a ring round them with a ballpoint pen. What's the matter with you that I can remember and you can't?'

Very calmly, not showing any of the excitement he felt, Wexford asked if they had that particular volume of the Yellow Pages with them in the flat.

'Of course we don't.' Anne Rokeby was scornful now. 'But no one ever throws those things away, not even when you get a new one. It'll be in the hall cupboard at the cottage unless your people have disposed of it. It'll be there with rings round all those builders' names, of course it will.'

* * *

113

It was a relief to be away from those bad-tempered, unhappy people. Wexford walked a little way down the road towards Paddington Green, recalling the song about Pretty Polly Perkins and her lover the milkman.

I'm a broken-hearted milkman, in grief I'm arrayed
Through keeping of the company of a young serving maid,
Who lived on board and wages the house to keep clean
In a gentleman's family near Paddington Green.

The gentleman's family could have lived in one of the remaining Victorian houses sandwiched between the newer building on the eastern side of the green. St Mary's Church was beautiful, the kind of place people called a 'little gem' and he remembered reading somewhere that in exchange for being allowed to build the Westway so close to it and across its land, the church had been given a donation sufficient to restore it to its former glory. Its clock struck noon with the kind of chimes that are usually called 'silvery' but sounded more golden to him, they were so rich and harmonious.

He sat down on a seat on the green and phoned Tom.

Lucy would go to Orcadia Cottage, Tom said, and meet Wexford there to explore the phone books. Was it too far to walk? All the way up the Edgware Road, turn in at Aberdeen Place, he calculated, but maybe a more interesting way would be to try the hinterland of Marylebone. Church Street with its antique shops detained him briefly, but after a minute or two of being amazed by Alfie's windows, he walked through to Lisson Grove (where Eliza Doolittle lived, he recalled) and on up Grove End to Orcadia Place.

Two people, not police, were outside, looking at Lucy's car. They moved away when they saw him and transferred their attention to the house itself. One of them was the fat young woman with the pushchair, though she was without it this morning and holding the hand of its usual occupant. He went up to the front door and having no key, rang the bell. Lucy answered it and he was about to step inside when, quick as a flash in spite of her size, the young woman was at his side.

'If you're going in, can we come?'

'I'm afraid not,' he said. 'Sorry but no.'

Lucy said, 'You shouldn't even be in the garden. There's nothing for you to see and I'd advise you to go home.'

Wexford thought the girl would retaliate — he dreaded a racist comment — but she said nothing, contenting herself with a glare at Lucy's cornrows, and went reluctantly away, the child whose hand she was clutching, starting to grizzle. He closed the front door behind him and turned to survey the welter of phone directories lying on the hall floor. Lucy started to pick them up.

'I'd have said that one of those Rokebys is the sort of person who never throws anything away, but they appear to have thrown away the crucial one. There are three copies of the Yellow Pages but not the marked copy. Mind you, I've only looked in the hall cupboard.'

'It may be somewhere else in the house.'

They set about searching likely places and unlikely ones, a drawer at the base of a wardrobe, the drawers in a dressing table, bookshelves in case the missing directory had been placed among oversized books, the four cardboard crates packed with ornaments and crockery which the Rokebys had perhaps intended to take with them to St Mary's Grove but in the event had left behind. On top of the fourth of these, the last one they searched, was the missing Yellow Pages. But when Wexford lifted it out he found that the pages in the first half of it had been torn out.

'And that's the bit with the 'Builders' and 'Contractors' in,' he said.

'It has to be the one, sir. But the pages are gone. It's no use to us.'

'I'm not so sure. Have a look at those crates. All the stuff that's packed inside them is wrapped in newsprint. Not Yellow Pages, I know. But suppose they ran out of newsprint when they came to pack a fifth crate and used Yellow Pages for want of anything else.'

'Except that they didn't.'

'Lucy, will you drive me back to St Mary's Grove — do you know where that is? There's just a chance . . . '

No sightseers remained outside Orcadia Cottage. It had begun to rain, a thin drizzle. 'If it

116

doesn't work out the way I'm hoping,' Wexford said when they were in the car, 'at least we know about Subearth structure and it's possible that may be all we need to know.'

'What do you think we're going to find, sir?'

Instead of replying Wexford said, 'You've been to that flat the Rokebys are living in, haven't you?'

'Just the once, sir.'

'Did you notice how few ornaments there were about?'

Lucy shook her head. 'I don't remember.'

'Let's hope that the ones they brought with them they never unpacked.'

This proved to be the case. The Rokebys were far from pleased to see Wexford again and positively hostile to Lucy. 'Two of you?' Anne Rokeby said. 'What are you going to do? Arrest us?'

'Did you bring a crate of china or crockery with you when you came to this flat?'

Rokeby said, 'And if we did? Did you think it wasn't china but another body?'

'This isn't a joking matter, Mr Rokeby,' said Lucy. 'Since you appear not to have unpacked it, we'll see that crate, if you please.'

It was full of pieces of what might have been a dinner service and each piece was wrapped in a sheet from the Yellow Pages. Lucy began unwrapping them, doubtful until she reached the third layer from the top. The next piece she brought to light, a sauceboat, was wrapped in a page on which the name K, K and L Ltd had a ring round it in ballpoint.

117

'We seem to have found what we're looking for, Mr Rokeby,' said Wexford. He smiled. 'When we have unwrapped all twelve dinner plates and all twelve soup bowls we'll leave you in peace.' My God, he thought, I'm catching cliché-itis off Tom. I'll be praying next . . .

'Eighteen!' said Anne Rokeby. 'I used to wash them all with my own hands in soap made for delicate fabrics,' and she burst into noisy tears.

★   ★   ★

From the sheets of yellow paper they noted eight separate firms of contractors, including Subearth. 'Oh, yes, Subearth,' said Rokeby. 'I remember now. I mentioned them to Colin Jones and he knew all about them. Recommended them actually.'

Wexford asked the Rokebys' permission to take the relevant pages away with them and this was grudgingly granted. Anne Rokeby had stopped crying and was muttering an explanation of her conduct, though no one had asked for it. Seeing her beautiful dinner service, which she never expected to use again, had set her off so that she lost all control. It was enough to break her heart.

'Have you got a dinner service, sir?' Lucy asked when they were heading for West Hampstead.

'I don't know. I expect we had one once. Certainly not the eighteen-piece kind.'

'I shall never have one,' said Lucy. 'I shall

never have anything you can't put in a machine to wash it.'

Wexford laughed. It was Wednesday, a good day to start phoning up builders, well before they all started knocking off for the weekend. How many of those who came to size up the potentials of Orcadia Cottage, he wondered, had opened that manhole and looked inside. Ninety-nine out of a hundred people who had done that would have told Rokeby and then told the police. But one would not. One would have made use of what he had found.

13

Subearth Structures operated out of a Victorian house in the backwoods of Kilburn, round which lean-tos and sheds clustered. The house, when first built, must have been extensively encrusted with mouldings of fruit and flowers and leaves above its front door and all its windows. Most of this decoration had by now cracked or crumbled or fallen off and an attempt had been made to smarten up its appearance by painting the entire façade with a thick matt white paint. Recalling his ice-cream metaphor when he saw the houses of The Boltons, Wexford thought this place was like an ice that had half melted.

As in all builders' yards, piles of sand, shingle, bricks and tiles cluttered the place and a concrete mixer ground away monotonously. Lucy had already spoken on the phone to Brian George and it was he who came out of one of the sheds to meet them. Invited to come inside, she and Wexford followed him into the ice-cream house and into a kind of sitting room. Its walls were painted a bright turquoise. A cheap red hair-cord covered the floor and the chairs were upholstered in brown plastic. If this was where he brought potential clients, Wexford thought, it was a wonder any of them continued with their purpose of installing an underground room. On the turquoise wall hung framed photographs of various breeds of dog as might be in a vet's waiting room.

'Now I wasn't actually working here when Mr Rokeby asked us to make a survey.' Brian George said this as if he might have been half-working there or working perhaps, Wexford thought, only in spirit. 'You'll want to talk to someone who actually was working here.' George nodded as if to confirm this careful assessment of the situation. 'I think Kev would be your best bet, that is Kev Oswin. Kev actually went to Arcadia Cottage — funny name, that, isn't it? Cottage, I mean. I'd call it a big house myself. But as I say, Kev went to Arcadia Cottage to size up the situation and your best bet would actually be to have a word with him. If you'll excuse me I'll go and root him out.'

Once he was out of the room, Wexford said to Lucy, 'Was he like that on the phone?'

'Exactly like that.'

She picked up a trade journal from a coffee table and Wexford retired into his thoughts. He had had a long talk on the phone with Dora the previous evening and an even longer one with Burden. Jason Wardle was still somewhere at large. Calls to all his known relatives and friends had achieved nothing. He might be abroad. He had had days in which to leave the country by air, or more probably, because simpler, by Eurostar. Sylvia's car had not yet been found.

'His parents seem to know no more as to his whereabouts than we do,' Burden had said. 'They're rather old to be the parents of a twenty-one year old. James Wardle must be getting on for seventy. He's been retired for years and they live in rather an isolated place on the

121

outskirts of Stringfield. They claim not to have seen him for a month. Unless they're very good liars, they genuinely don't know where he's been living in that time and they knew nothing about Sylvia. As far as they knew — this is what they say — he had a girlfriend he met at the University of Myringham that he later dropped out of. They had the girl's name and we've seen her, but I'm as certain as can be in these circumstances that she hasn't seen him for several months and has no idea where he is.'

Dora had more to say about Sylvia herself than the hunt for her assailant. 'She seems pretty well, Reg. I've borrowed Mary's car and I take her back to the hospital every day to have the wound dressed, but tomorrow will be the last time. Ben's gone back to school for the last week till the end of term but Robin's with her. She seems to like my being there and that's maybe because I haven't said a word about her having a — well, a love affair with a boy young enough to be her son. I've wanted to but I haven't. I thought of you and what you'd want and I didn't say a word.'

'Thank you for that, darling,' he had said and was pulled out of his reverie by Lucy saying, 'What's happened to him? We've been here ten minutes.'

'Wait a bit longer,' Wexford said, 'and if he hasn't come by a quarter past we'll go after him.'

At fourteen minutes past Brian George came back with a very short very fat man he introduced as Kevin Oswin. Oswin was as taciturn as his employer was verbose. When

Wexford asked him if he had gone to Orcadia Cottage to look over the place with a view to making an underground room, he returned a single 'yes'.

'And how did you set about doing that?' Lucy asked.

'How d'you mean?'

'Did you walk round the place, take measurements, look in the cellar?'

'There wasn't a cellar.'

'The coal hole then — did you look in the coal hole?'

Oswin was silent for a moment, then he said, 'No.'

'Mr Oswin,' said Wexford, 'could you be a little more explicit?'

Oswin stared, perhaps unaware of the meaning of the word.

'Say a bit more about it, I mean.'

'There's nothing to say, but if that's what you want, OK.' Oswin suddenly became voluble, but speaking slowly as if to people who understood English only with difficulty. 'I said to him, Mr Rokeby, that is, that the whole front garden would have to be dug up. Right? Excavated.' He rolled his mouth round the word. 'All the trees have to go, the hedge, the lot, them pillars with the birds on.' The pause was longer this time, ending in a sigh. 'He said, what about the back, and we went out the back and I said to my bruv I said that it wasn't on.' So much talk appeared to have exhausted Oswin and he closed his eyes.

'Your bruv? You had your brother with you?'

'Yeah, my bruv Trevor.' He added importantly,

'Trev's like self-employed, got a car-hire company, but he's about here somewhere. He come with me to look at the place, but he stayed outside to have a fag. Terrible heavy smoker is Trev. I went inside with Mr Rokeby and had a look round for what that was worth.'

'Why wasn't it a practical proposition?'

'It'd have meant excavating under the roadway at the back and that wouldn't be allowed. Westminster Council wouldn't have that. Wouldn't be allowed. Got that? Not allowed.'

'But you didn't look into the coal hole?'

'Never knew there was a bloody coal hole till I saw it on the telly. Right?'

It must have been Trevor that Wexford caught a glimpse of as they were leaving Subearth's premises, an equally fat if slightly taller man than his brother, standing by the concrete mixer smoking a cigarette. He wore a suit and tie and appeared to be paying no more than a social visit. 'Who do we see next?' he asked Lucy.

'Groundhog and Co. have gone out of business, sir. The recession's been too much for them. Perhaps we ought to talk to the boss sometime, but don't you think we could see those that are still operating first?'

'All right, then.' Wexford was looking at Lucy's list. 'How about K, K and L? They're in Hendon and that's not far away, is it?'

Not a builders' yard this time but a shop in one of those parades that break the monotonous rows of semi-detached houses on arterial roads. In this one was the usual sequence, newsagent, hairdresser, building society, dry cleaner, but instead of the bathroom shop, K, K and L, Below Surface Home Extensions. A rather gloomy-looking young woman in a black trouser suit showed signs of being more helpful than Brian George and Kevin Oswin.

'Our Mr Keyworth was down to do the survey,' she said without looking anything up or having recourse to the desktop on the counter. 'He was due to go over there in August twenty-o-six and he was just leaving in the taxi when Mr Rokeby phoned and said not to come because the planning people refused his application. There'd been a lot of opposition from the neighbours.'

'And you are?' Lucy asked.

'I'm Ms Fortescue.' Wexford thought her reply quaint for present day usage. Perhaps she read his mind for she added, 'Louise Fortescue.'

'Why a taxi? Doesn't Mr Keyworth drive?'

'He'd lost his licence.' She added vindictively, 'Driving massively over the limit.' As if she still needed to assert Keyworth's superior status: 'It wasn't a black cab. His next-door neighbour's got a car-hire company. They only drive Mercedes.'

'Well, Ms Fortescue, would you mind telling us how you happen to have such a precise memory of something that happened — what? Three years ago?'

'Three years, yes. That's easy. Me and Damian — Mr Keyworth that is — we were engaged. I remember everything about that week because we were planning our wedding. I'd even moved in with him to his new home in West Hampstead

— he'd only been there a bit over a year — and the day after he was due to go to Orcadia Cottage I broke it off. The way he behaved I couldn't do otherwise. I moved out that night. Luckily I'd kept my flat. She turned her face away. 'It was me broke it off, but I've never got over it.' Her voice broke a little. 'I'm sorry.'

Meeting each other's eyes as they walked to the car, Wexford and Lucy just overcame the desire to laugh. 'I was engaged once,' said Wexford.

'So was I.'

'I didn't marry her. She married someone else and so did I.'

'And I didn't marry at all. Poor Miss Fortescue, she's taken it very hard. What exactly are we looking for, sir?'

'I wish you'd call me Reg.'

'I'll try,' said Lucy, 'but it will be difficult. What are we looking for?'

Wexford got into the passenger seat. 'Well, someone like Ms Fortescue. Someone who knew about the set-up at Orcadia Cottage because she or he had been told about it.'

Lucy turned into the Finchley Road. 'You mean that the theory is that one of these people who made a survey knew about the coal hole and possibly the cellar, but isn't going to say so? They discovered it at the time and either went back when they knew no one would be at home or else told someone else about it.'

'Something like that. We still have J. Peterson and Son to see, and Underland Constructions.'

'They know we're coming.'

J. Peterson had a small office over a hardware shop in North Finchley. The room was tiny, no bigger than the average suburban bathroom. It contained nothing but a desk, two chairs and the ubiquitous laptop. No pictures were on the walls, no maps, no posters, no curtain or even a blind was at the narrow sash window. The atomosphere wasn't far off that of a prison cell.

'We do most of our business online,' said a harassed-looking man who gave no sign that he had expected them. 'The client gets on to our website and books an appointment and we contract out to a building firm.'

'You keep a record of that?'

'The builders have an architect who would do a sort of design and if the client likes it and accepts the estimate it'll go ahead. We'll have a record on the computer if this client — what's he called? Rokeby? — if he accepted the estimate.'

'He didn't,' said Lucy.

'Then I can't help you.' The man sounded pleased.

Underland Constructions might have answered Lucy's call and agreed to see her and Wexford, but only one man appeared to be in charge of the big sprawling builders' yard in Willesden. The place looked as if it were being dismantled. Two of the sheds were empty. The office with 'Reception' over the door had no one behind the counter.

'We're shutting up shop,' the man said. 'Been struggling for the past year but in the end it's been too much for us. I don't suppose I can help you. What was it you were wanting?'

Lucy told him.

'You don't want us. You want our architects. They did all our designs for us. Not any more, of course, but they're still in business. Doing all right, as far as I know.'

He went into the office and came out again with a much-thumbed card. Lucy read what was on it aloud to Wexford when they were back in the car. 'Chilvers Clary, Architects, and then there's a string of degrees or whatever after Robyn Chilvers and Owen Clary. They have an office in the Finchley Road. Shall we go straight there?'

'Pity it's such a long time ago,' Wexford said. 'I doubt if Robyn Chilvers will have had her engagement broken on the relevant day. Still, even if they'd forgotten about it and haven't kept records, reading all this Orcadia Cottage stuff in the papers will perhaps have jogged their memories.'

'Yes, perhaps.'

'All the time, though, we come up against this stumbling block. In order to do a survey or make a design, whoever he is would have had to examine the coal hole, probably go down into it. And if he or she did and was honest they would have seen what was in there and gone to the police. And if they're not honest and did see what was in there they didn't go to the police and they're not going to tell us now.'

Some years before Wexford had got out of a tube train at Finchley Road Station and walked up the hill towards West End Lane. Investigation of a Kingsmarkham murder with London connections had brought him there and he had thought the Finchley Road rather a pleasant place to shop and perhaps to live in. It had gone downhill very badly since then. A huge shopping mall, already dilapidated, had spoiled the western side of the street, while opposite shops and restaurants had closed, their windows boarded up. Chilvers Clary was still there and so were a massage parlour and a betting shop. The massage parlour was called Elfland and in its window were photographs of very pretty young women dressed as fairies with feathery wings and holding bows and arrows. It looked respectable and rather dull.

Those adjectives might also have been applied to Chilvers Clary, Architects. It also appeared less than promising. But for Wexford and Lucy a small breakthrough was coming. It was very small, but it let in a chink of light. Lucy said afterwards that she could have hugged Owen Clary, not a very unlikely impulse, Wexford thought, for Clary was a very handsome man, about thirty-eight with olive skin, black hair and classical features, dressed in an immaculate dark grey suit.

'My partner is out on a job,' he said. 'Incidentally, Robyn is also my wife. But I don't think she could help you, whereas I can. Well, up to a point. All this newspaper coverage has brought it back to me. I well remember going to Orcadia Cottage in summer 2005 it would have been. I went on my own the first time and the second time with the chap from Underland. Mr Rokeby let us in, but then he and his wife had to go out. I didn't know but I guessed there was some sort of cellar under the house and it seemed to me that this would be halfway to the underground room Mr Rokeby wanted. Of course I didn't know then that the planning authority would turn down his application.

'The Underland chap and I shifted this great tub of plants off the manhole cover in the patio. That was the first we knew of it that there was a manhole cover. Now that was all I wanted to know, that there was a cavity underneath the patio, I wasn't bothered about going down there or even looking down there at that juncture. In fact, to be honest with you, I was rather dressed up and I didn't fancy going down into what I knew would be a filthy hole.

'I asked the Underland chap if he had a pair of steps or a ladder with him in his van and he said he had. 'Go down there and take a look if you fancy it,' I said to him and I went back into the house to see if there was a way down from inside into that cavity.'

'You remember all this very clearly, Mr Clary,' said Lucy.

'I've a good memory. Anyway, as I say, a lot came back to me when I saw the pictures of Orcadia Cottage on television. Do you want to hear the rest?'

'If you please,' said Wexford.

'I thought there might be a trapdoor in the kitchen floor or in the hallway, but there wasn't. It seemed to be quite strange that there could be a coal hole in the back for solid fuel to be shot down and no way of getting it up from the inside. I was quite a long while inside there feeling around, tapping the walls and so on, but eventually I went back outside. I thought that if we go ahead with this — I wasn't going to take any further steps until Rokeby had got his planning permission — I'll find out from him the answer to this riddle.

'The Underland chap was outside, sitting on a garden seat on the patio. He'd put the tub back himself on the manhole cover. He'd gone down there, he said, he'd had a look, but there was just a big sort of coal storage space. I said to him I was doing no more until Rokeby had heard about his planning permission and he agreed with me and we left.'

Lucy said quietly, 'How did he look, Mr Clary?'

'What do you mean, how did he look?'

'Was he just the same as before you went into the house?'

'I didn't notice.'

'Can you give us his name?' Wexford asked.

'I don't think I ever knew it,' Clary said. 'I called him Rod.'

'We may want to see you again,' said Lucy and she made this routine undertaking sound rather menacing. A threat rather than a promise. 'I don't believe a word of it,' she said to Wexford on the Finchley Road pavement.

He laughed. 'I know what you mean, but I couldn't say I don't believe a word of it. I believe he went there and I believe they jointly shifted the manhole cover. And it's not incredible that Clary didn't want to get his nice elegant suit dirty. But that 'Rod' went down that hole

131

without finding those bodies or showing any sign that he had had sight of the most revolting and macabre sight he had ever had — that I don't believe. That he came up again and walked out on to the patio and waited for Clary to come out, that I don't believe either. Wouldn't he, however tough he was, have run into the house and shouted out about what he had found? Wouldn't he maybe have thrown up? At any rate, it would have shaken him to the core. But it didn't, or Clary says it didn't.'

'What happened then?'

'On his own showing, Clary was in the house a long time. Long enough, I think, for 'Rod' to close up the manhole, put back the tub and drive away.'

'But you said he'd be shaken to the core.'

'Not so shaken he couldn't drive round the corner and sit there to recover. I suggest he lifted up the manhole cover and when he saw what he did see from the top, he didn't fetch a ladder from his van. He saw, he understood what he saw — nothing like what it would have been had he gone down there — put the manhole cover back and dragged the tub back and drove away. God knows what Clary did next. He wasn't, or thought he wasn't, strong enough to lift the tub himself. Besides he was in his nice suit. 'Rod' wasn't a mate of his but just a builder who might or might not be helping with the construction of an underground room. Clary had already made up his mind to do no more until the planning permission did or did not come through. No doubt he went back to Finchley Road and forgot all about it until three years later when those bodies were discovered.'

'Those bodies and a fourth one, sir — er, Reg.'

'Yes, the mystery is, why did he do nothing when those bodies came to light six weeks ago?'

★　★　★

Wexford was due up at 'the big house' for dinner with Sheila and Paul and the children. He was looking forward to it. Being on his own in the evenings didn't suit him. When he looked back over his life, he realised how seldom he had been alone at home. He had gone out, been repeatedly called out, kept out most of the night sometimes, and Dora had been on her own, but he hardly ever had. Not since he was young and single, and that was longer ago than he cared to remember. It wasn't cooking a meal for himself that he minded because 'cooking' mostly meant scrambled egg on toast or sausages and chips heated up from frozen, it wasn't lack of anything to do because reading was always there to do and always done; it was being without company, preferably Dora's. He, who in his youth had had one girl-friend after another, later on had had to curb his roving eye, had now become entirely monogamous. That was excellent, completely satisfactory, but still he was lonely without her.

As he dawdled about the little house, wishing for a quick passage of the hour which must elapse before the children came to fetch him — they insisted on that — he sat down by the window that looked out over the Vale of Health.

133

It was a still quiet evening of hazy sunshine. He thought about the various men who had come to Orcadia Cottage to build (or not to build) a subterranean room. Kevin Oswin, Damian Keyworth and the Underland architect Owen Clary with his plumber who might or might not be called Rod. Oh, and there was one other that they knew almost nothing about, Oswin's 'bruv', the man called Trevor. He was surely as important as Rod, yet it seemed he wasn't a builder and as if he had just gone along for the ride.

Although he knew how cautious he must be in constructing scenarios, Wexford nevertheless began imagining one of those men — perhaps because of their superior knowledge of under-ground structures — having his attention alerted by that tub which concealed a manhole cover. It was only conjecture. It was true, though, that he might have mentioned it to Oswin or Clary, but it had never registered. And, anyway, which one? Rod or Trevor? Was it possible that one of them had come back later, perhaps when it was known when Rokeby would be out or away on holiday, and looked for himself? It was not only possible, Wexford thought, it had to be. Not necessarily those two, but one of those, Damian Keyworth, Kevin Oswin, Trevor Oswin, Owen Clary or Rod, one out of five men, whatever he might now say, had come back and explored where up till then no one had looked.

Unless, of course, it was Rokeby himself all the time. In that case, why had Rokeby called the police when he opened the manhole and found its contents? Because someone else had found them and tried to blackmail him? That would take some working out and needed time. Just now Wexford hadn't time. He heard the front door open and the little girls' feet on the stairs.

'Grandad, Mum says you're to come as you are.'

This was Amy. Anoushka had already jumped into his arms.

'What does it mean, Grandad, 'come as you are'? How could you come as you're not?'

He laughed. He was enormously pleased, because he thought Amy had inherited this from him, this way of enquiring about everything, allowing no hackneyed phrase to go unquestioned.

'It means to come in the clothes you're wearing. Not to change.'

'It's stupid.'

'No, it's not. It's everyday usage. It's good to question, Amy, but it's not good to be too censorious. OK, I'll tell you what that word means later. Let's go. I want my dinner.'

14

It was a week later. He had intended to drive back to Kingsmarkham for the weekend, but Dora phoned when he was thinking of leaving and told him she would be renting a car and bringing Sylvia with her.

'She isn't going to drive, is she?'

'Of course she isn't, Reg. I *can* drive, you know. Maybe you haven't noticed or being a man have chosen not to notice, but I passed my driving test very nearly half a century ago.'

'All right, all right.' He started laughing, noting that this was a rare occasion of laughing for pleasure and not because something was funny. 'I've missed you a lot.'

'Good,' she said. 'Excellent. Sylvia and Mary will be staying with Sheila just in case you thought you might have to make up beds.' Dora paused. 'Can you make up beds, darling?'

'I must have done long long ago in the Dark Ages but I don't recall.'

Knowing that Dora would soon be back brought him a warm feeling of satisfaction and contentment. To walk at least part of the way to Tom's office in Cricklewood would be pleasant on this fine July morning and good to think he would have no slow and tedious drive through the southern suburbs this afternoon. Tom was waiting for him with the latest on their investigations into the name 'Francine'.

'Not that there's anything you could call a discovery. I've had three nerdy types getting the best they can out of the Web and you'd be surprised how many women there are in this country called Francine. You'd expect them all to be in France, wouldn't you?'

'Maybe not in these cosmopolitan days.'

'Of course, the majority are the wrong age. That is, most aren't between twenty-nine and thirty-four. That's because we're counting on the girl whose name was on the piece of paper being between seventeen and twenty-two when it was written. But that's really only a shot in the dark.'

'You mean that the young man would have been that sort of age himself and would therefore only know a girl of that age?'

'I know that doesn't have to be the case, Reg. I said it was conjecture.'

'If you get to see any of them or speak to any of them what are you going to ask her?'

Tom hesitated. 'Well, I've spoken to one so far. Just one. She lives up in Middlesborough. Her name is Francine Miller and she's thirty, a nurse and not married. I asked her if she had ever been in a house in a street in St John's Wood, London, twelve years ago. She knew at once what I meant. I suppose everyone in the country does. 'Orcadia Cottage,' she said. 'It's about that, is it?' I didn't dare think she was the one. Of course she's not. She'd just read about it and seen it on TV. She wasn't even in London twelve years ago but still at school in Berwick. One interesting thing — if it's interesting — is that the preponderance of Francines under the age of twenty-eight is much less than over thirty. I'm not putting that very well, but you know what I mean.'

'People stopped calling their daughters Francine,' said Wexford. 'The name had begun to go out of fashion. But we're not looking for little girls anyway, are we?'

'I don't think so.' Tom sounded despondent. 'Of course I can't be sure Francine Miller was telling the truth. On the other hand, being a realist, I'm not imagining a girl of eighteen popping down to London on a day trip from the north and putting three dead bodies into a manhole in the classy district of NW8.'

Wexford smiled. It was the first time he had heard Tom — a stolid man without a sense of humour — say anything even remotely satirical. ''Francine' was written on that bit of paper alongside what is presumably a pin number and 'La Punaise'. Because *la punaise* means a pin we've assumed it's a cunning way of reminding the owner of the address book what her pin number is, but to anyone else who sees it it suggests a restaurant. I suppose it isn't or wasn't a restaurant, was it?'

'We've been there and done that,' said Tom. 'There isn't a restaurant called that anywhere in London and there wasn't in the late Nineties. Our best bet is that Francine was his girlfriend who was a student of French and he wrote down *la punaise* for her to translate it.'

'And when she'd translated it the two of them plundered poor Harriet Merton's bank account.'

'That must have been a Eureka moment.'

138

'What about the jewellery, Tom? Are we' — Wexford quickly translated that 'we' to 'you' — 'are *you* any further on that?'

'Lucy's shown it all to Mildred Jones and Mildred says, yes, it might be or it might not. It's not as if she was ever likely to be able to identify it and Anthea Gardner had never seen any of it.'

Wexford asked if he might see what printouts there were on the 'Francine' progress and a young DC called Miles Crowhurst brought him a file bulging with information. But most of it was negative. Francine Miller might be called the star attraction. Not for the first time, Wexford was wondering if enough had been done towards searching the memories of the Mertons' neighbours in the Orcadia Place — Melina Place-Abercorn Place-Alma Square area. But when he raised the subject Tom always said most of the people hadn't even been living there twelve years before, and those residents who had had been questioned in the first few days after the discovery of the bodies. The three largest houses in the vicinity had been sold and divided into apartments and only four separate dwellings remained where it might be helpful to question the residents again.

'Do it if you like,' Tom said, and added a little awkwardly, 'Better take a DC with you. I mean, how about Crowhurst?'

Because he had no standing of his own, Wexford thought, but without bitterness. After all, Tom might have said better go along with Crowhurst. Tom evidently had no intention of coming along himself.

'If you've no objection,' Wexford said, 'and if Miles Crowhurst is free, I might go along there now.' And then home to prepare for the coming of Sylvia and Mary . . .

'None at all,' said Tom, adding rather oddly, 'Be my guest.'

It was a while since Wexford had been near Orcadia Cottage. The roses were over but poppies and zinnias were out, together with a bed of stately dahlias, orange, pink and almost black, fuchsias bearing a thousand tiny red bell-shaped blossoms, and mauve and white Michaelmas daisies. And the sightseers seemed to have grown tired of their daily nothing-to-see vigils and gone home. Someone had hung a child's sock on the beak of one of the stone falcons. The property of the plump child so often here in its pushchair? The day was sunny yet hazy, utterly still and with no chilly breath to spoil the mildness.

Their project — Wexford's and Miles Crowhurst's — was a house-to-house inquiry of a limited kind. Only three households were to be questioned and these investigations were to be more in the nature of conversations. What did the Milsoms of Alma Square, David Goldberg of Melina Place and John Scott-McGregor and Sophie Baird of Hall Road know of Martin and Anne Rokeby? Would they even have known of their existence before those hideous discoveries were made under their patio?

The Milsoms were a retired couple living in a house far too large for them. Peter Milsom had answered Wexford's phone call with an immediate refusal to see them, but an intervention from

140

his wife (a whispered, 'It will only take a few minutes, Peter') changed his refusal to a grudging acceptance. Any hope Wexford might have had that Bridget Milsom had some small piece of useful information to give them was quickly dashed. They knew the Rokebys, but only to 'pass the time of day'.' 'I sometimes had a chat with Anne in the street,' Mrs Milsom told him. She spoke as if one or both of the Rokebys was dead. She had never been inside the house. 'I never really knew that Orcadia Cottage was there, what with the walls and the shrubs, you could barely see it from the road.'

'We had an anniversary party,' Peter Milsom said. 'They came to that. I think that was the last time we saw them.'

Nearest of these dwellings to Orcadia Cottage was David Goldberg's tiny house wedged between two bigger ones in Melina Place. A middle-aged man who looked ill and walked with a limp, he lived alone and told them he hadn't been outside the front door for eighteen years. His cleaner brought in food for him and anything else he might require. He had lived in his house for all those years but had few friends and had managed — as people in London can — to know none of his neighbours beyond 'passing the time of day' with them. The only people he seemed to know were John Scott-McGregor and Sophie Baird of Hall Road, by coincidence the next couple on Wexford's list. Of what he called 'the Orcadia Place business' Goldberg knew from television, which he seemed to watch obsessively and which Wexford could hear now.

Scott-McGregor had agreed on the phone to an interview but had told Crowhurst it would be useless: they knew nothing about 'those people'. Theirs was one of the newer and smaller houses in this part of St John's Wood, a 1950s redbrick of uninspiring design. And its occupants, Wexford thought, looked the kind of people who would never want to draw attention to themselves. They were strangely alike, both in their late thirties, of medium height, mousy-haired and with unmemorable features. Before she let them in, Sophie Baird greeted them on the doorstep with a little speech as to why, though her partner ran a removal company and she worked as a chief executive's PA, neither of them was at work that day. Once they were in the living room, a place which for dullness matched its owners, Wexford let Crowhurst take the initiative. He began by speaking of Orcadia Cottage, but Scott-McGregor cut him short.

'We know all that. You'd have to be deaf and blind not to know it.'

'What we would like to talk about,' Miles said, somewhat taken aback by this sharpness, 'is if you have any knowledge of the house. If, for instance, you had ever been in there or in the patio at the back.'

Sophie Baird said, 'Inside Orcadia Cottage, you mean?'

'That's right. Inside the house or in the patio while Mr Rokeby lived there.'

'I went in there to a sort of house-warming party when the Silvermans moved in,' said Sophie Baird. 'That would have been — well, at least ten years ago. Long before John moved in with me.'

'You were friends with these people? The Silvermans, I mean?'

'Not really. They were American and you know how Americans are, very friendly, speak to everyone. Devora and I, we got talking in the street, something about where was the best butchers and the next thing was they were asking me to their party. I wanted to see the inside of the house again.'

'Again?' Wexford was suddenly alerted.

'Oh, yes, didn't I say? My parents owned this house and *I* lived here till I was eighteen. My father had this house built.'

'But Orcadia Cottage? Your parents knew the Mertons?'

Sophie Baird looked at Wexford as if she thought he must be deaf or perhaps senile. 'Oh, yes, didn't I say? I'm sure I said. They were *friends*. My dad and Franklin were partners in a firm of accountants in the City. We were often in Orcadia Cottage. I was sure I'd said.'

'No, Ms Baird, but never mind. Would you like to tell us what you remember about it?'

'Well, I went there when I was a child, but mostly my dad and mum went there for dinner or drinks, that sort of thing. Only Mum got so she went off Harriet — that was Mrs Merton — and said Dad could go alone, she wasn't going to. I suppose the last time I went there would have been in about nineteen eighty-two or three.'

'Can you remember the house?'

'I'll tell you what I do remember.' Sophie suddenly became animated. She looked quite pretty, showing white even teeth in a broad smile. 'I remember the cellar. I'd never been in one before. I was about eight. Harriet was going down into the cellar to fetch something and I said could I come and we went down the stairs from the hall. She was never very nice to me, I don't think she liked children, but she let me go down there with her and she showed me the coal hole. They didn't have coal there any more . . .'

'The stairs,' said Wexford. 'The stairs went down from the hall?'

'That's right. One flight went up and another went down to the cellar. Haven't you been in there?'

Neither Wexford nor Miles Crowhurst answered her. 'Did you go out into the patio?' Wexford asked and almost before the words were out Scott-McGregor interrupted, 'What is all this in aid of?'

'We won't be long, Mr Scott-McGregor. Believe me, Ms Baird's information may be very useful. Did you go out to the patio, Ms Baird?'

'Not that time. I went another time. The first time I went there was this manhole with a cover on it. Is that the sort of thing you want to know?'

'Yes, please.'

'Well, the second time — I was about ten — there was a pot with plants on it standing on the manhole cover so that you couldn't see it. Did you know that Harriet was the girl in Simon Alpheton's painting? She didn't look much like it when I knew her.'

144

'Ms Baird,' said Miles Crowhurst, 'you have been most helpful. Thank you very much.'

Scott-McGregor turned to her. 'Well,' he said in a nasty tone, 'you are a marvel. It'll soon be ten quid to speak to you.'

'It makes you wonder,' said Miles when they were back in the car, 'why a woman stays with a guy who talks to her like that. And she seems to have been with him quite a while.'

Wexford opened the passenger door. 'I must go back for a moment. There's something I didn't ask. He won't like it, but that can't be helped.'

'Francine,' said Miles.

'Francine.' Wexford went quickly up the path. It was Sophie who answered his ring, still smiling from her recent success.

'Have I ever heard the name Francine? I was at school with someone called that. Francine Jameson. That's the only one I've ever known.'

'How old would she be now?'

Sophie pulled a face. 'Oh, dear, she was my age. She'd be thirty-seven.'

'Where can I find her?'

She gave him an address in Hampstead. 'We all met up at a school reunion about two years ago and she was there then. Is that what you want? Oh, good. I am doing well today, aren't I?' She spoke as if getting anything right was a rarity with her or perhaps that it would be rare for anything she did to be acclaimed.

He hardly knew what it was about her that made him feel he would want to talk to her again or she would want to talk to him. He had already

145

turned away, was already halfway down the path when, for the second time he went back. 'In case you need to talk to me,' he said and gave her his card.

Returning to the car, he noticed that Crowhurst had parked it between two vans, one removal size, the other large enough to carry perhaps eight people. He wondered how well Scott-McGregor's manner went down with his clients who were having their double beds and refrigerators moved.

Go home before you go to Gayton Road, he told himself. Go home and see Sylvia. Francine has been living there for at least two years and probably much longer. She won't run away in the next few hours or even by tomorrow morning. There's nothing to stop me going to find her on a Saturday. Miles drove him as far as Pattison Road and he said he would walk the rest of the way. Here, at this very point, where the Finchley Road runs up towards Golders Green, he had calculated was where Walter Hartright had met the Woman in White for the first time.

That was a novel he had loved since he was a teenager. Do young people ever read it now? Does anyone read it? Asking himself these questions was depressing. Round here was all countryside when Wilkie Collins wrote it, the Heath and pastureland extending nearly all the way down to what was then called the New Road. Tomorrow, after he had seen Francine Jameson, he would walk along the Spaniards Road to Highgate, go down the hill and find where Dick Whittington, as the sun came up, had turned and seen the streets of London paved with gold. When he was at school they had sung the round

Turn again, Whittington,
Thou worthy citizen,
Lord Mayor of London.

He let himself in to the coachhouse and Sylvia, pale-faced and shaky but well, came down the stairs and threw herself into his arms.

15

They passed the evening at Sheila and Paul's with the three children there. Sylvia had little to say about Jason Wardle's attack — his name wasn't mentioned — and her parents were careful to avoid the subject altogether. No doubt the sisters had thrashed it out when they were alone, but Wexford didn't want to know. If it could never be forgotten perhaps it could be put behind them. When Wardle was found things would, of course, be different; if he was ever found, if he hadn't disappeared abroad somewhere.

Wexford expected to sleep soundly that night and did so until the small hours. Then, when he awoke, it was to a realisation that was more a nuisance than an anxiety, but trivial things become anxieties at three in the morning. He couldn't talk to Francine Jameson because he was no longer a policeman. He no longer had a warrant card and he baulked at calling Tom on a Saturday and asking for Lucy or Miles to come with him — correction: ask Lucy or Miles to go to Gayton Road and take *him* with *them*. Could he instead present himself as a friend of Sophie Baird enquiring after her old friend? Hardly. She would simply phone.

It took him an absurdly long time, well into daylight, to decide on the simplest solution. Tell the truth. Tell her his name, what he had been and what he now was, adding that if she didn't want to talk to him or even speak the word 'no' to him, all she had to do was shut the door in his face. He got up at five and looked up her number in the phone book. She was there. Later on, at nine, he phoned the number and was asked to leave a message. Instead of that, he would go there, he thought. It was only a short walk away.

Before leaving he called Subearth Structures and asked Kevin Oswin for his brother's address and phone number. Kevin was strangely cagey about giving Trevor's address, but was eager enough to provide the phone number. It was no longer as easy as it had once been to discover the district in which someone lived from the three digits of an exchange. Wexford decided it wasn't important. Mobiles were gradually taking over from landlines and young people he knew relied entirely on their cellphones. He tried Trevor's number. After a dozen rings a woman answered and sounded as cautious as Kevin. But she gave Wexford Trevor's mobile number and when he called it the phone was answered at once.

'Don't remember much about it,' he said discouragingly. 'I only went along with Kev in the Merc because I'd nothing better to do. I never went in the house. The owner — don't recall his name — he and Kev were talking, arguing the toss; they come outside and went in again. I hung about in the lane and had a fag. Had a couple, they was so long about it.'

Wexford heard the unmistakable click of a cigarette lighter and Trevor's indrawn breath. He coughed, said, 'Kev never done the job. The place would have fell down if he had, he said. That was it. Then we went home.'

'Where's home, Mr Oswin?'

'Never you mind. All I'll say is, somewhere in West Hampstead. An Englishman's home is his castle — maybe you've never heard that. It means that's my business.' Trevor was overcome by coughing and the phone went down.

★ ★ ★

Dora was taking all three children on the London Eye, a downhill walk to Finchley Road, then on the Jubilee Line to Westminster. His own walk was shorter and by the time he reached the house whose number Sophie Baird had given him, he had convinced himself she wouldn't be in. He rang the bell and rang it again. The sound of footsteps from inside surprised him.

'Ms Jameson,' he said, 'My name is Wexford, Reginald Wexford, and I'm a former detective chief inspector. I'd like to ask you some questions, but before I do I have to explain to you that I have no official standing and no right to ask you anything.'

'Do you have any identification?'

'Yes, of course I do.' There on the doorstep he produced his driving licence, senior railcard and, although he had forgotten it was in his pocket, his passport.

She smiled, perhaps because she had seen that the passport still described him as a police officer. 'Come in. It's a bit of a mess.'

Almost everyone who invited you in said that. The ones who didn't were those who were in most need of saying it, the squalor-mongers and the compulsive rubbish hoarders. Francine Jameson's little house was clean and as tidy as most people's. In the living room a little boy of about two was sitting on the floor building an elaborate structure from Lego. At sight of Wexford he got up and went to his mother, clutching her round the knees. She picked him up.

'I'm afraid William is rather shy.'

He said, 'Hallo, William,' in that enthusiastic tone he had long ago learnt that children love, and sat down in the chair Francine Jameson indicated. She was a rather tall, slim woman with dark hair tightly drawn back and tied in a ponytail.

'What did you want to ask me?'

'You will have heard about the — er, discoveries at Orcadia Cottage in St John's Wood.' She looked a little bewildered. 'The place where' — he didn't want to say too much in front of the child — 'there were some unpleasant discoveries made under a manhole in the patio.'

William said, 'Patio,' and then, 'patio, patio, catio, matio.'

'Yes, darling, you *are* clever,' said his mother and to Wexford, 'I read about it in the paper. What has it to do with me?'

'Have you ever been to Orcadia Cottage?' She shook her head, mystified. 'Do the names Franklin and Harriet Merton mean anything to you?'

'I've never heard of them.'

'*La punaise?*'

'It's French. It means a pin.'

'Yes, but it's quite an unusual word. Would you mind telling me how you come to know what it means?'

'I wouldn't mind at all.' She laughed. 'I teach French. That's what I do. I teach French at Francis Holland.'

It must be a school, he thought. He got up, thanked her. 'Do you happen to know anyone else with your first name?'

'Francine? I don't think so. Only my mother.'

'And preferably your sort of age.'

'I've got it because my mother's French and it's her name. She's called Francine Seguin and when she and my father were divorced she reverted to her maiden name. But you don't want to hear this. You're looking for a young woman and my mother's nearly seventy.'

'Does she live in this country?'

'In Highgate,' said Francine Jameson, 'but I can't see how she'd be any help to you.'

Wexford, walking up the hill again, was inclined to agree with her. She lived in Highgate, though, where he was going. Abruptly, he turned back and struck out across the Heath past Hampstead Ponds. Not that he would look for Francine Seguin. There was no point. Unless there was in existence a society composed of women called Francine — a most unlikely contingency — and if there was Tom Ede would know about it by now. It might be that finding their Francine, the Orcadia Cottage Francine,

152

wasn't necessary. Better by far to get back to finding the builder who had put to use the knowledge he had picked up of the patio's subterranean layout.

Walking, he had decided when he first took it up in a serious way, was the best occupation for thinking. Better than sitting in an armchair where your thoughts tended to send you to sleep, better than in bed at night when the post-midnight madness distorted your mindset. He assembled his thoughts as he walked briskly across the open heath, forced to the unwelcome conclusion that so far, after innumerable interviews, Internet incursions and repeated assessments of information, they had really discovered nothing about the occupants of the tomb except what had been almost obvious from the start, that the older woman in there had been Harriet Merton. From the start, too, they had known — or DNA had revealed — that there was some sort of blood relationship between the two men. Was that all?

Well, they also knew that three of the bodies had been there for twelve years and one for only about two. Lucy had said that Clary had a good many questions to answer, but so did the Underland company. Would they have records of workmen they had employed, even casual labour? That didn't matter, he thought. Clary would know, Clary and perhaps that unknown quantity his wife Robyn Chilvers. They must make in-depth interviewing of those two their priority, he thought. Monday morning's task. If only Tom Ede would agree . . .

★ ★ ★

'I can't talk to Mother,' Sylvia said. 'Well, I mean she won't talk to me about what happened and if I mention Jason she clams up or changes the subject in a very obvious sort of way.'

'Do you want to talk to her about it?' Wexford asked.

'I want to feel I can, not that I have to pretend I was attacked by someone I didn't know, which is how it is now. Or pretend I wasn't attacked at all. Mother is horrified that I had a relationship with someone seventeen years younger than myself, but she wouldn't be if I was the man and Jason the woman. And she thinks I was — well, exposing Mary to some sort of corruption but I wasn't, I was very careful with Mary. Every time Jason and I — well, when we met — Mary was with Mary Beaumont; she's always spent a lot of time with her, she loves her a lot. That's why, when we were in the car and I could tell a row was about to happen, I let Mary out of the car and watched her run into Mary Beaumont's. I saw her jump into Mary's arms. Mother thinks I sort of pushed her out of the car and left her in the road, which isn't so at all.'

'I think you have to ask yourself whether you wouldn't rather have a mother with strict principles than an amoral one.'

'To tell you the truth, I sometimes wonder.'

'Where do you think Jason is now, Sylvia?'

'If I knew I'd have told Mike. I wouldn't shelter him.' Sylvia reached for her glass of wine. 'He wanted to marry me, you know.'

154

'Yes, I gathered that.'

'The thing was — and you'll have heard this from countless men in this sort of situation — the thing was when I said no, I didn't want to be married, he said that if he couldn't have me no one should. He said it over and over and I took no notice, and the last time he said it he stabbed me.' She gave a little nervous laugh and put her hand up to where the dressing on her scar pushed out the fabric of her sweater. 'He said he wasn't aiming for my heart because I had no heart. I'd like to have told Mother all that, but it's impossible to say things to someone who won't receive them.'

'I shall take you home myself next week,' Wexford said. 'I want to have a talk with Mike.'

'Not about me?' Sylvia looked alarmed. 'I've told him everything.'

'Not about you. About this case I'm supposed to be helping with up here, though there's no sign I've done any good so far. Talking to Mike may help me.'

★   ★   ★

But first must come another talk with Owen Clary and his wife. Tom Ede agreed, but rather grudgingly, Wexford thought. He could tell that Tom was already finding his methods eccentric. There was, Tom suggested, too much imagination involved in this constructed scenario of Clary and 'Rod' at Orcadia Cottage. What evidence did Wexford have for what he alleged Rod had done while Clary was inside the house?

155

'I don't have any evidence. If I did I wouldn't need to talk to Clary or Rod because this business would be nearly solved. You say I'm acting on my imagination and you may be right, but I see it as acting from my knowledge of human nature. I just don't think we should let it go without at least talking to this Rod.'

'Well, as I say, you do that small thing. I'll get Lucy to go along to Clary's home and you go with her if you want.' It was a subtly different form of words from what had been said to him before. This time he was accompanying her, not she him. But that was the way it was bound to be, Wexford told himself.

'I said at the time that I didn't believe a word of what Clary said,' Lucy said when they set off for the tall block of Maida Vale flats where Clary and his wife lived. It was she, Robyn Chilvers, who had told them on the phone that she would be glad to see them. Her husband would be there too, of course. It so happened that both would be working from home that day while the heating was being serviced in their Finchley Road offices.

Handsome men don't always marry good-looking women. Indeed, it is a phenomenon Wexford had often noticed that tall, elegant men with hawk's profiles like Clary commonly pair up with dumpy women with fat cheeks and small eyes and 'difficult' hair like Robyn Chilvers. It was even stranger that while he seemed a subtle and devious person, she immediately gave the impression of frank and open straightforwardness.

Their home was a black and chrome and ivory-white minimalist penthouse, a huge picture window affording a view across north London to the distant Harrow-on-the-Hill. Wexford and Lucy sat down on a very uncomfortable armless black sofa. Clary stood looking at them while his wife bustled in with double espressos in black cups on a white tray.

'I've told you everything I remember about that visit to whatever that so-called cottage is called,' Clary was saying rather sourly. 'You should be asking Underland for the name of their plumber, not me.'

'Except that they have gone out of business,' said Lucy, trying not to make a face at the first taste of the coffee. She said to Wexford afterwards that she thought it was taking the roof of her mouth off. 'They know nothing about a plumber called Rod who worked for them three years ago.'

'Well, I'm sorry but I can't help you.'

'But you can, darling,' said Robyn Chilvers. 'Rod, you said? He didn't just work for Underland, he did a job for us. Don't you remember when the dishwasher leaked? It can't have been more than a year ago. He'd done a job for us before and I had his phone number and I called him and he came within the hour. He was very efficient.'

'You mean that's the same man? I suppose I do remember, Robyn. I just didn't connect the two.'

'Do you still have that number, Ms Chilvers?'

'I'm sure I do. I'll get it.'

She was rather a long time. While she was away Clary paced up and down the room. Like a panther, Wexford said to Lucy afterwards. They sat there on the rock-hard seat, staring out at

157

London's houses and church spires and blocks and trees and green spaces while Clary walked up and down in silence. Robyn Chilvers returned at last with a yellow Post-it on which she had written *Rod Horndon* and a mobile number. Clary turned round and instead of looking displeased, which was what Wexford expected, bestowed on his wife a smile of approval and patted her affectionately on the shoulder. Once they had said they were leaving, he became warmer and more expansive, apologising for not being able to give any more help.

'I am beginning to think,' Wexford said later, 'that whatever happened the first time, the second visit Clary with Rod paid to Orcadia Cottage was quite different from the way Clary says it was. Why were there two visits anyway? Clary must have had some idea of what he was going to be looking at. Why not take a plumber with him the first time? The second time Rokeby and his wife were out. I'm wondering if this was very much to Clary's advantage. If maybe Rokeby named several days on which Clary could come, but said that on one of them he and his wife would have to go out — and that was the one Clary picked. Will you call that number, Lucy? It's a bit dodgy for me to do it.'

'Why? Oh, I see. Yes, of course I will. You mean he can't very well refuse to see me but he could you?'

'Something like that,' Wexford said.

* * *

158

People change their mobile numbers and this was what Rod Horndon had done. Lucy wasn't going to be defeated by a little difficulty like that. She explored phone books, electoral registers and finally found Horndon where she hadn't really expected him, on his own website. He and a friend, it appeared, had started their own building company — 'Small but Specialist' being their way of describing themselves — which had weathered the recession. To his amusement and some admiration, Wexford saw that they traded and relied on the slogan, 'We Keep our Promises' and boasted that they never failed to come on the day and at the time they said they would.

'I can see that would be a useful gimmick,' Wexford said. 'Original if not unique.'

'I might even use them myself,' Miles Crowhurst said. 'Not to have to wait in all day for builders and then have them not come, that would be something. I could get them to put in my new bathroom.'

'Never mind your bathroom,' said Tom. 'Just phone this Horndon. You've got three or four possible numbers there.'

But Rod Horndon, according to his teenage daughter, had gone on holiday with her mother to the Caribbean and wasn't expected back for another two weeks.

'I wish I could take my wife to the Caribbean,' said Tom in a gloomy tone. 'Chance'd be a fine thing. Plumbers are always rolling in money. If I had my time over again I'd go in for the pipework. The Met wouldn't see me for dust.'

16

Mary made a scene when Sylvia told her they were going home. She wanted to stay with her cousins and behaved uncharacteristically (according to her mother) when told they would be leaving on Friday afternoon with Grandma and Grandad. There was some crying and stamping of feet.

'Why not leave her here?'

Sylvia hugged her sister. 'Would that be all right? Wouldn't you mind?'

'Ask Gudrun. If she's happy about it I shall be.'

So Mary was left behind with Amy and Anoushka in the care of their nanny who told them that it would be a pleasure as Mary was much less naughty than the other two. 'Grandad,' said Amy, 'do you think she'll learn to be as naughty as us in just one week?'

Wexford said he wouldn't be surprised. He drove Sylvia back to Great Thatto, reaching there at about five in the afternoon, and he and Dora went into the house with her. Dora was trying, and had been trying during the last part of the journey, to persuade her to come home with them and stay for the three nights before they returned to London.

'I really do want to be on my own for a while,' Sylvia insisted. 'Ben's coming home just for Sunday, and on Monday I mean to start back at

160

work. I'm perfectly well. I shouldn't skive off any longer.'

Dora said rather petulantly, 'You never told me social services expect you back so soon.'

'They don't. I hope they'll be pleasantly surprised.'

Wexford was to remember those words. No Mary, no other Mary, no pre-school class head, no workplace chasing her. It would add up . . .

He dropped Dora at their own house and went to return the rented car to the car hire place in the High Street. Next morning Sylvia phoned to say all was well and she was fine. Wexford took the call and he thought she sounded very tired and rather nervous, but wasn't that normal? She had been through a lot. He was due to meet Burden for a drink in the Olive and Dove at six and Dora was determined to spend the evening at the Old Rectory with Sylvia. She would cook their dinner and had suggested that her daughter should invite more people and make a small homecoming party of it. She had even named two or three old friends of Sylvia's and had suggested — Wexford warned her not to — that Neil Fairfax, Sylvia's ex-husband, might be among them. Wexford expected Sylvia to explode but her reaction was uncharacteristic. No, that wasn't a good idea. No, thanks, no dinner would be needed, she wasn't eating much, and really it would be better if her mother didn't come at all. She meant to go to bed early and watch television.

Wexford left for the Olive and Dove, promising to get home early. He suspected that Dora would make a fresh onslaught on Sylvia once he was out of the way, and he understood. He could tell how worried she was and that perhaps she had reason to worry. She had always been a deeply concerned mother if rather too prone to interfere in her daughters' lives. But he could understand that too.

Even though he had never been away from Kingsmarkham for long since his retirement, those five or sometimes twelve days in London at a stretch, he noticed each time he went home the small changes which had taken place in his absences. Last time, for instance, a big old house in York Street, not protected by listing, had been pulled down, leaving a desolate building site behind. This time a whole row of new trees, sturdy hornbeam saplings, had been planted along Orchard Road. He noticed these things particularly because of his new walking regimen. It scarcely occurred to him to use any other means of getting from his house to the Olive and Dove, whereas, once and not long ago, he would have had to make a determined effort not to take the car and to tell himself that he was only walking so that he need not avoid alcohol.

Burden was already there. Wexford sometimes thought how awkward it was for Englishmen to greet each other, even in the case of close friends. Continental Europeans would have shaken hands or even embraced. Arabs and many Asians would have embraced and kissed, even to that extraordinary fashion he had only seen on the screen, of kissing on one cheek, then the other and then the first one again. Secretly, in those wakeful, vaguely mad times of the night, he thought that he would quite like to embrace Burden when they met after an absence, though he drew the line at that triple kissing. Thinking of telling Burden this and his reaction — a kind of incredulous but well-veiled horror — made Wexford laugh out loud.

'What's funny?' Burden brought their two red wines to the table.

'Oh, nothing.'

'My grandma who lived until I was about eight used to tell me about some comedian on the music halls when she was about eight herself. His name was Ernie Lotinga — isn't it strange I can remember that, all those years ago? Anyway, his catchphrase when he'd cracked a joke was to put on this deadpan face and say, 'I don't see anything funny to laugh at.' Apparently it rocked them in the aisles.'

'I've heard of him,' Wexford said. 'He was T. S. Eliot's favourite comedian.'

Burden wasn't interested in that, as Wexford had known he wouldn't be. 'How are you getting on with the bodies in the coal hole?'

'Not very well. We can still only identify one of them and she was pretty obvious from the first. How would you find a woman who is probably about thirty, not particularly honest unless she's changed a lot, most likely a Londoner, speaks French or is French, of the name of Francine?'

Burden suggested all the methods Tom Ede had used. 'But I suppose there are a lot of them?'

'Too many. You see, I've said she's probably about thirty and she won't be much younger, but she may be a lot older.' He told Burden about *La*

Punaise and the woman's name written on the slip of paper. 'Although the assumption is that he intended to ask this woman for a translation, there's nothing to tell us that she was his sort of age. She might be his former teacher or a friend of his mother's or a neighbour.'

'She might be a murderer.'

'It has crossed my mind.'

'You could advertise for her. If she killed them she won't reply, but you've no reason to think she did, have you?'

'None. Advertise for her how? She would have to be — well, distinguished by her association with Orcadia Cottage on the lines of 'Will Francine who had a connection with Orcadia Cottage, Orcadia Place, London NW8 twelve years ago, please get in touch with the Metropolitan Police . . . '? You can see what that could lead to, the real Francine not replying because although she was asked to translate something twelve years ago, she had never heard of Orcadia Cottage until the bodies were discovered in the vault and she read about it in the papers. And hundreds of false Francines making all sorts of crazy claims.'

'You could mention the translation, but you don't really know why her name was on the same piece of paper with that French word? You don't really know that, do you? He, whoever he is or was, might have written *La Punaise* on the paper because he thought it was a restaurant and the number could be Francine's phone number without the area code because he already knew those three digits.'

'I've told you, Mike, we don't really know. I can go and see this woman in Highgate, but she's no more likely to be *the* Francine than any of those Tom has checked on.'

Burden helped himself to an olive, speared on the end of a cocktail stick. 'So what are you doing? What will you be doing when you go back?'

'What we've been doing all along,' Wexford said. 'Dodging between a bunch of architects, builders and plumbers and possible Francines. Paying yet another visit to Martin Rokeby and another to Anthea Gardner and Mildred Jones, though as far as I can see they have nothing else to tell us.'

'Your Francine may be the young woman in — what do you call it? — the vault. Have you thought of that?'

'She would have had to be about twelve when the other bodies were put in there.'

'Why not?'

It had been a less rewarding encounter than he had expected. This was hardly Burden's fault, Wexford reflected on the way home. There was so little to go on, nothing that he and Tom and Lucy with a whole team of investigators hadn't already thrashed through. He had started with such high hopes and he believed Tom had had high hopes for him. Or perhaps that was something he imagined and Tom had never seen him as any more than someone to talk to about the case, to act as a kind of sounding board on which to bounce off ideas. All he had done was find a car and all Forensics could do was find

165

that that car had transported the body of Keith or Kenneth Bray, Gray or Greig.

Rain had begun to fall, thin as a mist at first but gradually increasing, so that he asked himself why he hadn't brought a raincoat or an umbrella. By the time he reached home he was soaked and he went straight upstairs to change before finding Dora.

'Walking has its pitfalls,' Wexford said, 'when you don't come to it till late in life. Have you spoken to Sylvia while I was out?'

'She phoned. She said she'd go to bed early and watch television and that was what she was doing. It was a relief to hear from her.'

He took hold of her hand. 'What have you been imagining now?'

She sighed a little. 'Darling, you remember a few years back Sylvia had that — friend. I don't want to say boyfriend and I just *can't* say partner. And he was violent to her and sort of imprisoned her and you and I went over and you knocked him down and got rid of him.'

'Of course I remember him.'

'Well, I've been wondering if she sort of attracts men like that, even if she wants men like that and if this Jason might come to her again, might even be with her now. So her phoning was an enormous relief.'

'If he came,' Wexford said, 'because she's come back and he knows it, she won't let him in.'

'Yes, but there's something I have to tell you. It's what she told me on the phone just now.' Dora freed her hand from his and closed it over the other one. 'He's got a key.'

166

Wexford said nothing. He sat very still.

'It's a front-door key. I asked her if the police know and she said, 'What would be the point of telling them?' Having a key doesn't mean he can get in if she keeps her front door locked and bolted, and apparently she does.'

Wexford picked up the phone and called Sylvia's mobile number. The message answered him. He called it again and this time she answered.

'Is your front door bolted on the inside, Sylvia?'

'I think so. I'm in bed.'

'Go down and check. Take your phone with you.'

She made exasperated noises, sighs and the kind of sound that accompanies the rolling of eyes. He heard her feet on the stairs. Her voice came after a brief silence. 'All right, Dad. I'm going to bolt the door now.'

'Let me hear it,' he said.

First one bolt, then the other, ground across, the upper one with a squeak, the lower with a kind of growl.

'All right,' he said. 'Tomorrow you will have the lock changed. You won't do it unless I make you, so I shall come over first thing in the morning and call a locksmith myself. See you at eight. Good night.'

'Good night, Dad.' She sounded very subdued.

* * *

'D'you want to come?' he said to Dora at seven.

'I don't think so, darling.' She was still half-asleep. 'Sylvia won't want an invasion.'

Fog had been forecast and, looking out of the window, he thought at first it would be unwise to drive. It was possible to see to the other side of the road, but no further. Still, when he had made himself tea, taken a cup upstairs to Dora and eaten a slice of toast and Marmite, the mist had begun to clear and a weak sun appeared.

The road to Great Thatto passed through some of the prettiest countryside in this part of Sussex, a place of high hills and deep valleys, thickly wooded but dotted here and there with thatched cottages and newer houses. The older dwellings had that self-conscious look of cottages which have been half-timbered, exquisitely thatched with enduring reed and painted in the correct local colours of homes owned by middle-class householders with pretensions. There was little traffic, due perhaps to the fog which came and went, settling in pockets where least expected and suddenly disappearing altogether on the outskirts of Great Thatto. Mary Beaumont was in her front garden, picking asters and gypsophila. She recognised the car and waved to him.

The Old Rectory had been Sylvia's home for years now, since her sons were little, and long before she and her husband separated and Neil left the house for her and their children. Wexford had been there innumerable times. Yet now, as he drove through the open gates and up the drive, as the untended trees and bushes gave place to a wide space, he seemed to see the house with new eyes. It was a very big house. Had he ever realised before quite how big it was? Built in the middle of the nineteenth century for the rector of a parish, it had needed to be large enough to accommodate the incumbent and his wife, five or six children and all the panoply of servants a Victorian household apparently required. Now it was home to one woman and a little girl. Occasionally, in holidays, when they weren't off somewhere with friends or exploring foreign parts, to that little girl's brothers.

She should sell it and move, he thought. Here, in beautiful countryside, a house of this size would fetch a fortune. But it wasn't for him to tell her what she must know already. Children of any age never take advice from their parents. It was a rule of life and perhaps might stand as Wexford's fifteenth law or something like that. He rang the doorbell and had the satisfaction of hearing her draw back the bolts.

'Oh, Dad, you're very punctual.' She kissed him, something which was by no means inevitable with her. 'I'd have got the locksmith myself, you know, if you'd told me to.'

'Oh, really? You amaze me.'

She laughed. 'Have you had breakfast?'

'A bit of toast.'

'Let me cook you breakfast. You've got so thin you can eat bacon and eggs sometimes, can't you?'

'All right,' he said. 'That will be nice. I don't suppose I can phone a locksmith before nine, but I can go and look some of them up in the Yellow

Pages. Where are your phone books?'

It was rather an untidy house. Children, especially teenagers are seldom neat and orderly and Robin and Ben tended to leave their property all over the house. Where they had used an item, rather than where it was kept, was inevitably where it remained. But that, Wexford thought, would hardly apply to a phone directory, the last thing needed by people in their late teens who conducted all their business on cellphones, BlackBerries or iPhones. He went back to the kitchen where Sylvia was breaking eggs into a pan on the Aga.

'No, sorry, Dad. It was before Jason — well, you know what. There was a leaking pipe in Ben's room and I took the Yellow Pages up there to phone a plumber and sort of describe what was happening. It'll be up there still, I expect. I'll get it when I've done your breakfast.'

Plumbers, thought Wexford, they got everywhere. 'I'll get it,' he said, destined to be enormously glad that he had insisted.

All the bedrooms in use but Ben's were on the first floor, Sylvia's very large and facing the front, Robin's and Mary's at the back and separated by a spare room, but Ben's was on the top, on the second floor and at the end of the passage. The last time Wexford had been in Ben's room was all of twelve years ago, maybe fourteen, when he had gone in to read the little boy a bedtime story. He opened the door.

He drew in his breath, but made no other sound. From a hook in the ceiling a man's body was hanging, its feet about a yard from the floor.

It was naked. Jason Wardle, Wexford thought. It had to be Jason Wardle. He had stood on a chair, adjusted the rope round his neck and kicked the chair away. It lay on its side beside the pendent central lamp, which he must have taken down in order to do the deed. Discarded clothes lay on Ben's bed.

Sylvia's voice called out, 'Dad, what are you doing?' and he heard her feet on the stairs.

Outside the room in a second, he slammed the door behind him and ran down to seize her in his arms. 'Don't go up there, don't,' was all he said.

17

Mobile phones make life a lot easier. This was Burden's opinion, offered after they had managed to redirect the homecoming Ben to his grandparents' house. 'Yes and no,' said Wexford, who privately believed that it was all right when the police had them but a restriction of freedom to other people.

'I shall never be able to live in that house again,' Sylvia had said when told what her father had found. 'I'd rather sleep in the street. When I think how I slept there last night and he — *that* — was — well, just above my head . . . '

'I shall take you home to your mother,' Wexford said, 'and Ben will come to you there.'

'I shall never come back here.'

'You should wait a while before making decisions like that,' Wexford said as they left Great Thatto behind and entered the road that passed through Thatto Wood. He was driving quite slowly because they had both had a shock and he braked hard when a deer ran across in front of them. 'It may be enough for you never to use that room again. Empty it of furniture and lock the door.'

Even as he spoke he thought of what that would mean, your *home* in which one room was forbidden, in a way haunted, because someone had hanged himself inside it. We don't use that room, it's been shut up for years. Something terrible happened inside there . . . 'No, I expect you're right,' he said, and he felt her shivering beside him. Of course she was in shock, severe shock, and that perhaps accounted for her showing no grief.

It was he who told his grandson Ben. He had allowed for the macabre imagination of the teenager and he wasn't surprised when the boy's eyes expanded in a not altogether horrified way. 'In my bedroom? Wow, but that's gross. Is he still there?'

'I shouldn't think so.'

If Jason Wardle had killed himself in Ben's bedroom to cause Sylvia distress through distressing her son, he had a poor idea of the psyche of his near contemporaries. Of course it would have been a different matter if Ben had actually seen the hanging body — or would it? Wexford wondered uncomfortably how inured these children were — he naturally thought of them as children — by what they saw on television and to a far greater extent on the Internet. Still, none knew better than he the difference between a dead body and the representation of one. Lady Macbeth couldn't have been more wrong when she said that the sleeping and the dead were but as pictures. The sleeping might be, but the dead were lost and gone, as if they had never been alive.

When Burden arrived Sylvia was with her mother in the kitchen, repeating what had become almost a mantra. 'I can never go back to that house, I never can. I can never go back there.'

After Burden had spoken to her Wexford took him into the living room. 'If she means it, that house won't be easy to sell. A suicide doesn't damage a house as much as murder, but it doesn't improve its saleability.'

'It's not in the same league as your Orcadia Cottage,' Burden said.

'No. I suppose Rokeby knows that. He'll be lucky if he ever sells that place. But back to Sylvia. I think she should stay here, don't you? It's big enough for all of them, but it's seldom they're all at home at once.'

'You never did like the Old Rectory.'

'No, I never did. Sylvia won't have to attend the inquest, will she?'

'I don't see why she should,' said Burden. 'You will. You found the body.'

'Well, it wouldn't be the first time. Or the hundredth, come to that. What I should like would be for none of that stuff about her affair with a boy of twenty-one coming out. So far all the papers have got is that Sylvia was stabbed and a young man the police wanted to question was missing.'

'It will come out, Reg. It's inevitable. You must grin and bear it.'

'I'll bear it, but I won't grin,' said Wexford. 'Anyway, it's Sylvia who'll have to bear it, poor girl. But, Mike, how long had he been in the house before he killed himself? I haven't mentioned this to anyone else. Had he come in before Sylvia returned, maybe days or even a week before? Thank God she hasn't thought of that.'

174

'That too will come out at the inquest. If it's known. If there's any way of knowing it.'

Wexford sighed. 'Let's go into the kitchen and I'll make you a cup of delicious instant coffee. Why does it taste like quite a different drink from the real stuff?'

'I shall just go back to pack up my clothes,' Sylvia was saying. 'Just for that. I shan't stay a minute longer than I have to.'

Dora laid her hand over her daughter's. 'I've told her she must live here as long as she likes, Reg.'

'I've come to tell her the same thing,' said Wexford. 'We can be in London for as long as it takes to sell the Old Rectory and buy somewhere else.'

Dora had made coffee and not the instant kind. They sat round the table and Burden explained to Sylvia what the inquest would involve, but that she wouldn't be required to be there. Then he told her that the media would want details from Kingsmarkham Police and that would mean from him.

'I will do what I can, Sylvia,' he said, 'but there's a limit to what I can do and then they'll come to you.'

'I know. I can stand it so long as I don't have to go back to *that house*.'

But she went back with her father in the late afternoon to fetch her clothes and Mary's. 'And Ben's and Robin's, Dad.'

'They can fetch their own when they like.'

'Oh, but I can't expose them to the horror of going there.'

'Believe me,' he said, 'they won't mind. They aren't going to feel it like you do.'

He saw her into the house, but before going in himself he walked round the garden. Wilderness was more the word for it, acres and acres of hayfields, unkempt hedgerows, patches of woodland and overgrown ditches. Half-in, half-out one of these, almost covered by brambles, he found Sylvia's car, the unwieldy four-by-four, its ignition key still inside. He'd tell her, but not yet. Tell Burden first and get someone to haul it out.

She was packing. In broad daylight, the front door open and all the windows, she seemed calm and steady enough. Every suitcase she possessed as well as two plastic sacks and a large cardboard crate were being filled. What a lot of clothes women had! The clothes they needed for utilitarian purposes he understood, but even here questions arose he couldn't answer. One raincoat, yes, but five? Two or three 'nice' dresses for parties, he was used to that, but fifteen? And skirts and suits and trousers, dozens of pairs of these and sweaters and 'tops' beyond counting. For a while he watched it all being packed, wondering where it was going to be put in his house, and where her daughter's clothes were going to be put and her sons', not to mention computers and sports equipment and guitars and trainers. He supposed he should be thankful that now music could be downloaded on to iPods there would at least be no CDs.

He revisited Ben's bedroom. The body had, of course, long gone. Strange that when murder or suicide had happened in a room that room was invested with horror and fear, even if that particular killing had left no traces behind, or none that couldn't be easily removed. A man had stood here with a rope in his hand, had climbed on to a chair and unhooked a lamp that hung on a chain from a hook in the ceiling. The only thought in his head was of ending his life and how he would do it, yet he had laid the lamp down gently, careful not to damage any part of it. He had taken off his clothes — why? — folded them and placed them on the bed. He had wished to be naked when he killed himself and that she should find him naked. Did it signify something? That she had loved his nakedness because he was young and strong? You don't go there when it's your daughter you're thinking of, Wexford thought. Perhaps he was naked only to expose himself as so in her power as to be helpless and entirely vulnerable before her. For Wardle had intended Sylvia to find him, not Ben, of course he did. He would know that she would go into that room to check that all was as should be before Ben next came home.

Wexford glanced round him at all the paraphernalia in the room, the 'stuff' necessary to a sixteen-year-old if he is to live according to today's teenage standards of what living meant. And he saw that computers and tennis racquets and musical instruments and trainers were only the half of it. Was his house to be invaded by amplifying equipment for use with that enormous guitar? It was all very well in this vast rectory where you could make intolerable noise in one part of it and hear nothing two floors and six rooms away. Now he knew why Ben had slept there and he laughed to himself, *at* himself, for his past mild indignation that his younger grandson had been exiled to this distant place.

For some reason he explored the whole house, going into every room as if he expected to find more hanging bodies. As in some horror film, he thought, where every door opened on to yet another grisly death's head. Of course there was nothing. He found the Yellow Pages Sylvia had said was in Ben's room, but turned out to be in the spare room between Robin's room and Mary's and went along to Sylvia's room where she was putting the last of her fifty-two pairs of shoes into the crate. It took a long time to carry it all downstairs and out to the car. It was a big car, but still the inside as well as the boot were filled. He thought as he squeezed in the final bag how much he disliked the idea — so much more than an idea now — of Sylvia and her three children all living in his house, living with these mountains of baggage, of which this car-full was only the start. They would spread their property over every square inch, make their horrible noise so that his kind, quiet neighbours would be forced to complain, play ball games in his garden, Ben and Mary constantly going next door to ask for their ball back. Of course the boys wouldn't always be there, but they would be there in their intolerably long holidays. And it would go on for months, months and months if not years.

He would not say a word. Well, he would say many words to Dora and she would say the same words to him, but none to Sylvia and his grandchildren. Of course he wouldn't. He was her father, their grandfather, their progenitor, and this was the kind of thing you had to put up with if you were a parent. Sooner or later it or something like it came to all parents and you were lucky if it didn't. He thought of the older brother, not the Prodigal Son who was a misbehaving spendthrift, but the older brother that his father reassured. 'Thou art ever with me and all that I have is thine . . . '

'It's a blessing we've got the coachhouse,' Dora said on the following Wednesday when they were on their way back to London.

On the Sunday Robin had come home from Cambridge in his old banger and shifted all his property and Mary's from the Old Rectory to Wexford's house in Kingsmarkham. Next day and the next Ben, in a friend's car driven by a friend, had removed all his property except the bare furniture from his own room and brought it to his grandparents'. Sylvia took over Wexford and Dora's bedroom, which she intended to share with Mary. Ben and Robin's property occupied so much space that it overflowed on to the landing and the overspill had to be put in the garage. Sylvia had taken the news of her car without any sign of emotion. That Jason Wardle must have driven it to the Old Rectory and abandoned it there perhaps only hours before hanging himself appeared not to affect her. It was only the thought of the house which upset her.

The mantra had varied and had now become,

'It's so sweet of you to let us live here. We're enormously grateful. I'm sure you really hate it. But you do realise I could never, never go back there.'

They had been in the coachhouse for just seven minutes when Sheila arrived, dying (as she said) to hear all about it. Dora told all and in the detail Sheila seemed to require. For his part Wexford said nothing. He was thinking how sad it was that Sylvia, whose lover had died by his own hand, showed no sorrow.

18

Two weeks had gone by and two days more. Wexford had been told there was 'no rush' for him to come back. Tom said to take his time and meanwhile here was something for him to think about: Forensics had discovered hairs in the boot of the Edsel and these afforded sufficient DNA to be compared with that taken from the older man's remains. Not much help, Wexford thought. All such a comparison could show was that the older man had put his head inside the Edsel's boot or that his body had been carried there. But perhaps it was a small step forward.

He walked into Tom's office to find the detective superintendent in a state of excitement. 'I've found her.' Tom was ebullient. 'She's the one. She ticks all the boxes.'

If there was a cliché Wexford hated more than 'level playing field' or 'kicking into the long grass' it was the one about ticking all the boxes. But he merely looked enquiring.

'Francine, I mean. Miles found her on the Internet, I don't know how. I'm more or less computer illiterate, it's a closed book to me. But he found her and she's coming in. I've talked to her on the phone. She knows all about Orcadia Cottage, she's called Francine Withers, thirty years old, had a relationship with a man called Keith Chiltern that ended when he disappeared twelve years ago.'

Wexford nodded. 'Where's she coming from?'

'High Wycombe. She manages a supermarket there. She's been married and divorced, no children. She's the one, Reg.'

'Why is she coming here? I'd have expected us — you, that is — to go to her.'

'We would have. She volunteered, said she'd like to come here.'

Wexford laughed, said there was no accounting for tastes and thus contributing a cliché of his own. As he had always feared, it was catching. Rather belatedly, Tom asked after Sylvia and Wexford kept his reply as short as he decently could. A young WPC brought in coffee. The tray had just been removed when Ms Francine Withers was announced.

The same WPC brought her in. She was of medium height, a little overweight, with blonde hair, black at the roots and a broad, handsome, over-made-up face, full mouth, straight nose and the kind of staring eyes that look as if their owner has just seen something shocking. As he must have looked, Wexford thought, when he walked into Ben's room and saw the hanged man. She had dressed carefully, that was apparent, but not very judiciously in a too-short skirt, tight jumper and the kind of cropped jacket that shows off the flaws in an imperfect waistline. Her boots were suitable for the depths of winter rather than a late summer day.

'Good of you to come, Ms Withers,' Tom said.

Francine Withers held out her hand, first to Tom, then to Wexford, and said she was pleased to meet them. 'I had to take the day off work,' she said, 'and I don't get paid if I do that. But I thought it was my duty to come. You have to be a good citizen, don't you?'

Neither Tom nor Wexford replied to this. It is the kind of question that makes seasoned policemen distrust the speaker.

'Now, Ms Withers,' Tom began, 'perhaps you'll take us back to when you first met Mr Chiltern. That was his name, wasn't it? Chiltern?'

'That's right. Keith Chiltern.'

'You were living in High Wycombe at the time and so was he?'

'Oh, no. I only went to High Wycombe when I got married. My husband came from King's Langley. I used to live in London, in Battersea, and so did Keith. I was friendly with this girl and she introduced me to her brother, that was Keith, and we started going out. He was in the building trade, Keith was. It would have been 1996 we started going out.'

Wexford said, 'Where was he living?'

'In Clapham. I don't remember the address, I only went there once. I had a room in Lavender Hill Road and he used to come there. I lived there till I got married in 2003. He was working on this Orcadia Cottage. It wasn't very big but very posh. The people who owned it went away and he said we could go and stay there, they wouldn't mind, while he did some work on the patio. There was a manhole thing in the patio and he was doing something to it. I don't know what, I didn't take much interest.'

'Just a moment, Ms Withers,' Wexford said.

'When exactly would this have been? Nineteen ninety-six or later?'

'I can't remember dates like that. It was summer. I reckon it must have been '96. The people who owned the place were called Merton, I do know that.'

'Tell us about the house. It was a brick house. Did it have any creeper growing over it? Roses, ivy, that sort of thing?'

She hesitated. 'There might have been a rose, I don't remember. I only went there a few times.'

Tom interposed. 'But you did go inside the house? You slept in the house?'

She nodded. Wexford noticed the little beads of sweat forming on her powder-coated upper lip. 'This manhole you spoke of — there's been a lot about it in the papers, hasn't there? A lot of photographs of it and of the patio?'

'I don't know. I don't read papers.'

'And you don't watch TV or look at pictures online?'

She didn't answer.

'And you never went into the manhole or the cellar? There was no way in from inside the house, was there?'

'No, there wasn't,' she said.

'No staircase down to the cellar in 1996?'

She blushed darkly. 'Don't you believe me?'

'Tell us about Keith — er, Chiltern, wasn't it?'

'Keith Chiltern, yes.' Her voice had become petulant. 'He had a car, a big American car. The detective on the phone asked me if Keith had a big American car and I said yes, he did.'

Wexford said with apparent lack of interest,

'What colour was the car, Ms Withers?'

'What colour?' She was growing indignant. 'I don't know. I don't remember. It's years ago.'

'Do the words *La Punaise* mean anything to you?'

She shook her head.

'Now the house, Orcadia Cottage. You said it was posh. How was it posh? Very modern furnishing, abstract paintings, blinds at the windows, polished wood floors, that sort of thing?'

'All that,' she said. 'Great big TV with a flat screen.'

'So you and Keith split up. You quarrelled?'

'I broke it off. I'd met Malcolm, that's my ex-husband.'

'And you never saw him again after — when?'

'Sometime in '98. I don't remember when.'

'All right, Ms Withers,' Tom said. 'Would you like to write down your full address in '96 and '97, the Lavender Hill address, and Keith Chiltern's address at the time. If you wouldn't mind, WPC Debach will take you into another office and give you pen and paper. We won't keep you long.'

She followed Rita Debach, casting a glance of venom over her shoulder. 'Well, Reg,' said Tom, 'my goodness, I dropped a real clanger there, didn't I? I was so sure too. It was summer, but she never noticed the creeper that covered the house. She never noticed the staircase.'

'The house was furnished in very modern style, abstract paintings et cetera. Flat-screen TV — had they even been thought of thirteen years ago?'

'What did she hope to get out of it, Reg? There's no money involved, no reward for being *the* Francine.'

'Fame, I suppose,' Wexford said. 'Or what passes for fame, these days. Name in the papers she never reads. Called as a witness in a trial? Face on her huge, flat-screen TV when the media get hold of her.' He started to laugh. After a second or two Tom started to laugh too.

'I wonder what she's writing down?' Tom said. 'All pure invention? Does she think we wouldn't check?' He added generously, 'I could tell you knew before I did. When did you know?'

'When she said Keith's name was Chiltern. She's from High Wycombe and she said her husband came from King's Langley. Those places are both in the Chiltern Hills and that — well, that told me.'

'Good for you. Go to the top of the class.' Tom picked up the phone and called WPC Debach. 'Rita? Bring Ms Withers back in, would you?'

WPC Debach came in alone. 'She's gone, sir. Disappeared. She didn't write anything on that bit of paper.'

Wexford said very seriously. 'She's allergic to paper, Rita.'

'We could charge her,' said Tom, 'with obstructing the police, but I don't think we ought to stick our necks out, do you?'

Wexford said, unsmiling, 'Better to keep a low profile.'

★   ★   ★

She could have found all the information she had in the media, he thought as he drove over to Highgate to talk to yet another Francine, the mother of Francine Jameson. Tom had spoken to her on the phone, giving Wexford clearance as his representative. If she had refused to see him she would have been well within her rights, but she hadn't refused, only said she couldn't imagine what information she might have for him. And so it turned out. She was French, called Francine, had given her daughter that name because she liked it. She had never heard of Orcadia Cottage until pictures of it appeared in the media. No one had ever asked her to translate *la punaise* into English. No one she knew had ever possessed a large, pale yellow American vintage car.

An empty afternoon stretched before him. If he went home to the coachhouse he knew he would find Sheila and Dora there, discussing Sylvia and the Old Rectory business. Rehearsals for *Ghosts* were still a week away and meanwhile Sheila had nothing to do but speculate with her mother as to whether Sylvia should sell the house, conquer her fears of the house, think in any case of buying somewhere smaller and — he guessed this bit — revise her ideas on older women having affairs with men the same age as their sons. Joining in didn't appeal to him. He drove across Highgate and parked in Shepherds Hill. Not having brought his A to Z guide with him, he had hazy ideas of the geography of this part of London. Alexandra Palace lay vaguely over there, Muswell Hill on the other side of the woodland and Crouch End at the bottom of the street where he was parked. He would walk, taking in the wood on his way.

London had surprised him. He had believed himself to have a fairly good knowledge of his capital city, but in the past six months he had seen he was wrong. For instance, he hadn't suspected there were so many rural spots like this wood. When he came to what he thought might be the end of it because he could see a street ahead of him, he found another wood on the other side of it and the street more like a country road. He turned to the right and walked along it, already beginning to wonder if he would ever find his car again.

The Orcadia Cottage case was never far from his mind, though Sylvia's troubles had distracted him. Tom hardly seemed concerned about what to Wexford was a great mystery. He could see how the young man possibly called Keith Hill or something like it, might have killed Harriet Merton, perhaps inadvertently by pushing her down those stairs; he could see how 'Keith Hill' might have killed the relative he either lived with or knew well, taken Keith or Ken Gray or Greig's car to transport his body and brought it to the vault; but how had he ended up there himself with his pockets full of valuable jewellery? Someone must have put him there before he could sell the jewellery. Francine? Some unknown killer? And why had he, who had removed a door and bricked up a doorway, not carried out the far simpler task of filling in the top of the manhole and paving over it? Because, although he meant to do it, had perhaps planned how to do it, someone had killed him before he could?

Wexford realised something else. For all their searching, they had found no one who had been related to 'Keith Hill' or had even known him; apart from those Miracle Motors people who had seen him once, no one who could even identify the older man by name. They had no idea where the two of them had lived or even if they had lived together, no idea of the sequence of the three earlier deaths, no hint of motive or means of murder. There were people out there, he thought, there must be, who had known one or both of the men well, yet no one had come forward when details of the bodies had appeared in newspapers and on television.

By this time Wexford had left the woods behind and come once more among houses. This must be Muswell Hill. It looked a pleasant place to live. He wandered around it, interesting himself in the different types of early twentieth-century domestic architecture, then trying to work out how he could return to his car without retracing his steps. It seemed to him that if he kept turning right he ought to find himself at the end of Shepherds Hill, but this strategy failed and he was hopelessly lost. If only he had turned right earlier, he was later to learn, and taken Cranley Gardens he would have come out into Shepherds Hill — but thank God he hadn't.

He had noticed that his car was very near Highgate tube station, but which line it was on he had no idea. If he could find a tube station somewhere down here he could look at a map, get in a tube train and somehow — he feared it might be a circuitous route — find his way back to Highgate.

He began looking for the red, white and blue circle with a horizontal bar across it that was Transport for London's sign, but saw none. There were buses but they all went to places he had never heard of such as Stroud Green and Manor House. Could a place be called Manor House? He asked a passer-by, an elderly woman, where the nearest tube station was and the result was to set her off on a violent denunciation of Transport for London for making this area an underground desert.

'That's what I call it,' she said. 'An underground desert. The nearest tube is Finsbury Park, if you can believe it.'

Wexford could easily believe it, as she seemed knowledgeable and he hadn't the faintest idea where Finsbury Park might be. He asked her how he could find Shepherds Hill and she gave him complicated directions through Crouch End. He set off to walk, looking for street names he thought he might have a chance of recognising. One of these, a street called Hornsey Lane, had its nameplate on the brick wall of a medical centre. The doctors practising there were listed on a sheet of whiteboard instead of the old-time brass plate and one of them caught his eye as this particular name always attracted his attention: Dr James Azziz FRCP, Dr Francine Hill PhD, FRCS, Dr William V. Johns FRCP.

Ah, well, another Francine. He had once

190

thought it an uncommon name but they were everywhere. The chances against her being the one they were looking for were huge. It was a tack they had better give up on but concentrate instead on the architect, the plumber and the builder's labourer. He walked along Hornsey Lane, getting more lost than ever, turned to the left and left again and found himself, maddeningly, back at the medical centre. Again he looked at the whiteboard, he looked at the plate-glass window, through which he could see patients sitting in a waiting room with the usual warning posters plastered all over the walls. *What is chlamydia? Has your child had the triple vaccine? Are you drinking more than two units of alcohol per day? Stroke disables and kills!* He turned away, took a side street and then a broad avenue he hoped might be Shepherds Hill.

Why couldn't he forget this new Francine? Something about her name stuck in his memory and wouldn't go away, though he had no idea what it was. One thing was sure, this wasn't Shepherds Hill. Suddenly, out of another side street, a taxi with its orange light on, appeared to save him. Francine, he thought, settling into his seat and dutifully putting on his seat belt, Francine Hill. What's different about that? It's just another woman with that Christian name. They are legion.

Rokeby must be seen again, however distasteful the man found it. Trevor Oswin — why was his home address treated as a secret? Why did the woman who was probably his wife give him Trevor's mobile number rather than tell him to call again when her husband was in? Perhaps it meant nothing. Would Rokeby remember him? Francine, he thought, Francine Hill . . . The taxi drew up behind his parked car.

★ ★ ★

It was only at three two mornings later that he thanked God he had taken the wrong turnings and thus — twice — passed that medical centre. Before that he had Dora to reassure, Dora who had now begun to see the disadvantages of handing over one's principal residence to one's daughter's family and being obliged to live in one's second home. He reminded her how hard it was to predict the future, how the best laid plans (but this one was too much like one of Tom's maxims) could go wrong, how people changed their minds in the course of time. She could bring some of her favourite things here, that would be easy, favourite books, ornaments, photographs.

'Yes, Reg, I know, but you feel the same as I do, don't you?'

'Of course I do.'

'If before they got married people had to go to classes where they learned about what children are like, how they go on being your responsibility until they've got grown-up children themselves and beyond, the world population would go down fast.'

'They wouldn't listen,' said Wexford, 'and anyway half the population doesn't get married any more.'

192

For the first time ever that evening he phoned an Indian takeaway which sent the order round on a bicycle. The phone number was on one of the gaudy flyovers that came through the coach-house letter box every day. 'Now that's something you couldn't do in Kingsmarkham.'

'If it doesn't taste nice I wouldn't want to do it.'

But it tasted very nice and they accompanied it with a bottle of Merlot. 'Incorrect, I'm sure,' said Wexford and he felt a real nostalgia for all those oriental restaurants he and Burden used to visit in what he thought of as 'the old days'. But he said none of that aloud. He had to make London more attractive to Dora, more accept-able as perhaps a whole year's domicile.

A sound sleeper, she went to bed early. She never minded light in their bedroom and slept through the bedlamp being switched on and off. He sat up for a while, reading Kinglake's *Eothen*, a favourite book about the Middle East one hundred and fifty years ago, a different world, just as violent but more romantic. Dreaming about the awe-inspiring Hodja who preached in the Great Mosque with a sword in his hand, he awoke at three with the name Francine Hill on his lips.

Of course . . . That was why he had known she wasn't just another woman with that Christian name. Hill was what mattered, Hill. The young man who parked his big American car in Orcadia Mews had given his name to Mildred Jones as Keith Hill. Francine was his wife or his sister, she had to be . . .

19

So much of what occurs to us as gospel in the small hours appears absurd in the light of day. That wasn't true here. Dr Francine Hill, Wexford thought, who is a partner in a medical practice in Crouch End or Muswell Hill. He wasn't sure which, but he knew he could find it again.

Tom was sceptical. 'Yes, well, how d'you know it's not par for the course? Just another Francine. She'll either say no she's not, or she'll be like the last one, wasting our time.'

'I don't think so. She's not just another Francine. She's Francine Hill.'

'I suppose it'll do no harm to phone her.'

'Will you see her if I can get her to come in?'

'Well, I will or failing me, Lucy.'

Medical practitioners may not advertise but their names may appear in phone directories. After some searching Wexford found *Hill, Dr F., The Group Practice, Hornsey Lane, N8*. After he had held on while *Eine kleine Nachtmusik* played, a receptionist said that Dr Hill took calls only from private patients on this line. She became less curt when Wexford said this was the Metropolitan Police and to ask Dr Hill to call him on this number. It was the first time he had had to say, 'The name is Wexford' with his Christian name, but without his rank — the rank he no longer held.

He was sitting in the small office where Tom

had put the false Francine and from which she had run away when things became uncomfortable. No doubt Dr Hill had a surgery — did they still call it that? — for much of the morning. It might be lunchtime before she phoned, if she phoned. Would she think this was about some driving offence? It was unlikely she would know it concerned a boyfriend she had or might have had twelve years ago. On the landline in the office, so as not to occupy his cellphone, he called Owen Clary at Chilvers Clary.

Clary was out but the receptionist put him through to Robyn Chilvers.

She greeted him enthusiastically as if he were an old friend whose call she had been waiting for. 'I'm so glad to hear from you. I've lost your number — yes, do give it to me again.' He did so. 'Yes, you remember that builder, plumber, whatever he is, you were asking about? Well, by an extraordinary coincidence he rang up, wanted to know if we'd any work for him. Poor chap, he sounded desperate. Of course I took his name and phone number, but I'd lost yours — how stupid can one get?'

'Had you any work for him, Ms Chilvers?'

'We've barely any for ourselves. I said I'd keep him in mind.'

Wexford wrote down the name Rodney Horndon and a mobile number. 'Thank you very much. Ms Chilvers, I don't suppose you know anything about your husband's visit to Orcadia Cottage? It was in the late summer of 2006. You may not even have been married then.'

She laughed. 'No, we weren't. We were

195

together, though. We were engaged, but I broke it off in the spring and we got together again in '97. But you don't want to know that.'

Did he? Probably not. But it reminded him of someone else: Damian Keyworth, whose engagement was also broken off at much the same time. 'Thank you,' he said. 'You've been very helpful.'

The landline receiver was scarcely in its rest when his mobile rang. As soon as he heard his caller, he thought of Cordelia — 'her voice was ever soft, gentle and low, an excellent thing in a woman'.

'My name is Francine Hill. You left a message for me to call you.'

'Yes, Dr Hill. I wanted to ask you . . . '

'Oh, I know what you want. I've been expecting you — I mean the police. I think I ought to have got in touch with you, but I kept asking myself what, in fact, I could tell you. I kept thinking I knew nothing of any importance, but then I don't really know what *is* important. Shall I come and see you?'

For a moment he was taken aback. Her willingness! Her enthusiasm! 'Yes, please. If you would. First tell me, you are the Francine Hill who was at Orcadia Cottage, St John's Wood, during the late summer or early autumn of 1997?'

'Oh, yes. Yes, I was.'

'And with Keith Hill, who drove a big yellow American car?'

'That was my then boyfriend's car. His name was Teddy Brex.'

196

He wasn't going to tell Tom how utterly unlike his conception of Francine — the Francine of the credit-card swindle, of *La Punaise* — she had sounded. That would be enough to make him doubt and for Wexford there was no doubt. She had agreed — indeed, had offered — to come to the police headquarters in Cricklewood in her free time at four in the afternoon. She would have no more patients until six.

Wexford occupied the time by accompanying Lucy to Rokeby's flat in Maida Vale. A thin drizzle was falling out of a leaden sky. The flyover looked leaden too, elephantine because of its weight and the heavy uprights which supported it. Someone had chained a bicycle to the railings outside the house where Rokeby's flat was. Up against the broken steps someone else had parked a pram which looked unfit ever again to transport a baby. Once again, forewarned of their coming, Rokeby was outside his front door.

'I can't stop you coming,' he said, 'but I've nothing more to tell you. I can't help that. There's nothing more.'

'Mr Rokeby,' Wexford said when they were inside among the fluted columns, 'people often say what you've just said, but the fact often is that they remember more events than they think they do, and those can be awakened if the right questions are asked.' Wexford glanced around the big room, thinking to himself that no interior can be uglier than that which was designed to be grand and sumptuous but is rendered mean by cheap carpeting and chain-store chairs and tables. 'Now the right question here my colleague Detective Sergeant Blanch would like to ask you.'

But her first question or inquiry was not that. 'Do you think we could have a light on, Mr Rokeby? The rain is making it very dark in here.'

A central light, suspended too low down, suddenly blazed, making Wexford blink. 'Thank you,' Lucy said. 'Now Mr Clary — you remember him?'

Rokeby nodded.

'Mr Clary, the architect of Chilvers Clary, came to see you in the summer of 2006 and a while later he returned, bringing with him a plumber called Rodney Horndon? Is that right?'

'He was a plumber and Clary said his name was Rod. I don't know if he was Rodney Horndon.'

'Apparently he was,' Wexford said. 'Now, he came to Orcadia Cottage when Mr Clary came the second time?'

'That's right.'

'Now, it was summer. Did you and your wife' — Wexford glanced at Anne Rokeby, who turned a stony face to him — 'go on holiday that year? You did? And would that have been before or after the visit of Mr Clary and Mr Horndon?'

Anne Rokeby spoke in a voice as cold as her face. 'Of course it must have been after. We could only go in the school holidays and they, as I suppose you know, start at the end of July.'

Undeterred by her manner, Lucy turned to her. 'How easy would it have been to get into your patio from the mews while you were away?'

'Very easy, as my husband never bothered to lock the door in the wall. I'd lock it and the very next time my husband went out that way he'd leave it unlocked. As far as I know,' Anne Rokeby gave her husband a bitter look, 'the key is lost.'

Rokeby ignored this. He burst out like a child pleading for a promised treat that has been long postponed: 'Please, when can we go back to Orcadia Cottage? Please don't make us stay here any longer.'

'You can go back whenever you like, Mr Rokeby,' Lucy said, 'so long as you'll put up with people standing outside the house and staring in and put up with us poking about the patio from time to time.'

'Thank God.'

Rokeby came out with them, pulling the door almost closed behind him. 'Going back will save my marriage. I somehow feel it will save my life.'

'It's nice,' said Lucy on the stairs, 'to feel we're pleasing some of the people some of the time.'

* * *

When Wexford was a child the 'lady doctor' had been a formidable woman. It was often only her vast bosom which distinguished her from the male of the species. Her grey hair was clipped short, her reddened face innocent of make-up and her feet splayed in brown leather lace-ups. Of course, he knew very well Francine Hill wouldn't be like that. He knew that doctors were as likely to be young and beautiful as women in

199

any other profession, but it was only after he had heard her voice on the phone that he pictured her as such. His imagination came far short of the reality.

If he had only seen her in the street he would have placed her as a dancer, a member of some corps de ballet. She was very slim. Her hair was dark brown, almost black, parted in the centre and drawn back into a knot at the nape of her neck. Her mouth was full and red, her eyes large and dark blue and her skin dazzlingly white; like the 'lady doctor' of his youth (though different in all other respects) she wore no make-up. She had on a knee-length black skirt and jacket with a dark blue and red scarf, flat pumps instead of high heels, no jewellery.

Rita Debach brought her into the office.

'Please sit down, Dr Hill,' Tom said.

Wexford guessed she would be the kind of doctor who asked her patients to call her by her first name.

'Now my colleague here, Mr Wexford, tells me you were familiar with Orcadia Cottage in 1997. You went there, I think, with a friend of yours?'

'I was eighteen,' she began, 'living with my father and my stepmother in Ealing. I'd just left school. Teddy Brex was my — well, I suppose he was my boyfriend.' She paused to consider. 'Yes,' she said. 'Yes, of course he was.'

'And he owned a pale yellow Ford Edsel car?'

'I don't know if he owned it.' She spoke diffidently and Wexford could tell she was doing her best to be as accurate as possible. 'He *used* it. He drove it. He told me it had been his

200

uncle's, but his uncle had gone to live somewhere in Hampshire or Sussex, I can't remember where.'

'Was it Liphook, Dr Hill?'

'Oh, yes, it was. Of course it was.'

'Where did you meet Mr Brex?'

'It was at a show — an exhibition, I mean. I went with a friend. Teddy was at this college and the art department had a show of students' degree work. He'd made a mirror and won a prize for it.' She looked up and her face suddenly glowed with life. 'It was the most beautiful mirror. It had a frame made of different kinds of wood, inlaid, you know — he was very gifted. He did wonderful work. He gave me the mirror but I couldn't take it home. There were — well, reasons why I couldn't. I left it in the house. I don't know what happened to it.' I do, thought Wexford, it's in Anthea Gardner's house. Francine Hill had been carried away by memories and now she shook herself. 'But you don't want to hear this. We got to know each other, Teddy and I, and we started going out. He was twenty-one. I went to his house . . . '

Tom interrupted, 'He was twenty-one and he owned a house?'

'He *said* it was his,' Francine Hill said. 'I know he wasn't always truthful. It was in Neasden. I don't remember the address, but I think I could take you there. His parents were dead but he had a grandmother. I never met her. He took me to Orcadia Cottage.'

'He didn't own that house as well?'

She looked at Tom steadily. It was a look

which said, I am telling you the truth. If you don't believe me perhaps we should terminate this interview because I am wasting my time. Tom nodded rather uncomfortably.

'He took me there,' she went on. 'Of course he didn't own the place. It obviously belonged to someone quite rich. He said that a friend he was working for had lent it to him. You have to remember I was only eighteen and I'd led a very sheltered life, exceptionally sheltered, I think, for someone of my age. I've thought about it since and I've thought he couldn't have had friends who owned a place like that but I believed it then. I couldn't have *placed* people — do you know what I mean?'

'Yes,' said Wexford, earning an interrogatory stare from Tom.

'It was most beautifully furnished. Lovely old furniture and oriental rugs and very fine porcelain. I looked in one of the wardrobes and it was full of expensive clothes, dresses and suits, women's clothes, and there were some men's, too, in another wardrobe. The drawers were full of jewellery, it looked valuable. Is this the kind of thing you want to hear?'

'We want to hear anything you can tell us about Mr Brex,' said Wexford. 'Was he employed? What did he live on? Oh, and what time of year was this?'

'It was autumn. The leaves were falling. You ask if Teddy was employed. Well, he was self-employed. He was a joiner.'

Tom asked — spuriously, Wexford thought, 'Why did he take you to Orcadia Cottage?'

Francine Hill looked at him again, another long look but incredulous this time. 'We were boyfriend and girlfriend. We wanted somewhere we could be alone.'

'You had been learning French at school,' Tom said. 'Teddy Brex asked you to translate a French word. *La Punaise.*' He pronounced it 'punish'.

Francine shrugged slightly, holding out her hands. It was the test, Wexford thought. Tom was putting her to the test. 'Perhaps,' she said. 'I don't remember.'

'We could show Dr Hill the piece of paper on which it was written down.'

Tom nodded, called Rita Debach to fetch the relevant evidence, as well as the jewellery which had been found in the vault. She took a long time. Meanwhile, Francine talked about her experiences in Orcadia Cottage. No, she had never been into the cellar, she had never been outside at the back, never seen the patio with the manhole. There was no staircase down to a cellar that she saw.

'Do you think,' Wexford asked, 'that Teddy Brex would have been capable of bricking up a doorway, plastering over the brickwork and painting the new area of wall?'

'Yes, I think so. I don't know why he would. It wasn't his house. But if you're asking me if he *could* have done it, yes, he could and he would have made a wonderful job of it. He was a perfectionist.'

The scrap of paper arrived, protected between two sheets of plastic. As soon as she saw it she

203

recognised the writing. 'Oh, yes. Teddy wrote that. I remember now.'

'Would you have anything in your possession,' Tom said, reverting to policeman-speak, 'which might have on it Brex's fingerprints?'

'After twelve years?'

'What happened to Teddy Brex, Dr Hill? You split up? One of you broke it off?'

Wexford could tell at once that this was a question she didn't want to answer. Tom sat stolid, the picture of the unimaginative cop, the kind that has given the sobriquet 'plod' to the whole genus. Yet Tom wasn't really like that. He would hardly have reached the rank he had if he had been. Could it be, Wexford speculated to himself, that he was the kind of man who, if he finds a woman attractive yet knows she must be unattainable, is made brutishly angry by his frustrations?

'Or you just drifted apart?' This time the sarcasm was barely veiled. 'It was just one of those things?'

The blood rushed into her white face, suffusing it with colour. 'I got ill. I was ill for weeks and couldn't meet him. I had troubles at home — my stepmother died. After that I never heard from him again.' Wexford sensed that this was something she didn't want to tell them. 'Once I was better I did try to get in touch, but I couldn't find him.'

She looked at the jewellery, the two strings of pearls, the diamond and sapphire necklace, the ring, the bracelets and the gold collar. 'I think this may be some of the jewellery in the drawer, but I can't really say. I don't remember.'

Silence. Tom called for Rita to come and remove the exhibits. Wexford turned to Francine Hill and asked her if she would show them where Teddy Brex's house was.

'I couldn't today.'

'Sometime on Thursday?' Friday was impossible. On Friday he would be in Kingsmarkham, at the inquest on Jason Wardle. 'Perhaps Thursday afternoon?'

'Would two on Thursday afternoon be all right?'

It would be fine, Wexford said, and thank you very much, Dr Hill, you've been very helpful. Rita Debach showed her out. The door had scarcely closed when Tom said, 'Snooty little piece, isn't she?'

'Oh, I don't think so.'

'I don't know what use you think seeing this fellow's house is going to be, but you can go with Lucy if you like.'

And if PC Debach were sent, Wexford would no doubt be going with her. A policeman's aide's lot is not a happy one, he paraphrased to himself, which led the increasingly cross Tom to ask what he thought he was laughing at.

'Nothing,' said Wexford. 'Sorry.'

20

They picked her up at her home in Muswell Hill, an unpretentious semi-detached house in the street Wexford should have taken when looking for a way back to Shepherds Hill — should have taken and thereby never found Francine Hill and the Crouch End medical centre. A young man with a baby in his arms came to the door with her to see her off. Wexford, already far more involved with her and her concerns than he usually was with a witness, was pleased to see what he took for signs of happiness and fulfilment. They kissed and she kissed the smiling baby.

It took her a long time to find the house. They drove round and round the little streets on the south side behind the North Circular Road. Wexford could understand her difficulty for they all looked the same. 'It was on a corner,' she kept saying and then, 'on a corner but with the turning on the left side of the house.'

Some front gardens were tended, some left to become wilderness, some repositories for bikes, motorbikes and the insides of engines. Some of the little houses, generally in semi-detached pairs, had pebble-dashed facades, some plastered and painted with contrasting colour trims and fake porticos. But most were run-down and all of them, despite being 'trimmed in jollity', looked what they were and who they were designed for, homes for the poor.

'I haven't been here since Teddy brought me in '97,' Francine said. 'I came two or three times. I didn't realise then how — well, how dismal it was. Look, that one' — she pointed — 'Number 83 on the corner. That's it. I'm almost sure. Would you drive down the turning? Yes, can you see over the fence? That carport. Teddy kept his Edsel under that.'

The house was occupied. Somehow — and all burglars know this — whether a house is occupied is always apparent from the outside. Not that the owners are at home or out, but that someone lives there permanently. Curtains hung at the windows, the plant in the pot by the front door wasn't in the best of health, but it was alive and the soil round its stem was damp. Lucy rang the bell. If Francine thought Teddy Brex might answer the door she was the only one of them who did. It was eventually answered by an old woman, a woman who looked as if she was in her hundredth year. Her face was a relief map, criss-crossed by roads and rivers, her eye sockets moon craters, her mouth a thin slash between escarpments. A wisp of hair floated like a puff of white smoke on her head. She said in a surprisingly strong voice, 'Who are you and what do you want?'

Lucy showed her warrant card, introduced Francine Hill and Wexford. 'We are looking for Mr Teddy Brex. May we come in?'

'He's not here. You can come in if you want, but only for a minute or two. I'm busy.'

Old people are expected to live in cluttered dwellings, the accumulations of a long life covering every surface, old faded cushions on the armchairs, antimacassars too, framed photographs in which the pictures have faded to pastel shades, footrests for old feet and among the clutter on a table top, a magnifying glass for old eyes. Number 83 whatever this road was called was very unlike that. The room they went into was almost stark, its walls grey and white, the ceiling a darker grey. Two armchairs, an upright chair and a television set, the uncurtained French window affording a view of nothing much beyond a large carport.

Lucy said, 'May we sit down?' and without waiting for an answer, did so. Politely, Wexford waited for the owner of this house, if she was the owner, to seat herself, which she finally did in a stiff, reluctant kind of way. 'May we know your name?'

'Mrs Tawton. Agnes, if you want first names the way all the young do these days.'

'Thank you. Are you related in some way to Mr Brex?'

''Some way', is it? I should say so. I'm his only relative. I'm his grandma.'

Only to Wexford perhaps did this come as a dramatic surprise. After so many false leads and so much fruitless speculation, here was incontrovertible fact. It was as if Teddy Brex suddenly became a real person. He not only had a 'relative' who might or might not be an uncle, he had a grandmother.

'But, let me get this straight. You don't know where Mr Brex is? You haven't seen him since when?'

Agnes Tawton had begun to look a little shifty. The direct stare with which she had favoured

Lucy now fell and she eyed the wrinkled hands in her lap. 'It'd be a good ten years. No, I tell a lie. More like twelve or thirteen.'

'Were you living here with him?'

'Not exactly *here*,' she said, and paused. 'My house is in Daisy Road on the other side of the North Circular. I used to sort of come and see him here.'

'But you're living here now? Are you the owner of this house?'

She didn't want to say. That was very apparent. 'I've let my place.' The words were forced out as if they came from a squeezed tube. She seemed to have forgotten their visit was to be restricted because she was busy. 'I've got tenants in.'

Wexford could see exactly what she had been up to. He and Lucy needed no further elucidation. She had put her own house up for rent and moved in here when her grandson had disappeared. It was the grandson who owned this minimalist house, the grandson who was Teddy Brex, alias Keith Hill . . .

She had followed Wexford's thoughts. 'It was a crying shame leaving this place empty after all he'd done to it, painting it and all after the wicked mess his uncle left it in. I paid the rates' — she meant the council tax — 'and for the electric and gas. If he'd come back I'd have got out. I wouldn't stop in what wasn't mine.'

Wexford couldn't help marvelling, almost admiring her. Here she was, somewhere in her nineties, working a splendid scam that wasn't really a scam. He couldn't see that she had done anything illegal. These houses were horrible and no doubt those on the other side of the North Circular Road were equally horrible, but in these days one of them, however mean and cramped and ugly, was near enough to central London to fetch a high rent.

'You mentioned Mr Brex's uncle. Who is he? Where is he?'

'Don't ask me. Living in Liphook so far as I know. This place belongs to him, not to Teddy, whatever Teddy thinks. It was like this. Teddy's dad and him was only half brothers on account of Jimmy the eldest one being born before their mum was married. The wrong side of the blanket, you might say.' Wexford nearly gasped. He had read the phrase, never before heard it uttered. 'She was Kathleen Briggs,' Agnes Tawton went on, 'and Keith was born after she married their dad. Teddy never knew it, it was a shock to him.'

'Did you say Keith?'

'That's right. That's the uncle. Keith Brex he's called.'

It was all falling into place. It was from his uncle's name that Teddy chose a pseudonym for himself, Keith from his uncle and Hill from his girlfriend. The connection between them being not a straight uncle-nephew relationship accounted for the DNA anomaly. Wexford asked Agnes Tawton if she would give a DNA sample, expecting a flat refusal. But she surprised him. He could tell such an act would make her feel important, something to tell her neighbours — neighbours perhaps in both locations.

'I don't mind,' she said.

Lucy asked her, 'Where do you think your grandson is?'

'In some foreign place, I reckon. The young these days, they're off all over the world, aren't they? God knows why but it's a fact.' Agnes Tawton stared at Francine and Francine gave her a small friendly smile. 'He never told me he was going, but he wouldn't. Too scared of what I'd do about him not painting my friend's toilet like he promised.'

Wexford could easily believe in any man being afraid of this old woman. He left it to Lucy to tell her about the arrangement which would be made to take her DNA.

'I'm not going to get turned out of here, am I?'

'I can't see why you would be,' Wexford said. A picture came before his eyes of those two bodies in the vault, though he had never seen them, the young man and the older man, related but not true uncle and nephew. Keith Brex and Teddy Brex. 'You say this house belongs to Keith Brex.'

'Yes,' she said. 'Not that you'd know it what with me never hearing a dicky bird out of him. It's not as if Liphook's at the other end of the earth, is it?'

So if Keith were dead and Teddy dead but in any case out of the running for ownership and there were no other relatives? If Keith died first would Teddy have inherited the house? Probably. He might not have been Keith's full nephew, but he had been his half-brother's son. He was dead, too, and had just one relative, this ancient woman. It wasn't for Wexford to tell her she

211

probably was the owner. It was in any case unlikely anyone would attempt to dislodge her.

'Right,' said Mrs Tawton briskly, 'you've got what you came for, so now you can go.'

* * *

Later in the day Wexford retailed the whole thing as he saw it to Tom. 'The young man's body in the tomb is almost certainly Teddy Brex's and the older man's his uncle Keith Brex. We shall know for sure as to the young man's identity when we get the results from Agnes Tawton's DNA test. The older man's identity remains unsure. Agnes Tawton was no relation of his, though we know he was related in some way to Teddy Brex.'

'Well done,' said Tom.

'But if he's not Keith Brex, who is he? I think he must be. Agnes Tawton says Teddy had no other relatives but herself. He was an only child, his mother was an only child and his father had just this one half-brother, not properly speaking a Brex at all.'

'Maybe we should look up this Keith Brex's birth certificate?'

'The chances are,' said Wexford, 'it will give the mother as Kathleen Briggs and the father as 'unknown'.'

'I think we should try. So what do we think happened to make them both and Harriet Merton end up in a hole under the Orcadia Cottage patio?'

'I have a theory, Tom, but it's not much more

than a theory. Teddy Brex was the lover — if that's the word — of Harriet Merton. For some reason I don't know and can't know she threatened to tell her husband something about Teddy that would be — well, detrimental to him. Maybe he wanted out and she said she'd tell her husband he raped her or tried to rape her or even that she caught him stealing her jewels.'

'Well, there was a lot of valuable jewellery on his body and beside it.'

'There was. They fought, perhaps physically and he pushed her down the stairs which *at that time led down into the cellar*. He left the body there, probably because as we know disposing of a body is the killer's main problem. Was Keith Brex's body already there? We aren't going to know, but we may conclude that Teddy also killed him. Before or after Harriet? We don't know. We don't know why he killed him. A possibility is that when he found out the house in Neasden belonged not to his father but to Keith Brex, so hadn't become his on his father's death, he murdered him in a rage.'

'And put the body in the coal hole?'

'I think so, bringing it to Orcadia Cottage in the boot of the Edsel.'

'Keith had been in it. We know that now, but dead or alive at the time we don't know.'

'When Harriet was dead he bricked up the doorway that led to the stairs, plastered over it so that it looked as if no staircase had ever been there.'

Tom nodded, looking pleased. 'The question remains, Reg, if he could remove a door and brick up a doorway so that it looked as if no doorway had ever been there, why didn't he fill up the hole underneath the manhole cover? We've asked ourselves this before. He only had to get hold of some paving stone, not much, and cement it into the hole, child's play to him. Why didn't he? If he had that would have made the contents of the tomb hidden for ever. No one would have suspected the existence of an underground tomb, let alone two bodies in it, and no fourth body could have been put there ten years later. Why didn't he?'

'And why did he end up there himself?'

With the manhole still there and the manhole cover still on it, Wexford thought when he was on his way home. Why? Teddy Brex's troubles would have been over if he had sealed the tomb at both ends. He imagined himself in Teddy Brex's shoes, imagined himself young and with a girlfriend like Francine Hill. Teddy had everything to live for. He had secured a house for himself. Not much of a house, true, in not a very desirable place, but a roof over his head and always saleable. He had evidently stolen Harriet Merton's jewels, which could have been sold for thirty or forty thousand pounds. He had Francine. But here Wexford paused. Did he really have Francine? That lovely clever girl would have seen through him, probably was seeing through him over the matter of *La Punaise* and the credit card. She was the last woman, he thought, to become entangled with a thief and a murderer. Though she was ignorant of all that side of him, young as she was, she had

214

seen or would soon see how unsuitable he was for her, how positively dangerous for her.

Would she have any idea of any of this? Was it worth seeing her again? Still, he was sure Teddy Brex had presented to Francine a sunnier and sweeter aspect of character than that which had led to violence, robbery and murder. He had given her the mirror, the mirror that ended up in Anthea Gardner's house. How strange people were! The mirror he had given told Wexford that Teddy Brex wasn't entirely a brutish thug but someone, however corrupted, with an appreciation of beauty and perhaps hope for a future he was never to see gratified.

Wexford stopped. He stood still for a moment. A new thought had come to him with something of a shock. One mystery was: why hadn't Teddy Brex paved over the manhole? Surely there was a second. Someone put the girl's body into the vault to join the others. Why hadn't that someone paved over the hole in his turn?

21

How many inquests had he attended in Kingsmarkham? Hundreds, maybe a thousand over the years. But this would be the first at which he was present as a witness, a member of the public, and not a policeman.

He came by train, unusual for him who took himself everywhere by car. It was bad enough having to go at all, let alone driving himself through those southern suburbs which always seemed endless, which had surely come to an end once Streatham was passed — but not a bit of it, for Norbury and Croydon and Purley were still to be struggled through. The train from Victoria passed through some of these places but passed through them airily as if they presented it no problems, as indeed they didn't. If cars ran on prescribed lines like trams, how easy it would be. Almost magically, the train sped out into a sort of near-countryside in the time it would have taken him in a car to get halfway through Brixton.

If there had been a ticket collector at Kingsmarkham Station as in the old days he would have recognised Wexford and asked him how he was, but there was no such friendly official, just a machine with a greedy mouth that ate up his ticket. He walked into town. For the first time in his life he was about to attend an inquest at which he felt a measure of guilt. None of this was his fault, but how much of it was his daughter's? Too late to change that now, pointless to speculate how Sylvia, one-time domestic goddess, had transmuted into this earth-motherly, sexually rampant, socially wild still youngish woman.

The coroner was new, someone Wexford had never seen before. Wexford gave his name as the private citizen he now was, and took the oath, swearing to tell the truth, the whole truth and nothing but the truth. Listening with half an ear to the inquiry put to him — he knew by heart what it would be — he glanced at the people in the public seats to see if he recognised anyone. He didn't, but one couple particularly caught his eye, a man and a woman in late middle age, sitting close together, holding hands tightly. It struck him that they dressed as no one of their age in London would dress, the woman wearing a felt hat and square scarf, the man a tweed jacket with leather elbow patches, check shirt and knitted tie.

He began to tell the court what had happened that day. 'My daughter had just come home from hospital. Because a set of her house keys was missing it seemed advisable to change the locks . . . ' The whole truth? The whole truth would be that he and she feared Jason Wardle had them and might use them to enter the house. He felt — he imagined surely — the eyes of the hand-holding couple on him. 'A locksmith was needed. I went upstairs to look for the telephone directory which had been left in my grandson's bedroom on the second floor.' An enormous house, it must sound like, a rich woman's house. 'I opened the door. The body of a man was hanging from the light fitting in the ceiling.' Cool, emotionless — nothing else was possible — he described how he went downstairs again and phoned Kingsmarkham police.

The coroner asked if he had recognised the hanged man and if he had touched the body, to both of which questions Wexford answered an unhesitating no. That was all. There was nothing more for him to do or say. He was thanked by the coroner and got down to find himself a seat in the back row of the public seats. A doctor he no more knew than he knew the coroner described Jason Wardle's injuries and the cause of his death, and then there was some evidence from a psychiatrist as to Wardle's mental state, this man's opinion being that he was bipolar. A faint strangled cry came from the woman in the felt hat.

There was some discussion between the coroner, the clerk to the court and the doctor and then the verdict came: suicide while the balance of Jason Wardle's mind was disturbed. It was over. He had been twenty-one years old.

Wexford intended to go home — that is, to go to his own house and see whoever might be in. But as he walked down the steps he saw the couple who had earlier caught his eye, waiting at the bottom. Surely waiting for him. He didn't know them, he meant to pass them by but, as he approached them, the woman called out in a strident, upper-class voice, 'Where's your daughter? I suppose she didn't have the face to come.'

'Vivien,' the man said. 'There's no point . . . '

'Yes, there is. I want to tell him so that he can tell her. He can tell her that if she were a decent woman and not a whore my son would be alive today. My son would be starting a happy life . . . '

'I'm sorry,' Jason Wardle's father said wretchedly. 'It's not your fault, I'm sorry.'

'I'm sorry too,' said Wexford. 'I'm very sorry for you both.'

'And what's the use of that?' Vivien Wardle was crying now, the tears running down her face. 'There may be a bit of use in telling her what I said. You do that. You tell her she's a disgrace to her sex and to her children. Those poor boys, that poor little girl. What must they think of their mother?'

Her husband succeeded in taking Vivien away. He almost had to lift her into their car, she was so convulsed with misery and grief. Wexford felt badly shaken. But still he turned in the direction of his house and began to walk up Queen Street. Dora had been right and he had been wrong, he thought. Keeping aloof from all this, taking no stand, avoiding judgement, that was all wrong. A parent should speak out, no matter what age his child was, no matter what reputation he had achieved as a tolerant and never moralistic arbiter. He had been too easy and too kind, too *respectful*. Perhaps to prove to himself that all that was changing, at least in this instance, he let himself into his house without ringing the bell first, without the prior phone call he would usually have made.

Sylvia was in the living room, lying on the sofa reading a magazine and drinking coffee. She sat up, said, 'Dad! You might have let me know you were coming.'

He looked at the clock. He hadn't meant to, but noticing she was still in her nightdress, a shawl round her shoulders, her long dark hair loose and in need of a wash, he looked and saw it was twenty minutes to midday.

'There's some coffee. Do you want some?'

'No, thanks. I'm not staying. I've been to the inquest on Jason Wardle.'

'Suicide, I suppose,' she said.

Something inside his head snapped. But he remained cool, his voice slow and steady. 'Sylvia, I have passed no judgement on you. I have purposely not taken a side against you. But now I have to speak out. Maybe it will make no difference. Mr and Mrs Wardle were there, Jason's parents.'

She said nothing, cast up her eyes.

'Don't make that face, please. You are a fine example, aren't you, a fine role model, for Mary?' Sylvia drew back from him, put one hand up to press against her chest. 'Mrs Wardle told me what she thinks of you. She holds you responsible for her son's death. I don't, but I will say that without your intervention in his life he'd be alive today. Damaged perhaps, mentally unstable, perhaps, but alive.'

'What about him intervening in my life?'

Wexford said brutally, 'Jason was twenty-one. You are a middle-aged woman with a son only two years younger. You are a social worker, quite a highly trained one, but you didn't spot the signs of mental instability in him or if you did you didn't care. You had what you wanted from him and then you dropped him. Mrs Wardle called you a whore — that wasn't pleasant for a father to hear.'

Mrs Wardle had cried and now Sylvia's defiance slid off her as the shawl slipped from her shoulders, and she too began to cry. He watched her for a moment, then he said, 'Stop. Crying doesn't help. Does it? It doesn't make you feel better, whatever people say,' and sitting down beside her he took her in his arms.

Hugging a large damp woman with greasy hair who smells of sweat is not a pleasant experience, even if she is your child. But thinking like that almost made Wexford laugh. That would never do.

'Time you went back to work,' he said. 'Time you cleaned my house.' He had noticed the dust. 'And had Mary back with you. Your mother or I will bring her back on Monday.'

'I'm sorry, Dad.'

'I ought to advise you to go and see the Wardles, tell *them* you're sorry, but I'm not into draconian punishments. Besides, they might kill you. Vivien Wardle looks capable of it. Now go and have a bath and get dressed.'

She looked at him with that little girl face she occasionally put on. It was no longer becoming. 'If I do will you take me out for lunch?'

This time he did laugh. 'Certainly not. What an idea! I'm going straight back to London.'

And there, looking in on Tom Ede before he went off for the weekend, Wexford heard that Rodney Horndon was back from his holiday in the Caribbean. They would talk to him next week. Although he had spent no more than a few hours at the inquest and after that in admonishing Sylvia, Wexford felt strangely out of touch with the events at Orcadia Cottage. He must go back there, but as he decided to go out again it began to rain, at first lightly and then in torrents, the wind getting up and blowing the rain in sheets. It was the next day, in the late afternoon, that he walked down to St John's Wood.

It was only September but already the leaves were starting to fall from the Virginia creepers. A few had dropped on to the pavements in Orcadia Place and they lay more thickly scattered over the cobbles of the mews. Most of the houses and all the walls carried their burden of the spidery tendrils and heart-shaped leaves, now tinted to a clear red or deep blackish crimson. One fluttered down and alighted on Wexford's shoulder as he wandered about, half-hoping for some inspiration to come to him from these walls and windows and gables and doorways which must have seen so much. As he came by her gate Mildred Jones's front door opened and she came out of her flat on to the doorstep, preceded by a tall, thin young woman with long fair hair. They spoke, but were too far away for Wexford to hear what was said, and the girl came down the path to the gate, Mrs Jones calling after her, 'I'll see you on Tuesday, then. Nine a.m., remember, and don't be late.'

Once she was out of earshot, Mildred Jones came to the gate, said to Wexford in a confidential tone, 'Latvian. At least I know she can't be an illegal.'

He looked inquiring. 'My new cleaner,' she said. 'Comes from Riga, she says. I don't care where she comes from so long as it's in the EU. But they're a bit thin on the ground. In the fourteen years I've been here I've had seven and they were from Georgia — and I don't mean Georgia USA — and Uzbekistan and Ukraine, to name but a few.'

'You mean they didn't have a right to remain?'

'That's what I mean, yes.' She seemed quite unaware that it was unwise to give these details to a policeman, but he was a policeman no longer and perhaps that was how she thought of him. 'The first one was actually deported. Then there was the first Georgian. Then there was the Ukrainian with the ridiculous name, the one that disappeared, and soon after that Colin and I split up, so you can see that was a hard time for me. But I will say for these Russians — they're all Russian to me — they're good cleaners.'

Wexford was curious, even though all this wasn't relevant to the Orcadia Cottage case. 'How do you find them? I mean, if they're working illegally in this country they can't advertise, can they?'

'Oh, some do. But what they mainly do is put a note through your door. Well, they just put notes through the doors in the whole street. They put their name — just their first name — and say they can do cleaning and ironing and shopping and give a mobile number. They never say how much they're asking, because they know you'll stick out for paying under the minimum wage.'

'Really?'

'Oh, yes. It's nearly six pounds an hour and I couldn't afford that. That one you've just seen, she asked for the minimum wage — it's amazing what they know about our laws — but I told her four pounds an hour was the most I'd pay and of course she knuckled under.'

'Of course,' said Wexford.

Did she notice his dry tone or was there some distaste in his expression? Whatever it was she said suddenly, 'Oh my God, I forgot, you're police, aren't you?'

'Not any more, Mrs Jones, not any more.'

She began to explain. 'Just because I live here — I mean, in St John's Wood — and because I go to South Africa every year, people think I'm rolling in money. Let me tell you, I got this flat under our divorce settlement and that was all I got. Colin got our place in the country and I never had a penny out of him. He sold that house and got enough from it to buy a place on Clapham Common. I have to live on my investments and you'll know what that means in a recession. It was all I could do to afford the air fare to Cape Town and then I couldn't go first class.' She drew breath. 'It's not as though Colin's short of a bob or two. The irons in the fire he's got you wouldn't believe. A share in a business in West Hampstead and a share in a betting shop.'

Soon after he left her the rain began. He noticed crossly that it hadn't been forecast. The south-east was due to be dry all day. He had no raincoat and no umbrella and the rain came in torrents. There were no taxis, there never were when you really wanted them, but there were trees to stand under more or less all the way. His feet had got wet through his shoes by the time he reached the coachhouse and water had run down the back of his neck inside his clothes.

* * *

He and Dora were spared a further visit to Sylvia, for Sheila took Mary home to her mother on Sunday. The little girl was happy enough to go. Her cousins were mostly at nursery school and her chief regret was at leaving Bettina the cat behind. Wexford thought with the slightly malicious amusement all parents sometimes feel towards a difficult son or daughter, that Sylvia was in for a hard time as *her* daughter did what she threatened to do and began nagging her mother for a kitten or a puppy.

He took Dora out to lunch and they went to the cinema. The evening was fine and not cold. Dora wanted to watch a favourite programme on television, so Wexford went back to Orcadia Place. Ever since he had left her when the rain started he had been thinking intermittently about the things Mildred Jones had told him. And, more to the point perhaps, the things she hadn't told him.

This was the first time he had been into the

precincts of Orcadia Cottage on his own and this time he opened the door in the rear wall and stepped inside on to the patio. Alone there, with no one in the house and no accompanying police officer, he turned to look at the door for what was really the first time. It was made of vertical wooden boards, painted black and it had a bolt top and bottom. Like Sylvia's front door which she never bolted unless forced to do so. Was this door also never bolted?

Scarcely a paving stone in the yard was visible. Day after day of rain and high wind had brought down flurries of leaves from *Ampelopsis* — he had looked up the botanical name for Virginia creeper — from neighbouring walls and roofs and they lay in a thick wet carpet covering the ground. How much worse it must have been before Clay Silverman had his own Virginia creeper cut down. Wexford hardly knew what he was doing there, perhaps only taking yet another look at the place in the hope of deriving some clue from it as to what had happened here twelve years and two years before. It wasn't only the identity of the young woman in the 'tomb' that was important but also that of the killer of the young man they were calling Teddy Brex. Examination of Agnes Tawton's DNA would establish if it was indeed Brex but get them no nearer to finding who had killed him. Surely he had killed Harriet and killed the man who was almost certainly his uncle but when they were both dead and lying underground, had someone else killed *him*?

Standing there against the wall in the dying

226

light, Wexford found himself utterly disbelieving this. Teddy Brex had killed Harriet Merton, presumably to stop her telling the police about his theft of her jewellery and her credit card and had killed his uncle for possession of a house and a car, both quite reasonable motives. What motive could someone else have had for killing him?

Wexford decided to take the lid off the manhole (Paulson and Grieve, Ironsmiths of Stoke) and have another look down into the depths. The hole itself, though now quite empty, might suggest something to him. He started forward, his leather-soled shoe slipped on the wet crimson carpet and he fell, slithering on the slippery leaves.

Luckily he was unhurt. He had broken nothing. Thanks to losing that weight, he thought, for he had fallen more lightly than he would once have done and would only have bruises to his knees and maybe his right hand. He struggled to his feet, not easy on that mat of sodden leaves, took a careful step forward and lifted the lid off the hole.

And then he saw. He understood what had happened to Teddy Brex.

22

'But that's only guesswork, isn't it?'

Wexford had been pretty sure Tom would say that. He felt like quoting Sherlock Holmes and saying that when all else is impossible that which remains must be so. In this case, though, all else wasn't impossible, only extremely unlikely. The extreme unlikelihood didn't bother Tom.

'This Teddy may have had all kinds of unsavoury mates. Birds of a feather flock together, you know. One of them may have been there and pushed him down the hole. Because that's what you're saying, isn't it? That he slipped on those leaves and fell down the hole?'

'That's what I'm saying. If that manhole hadn't been covered I'd have fallen down the hole myself.'

'Hmm. Well, we'll see. We've got the DNA results. There's no doubt now that it was Teddy Brex. There's very little doubt that the older man was his uncle or half-uncle Keith Brex. His birth certificate is what you said it would be, mother Kathleen Briggs, father unknown. But who was the girl, Reg?'

'That's what we have to find out.'

★ ★ ★

Rodney Horndon lived in a part of London Wexford had never visited before. His street was

228

one of those branching off the Fulham Palace Road where the houses were ranged in terraces, late-Victorian, rather forbidding because they were all the same, their brickwork was a dark red, the small areas in front of them not to be dignified by the name of garden but either paved over or used as a storage space for defunct machinery. Horndon admitted DS Lucy Blanch and Wexford to the house himself. His wife and daughter were at work, he said, though no one had inquired after them.

Once, Wexford thought, and not long ago the television would have been on. Instead the focus was on a large desktop computer where Horndon had evidently been playing a video game involving biker-like characters, bristling with weapons, blasting each other with sub-machine guns. The action had been paused at a point where a giant-breasted redhead in a kind of silver metal bikini and thigh boots filled the screen, her arms raised and her bulbous red mouth open in a scream. Horndon, a shortish man of 50 with a big belly, glanced at it as if to turn it off but evidently thought better of this course. After all, he could return to it after they had gone.

'I think you know what we want to talk to you about, Mr Horndon,' Lucy said.

'That Orcadia business.' He pronounced it more like Al-Qaeda. 'Don't know what I can tell you.'

'Tell us about the day you went with Mr Clary to Orcadia Cottage. The owners, Mrs and Mrs Rokeby, were away?'

'Don't know if they was away. They wasn't

there. They was out, that's all I know.'

Wexford said, 'You lifted a plant pot off the manhole cover and Mr Clary suggested you went down there?'

Wexford must have touched a sensitive spot for Horndon reacted indignantly. 'He thinks a lot of himself, does Clary. Dressed up in a nice suit, white shirt and tie and all. Of course he'd no intention of going down there. That was my job. 'Have you got a ladder or a pair of steps in your van?' says Lord Muck, all posh. Of course I had, never go out without them. 'I'm just going inside the house for a few minutes,' he says and he disappears.'

'So you went to your van and fetched the ladder?'

Horndon looked at Lucy and slowly shook his head. 'I wasn't taking no orders from him. It was my boss at Underland I was working for, it was him paid me my wages, not Clary. I didn't know what might be down there, did I? Could have been full of water. I've come on that before. A hole where they used to keep coal but don't no more and when you take a butcher's it's full of bloody water.'

Lucy, not acquainted with cockney rhyming slang, caught Wexford's eye and he mouthed, 'L-O-O-K, look. A butcher's hook.'

Evidently still puzzled, she turned back to Horndon. 'Are you saying you didn't go into the hole, Mr Horndon?'

'Yes, that's what I'm saying.' Horndon was quick to anger and he was growing angry now. 'Clary, he said to me, 'Go down in that hole *if you fancy it.*' That's what he said, *if you fancy it.* Well, I didn't bloody fancy it, right? I didn't want to get my things dirty no more than Lord Muck did. All right? So I put the flowerpot thing back where it was supposed to go and I didn't need no help from him. I sat down on the wall and when he come back I said to him I'd been down there and there was nothing to see. 'Was there stairs?' he says and I says there was nothing, it was empty.' Horndon seemed to recall at this point just what had been down there, what he might have seen. He didn't shiver. He curled up his nose. 'I hadn't no call to tell the truth to him, had I? He wasn't paying me.'

When the front door had closed on them Lucy said, 'That 'butcher's hook' business, what does it mean?'

'It's old now and half-forgotten but people still say 'porkies' when they mean lies. It's Cockney rhyming slang.'

'Reg, I really don't follow.'

'Pork pies for lies. You leave off the second noun, the one that rhymes and use the first one.'

'I see,' said Lucy. 'It seems very complicated.'

Wexford laughed. He got out of the car at Melina Place and walked down towards Orcadia Mews. There was something he needed to ask Mildred Jones, something which by an oversight he had neglected to take her up on before. Orcadia Cottage looked much as before but with two changes. A newspaper had been thrust through its letterbox and on the doorstep was a bunch of flowers, their stems in water inside a plastic container. 'I wonder what it bodes,' said

231

Wexford to himself in the words of Hortensio. He walked up to the front door and rang the bell. No one came. The newspaper must be a freeby stuck there on the off-chance, the flowers delivered to the wrong house.

'You're not going to arrest me, are you?' were the first words uttered by Mildred Jones when she opened her door to him.

Wexford wanted to laugh but didn't. 'I no longer have the power to do that, Mrs Jones, but if I did why would I?'

'Oh, I don't know. I've been so worried, telling you that stuff about what I pay my cleaner — you know. Every time the doorbell rings . . . You're sure it's all right?'

'Quite sure.'

'Come in then.' She was more affable than she had ever been and in a cream and black dress with pearls looked prettier than he had ever seen her. 'I'm going out to lunch but not for half an hour.'

She took him into the over-stuffed living room. 'No, I was aghast after you had gone. I'd been so tremendously indiscreet. Talking about paying my cleaner less than the minimum wage, talking about employing illegals. At least they hadn't been trafficked. I might have landed myself in prison, mightn't I?'

'Hardly, Mrs Jones.'

'Well, a massive fine then. Or would I have to do community service like those hoodies?' She didn't wait for an answer. 'You'd like coffee, wouldn't you? It will have to be Nescafé, the real stuff takes too long, and I have to be out of here at twenty-five past on the dot.' She went to the door, opened it and shouted, 'Raisa! Coffee!'

No 'please', Wexford noted. No polite form of request.

He decided — though it was irrelevant — that he disliked Mildred Jones quite a lot. In his previous life, his previous existence, he had seldom allowed himself likings and dislikings. Now he could. It was an advantage.

'Last time I talked to you,' he said, 'you spoke about a cleaner you had had from the Ukraine, I think it was, who had a strange name and who disappeared. What exactly did you mean by that?'

'Well, she left and didn't come back.'

'What was she called?'

'I don't know her surname. Her Christian name, if she was a Christian, was Vladlena. I called her Vlad like Vlad the Impaler I saw in a film on TV. I can't be doing with these fancy names. After all, what are they, these girls, the lowest of the low where they come from.'

Raisa came in with coffee on a tray. The coffee was in a willow pattern pot, the cups and saucers to match, silver spoons, lumps of brown and white sugar in a silver bowl and milk in a silver jug. Wexford wondered if the tray would have had such a civilised and elegant appearance if Mrs Jones had prepared it herself and decided that like hell it would. Raisa herself, slender, sharp-featured with long blonde hair, was the girl Mildred Jones had been talking to on the door-step when last he spoke to her. She smiled at him.

'Thank you, Raisa,' he said.

She was barely out of the door when Mildred Jones said, 'It doesn't do to talk to them like you knew her socially. Do it just the once and they start to take advantage.'

He wanted to say that he supposed she learnt to talk in that way to servants when she was in South Africa during apartheid. If he did that he'd never get another word out of her. 'Vladlena, Mrs Jones.' He was damned if he was going to refer to the girl as Vlad.

'Yes, well it was quite weird. She was here doing the ironing one morning . . . '

'Just when was this?'

'Three years ago, maybe a bit more. Like I say, she was doing the ironing. In the kitchen she was with the radio on. They always have to have the radio on, can't function without it. Doesn't matter what's on, music, talks, drama, anything, so long as they've got background noise. I went into the kitchen and the radio was on and the iron was on, standing in that metal rack thing at the end of the ironing board. And on the board was one of Colin's shirts with a great iron-shaped burn in the middle of the back.'

Mrs Jones took a gulp of her coffee. 'I must go in five minutes. Well, like I say, there was this burn and half the ironing in a pile yet to be done but no sign of her. I called out but she wasn't in the house. Then I saw her coat was gone. It was plain to see what had happened, she had burnt Colin's shirt and got frightened — with good cause, I may add — and just fled without saying a word to me.'

This wasn't quite what Wexford had hoped

for. It was hardly a disappearance. 'Did you ever hear from her again?'

'It's funny you should say that because I did. A long time later, months and months, I saw her go into Mr Goldberg's house. Do you know where that is?'

Wexford remembered the reclusive man whose food was fetched in for him by the cleaner. 'In Melina Place.'

'Right. She was going in there as bold as brass with two shopping bags. I went up to her and said I'd seen the shirt with the burn mark and she'd have to pay for it. I wasn't going to let her get away with it. Well, the next thing I knew was David Goldberg was on the phone to me. He never goes out, he's not quite all there.' She tapped the side of her head. 'But pushy like all Jews. And he can use a phone. The rudest person I've ever spoken to. Well, I didn't speak to him. He spoke to *me*. How dare I accost his cleaner — accost was the word he used — who did I think I was, poking my nose in where I wasn't wanted, interfering — I won't say the name he called me — et cetera, et cetera. Vladlena had gone, he said, she'd left that day because she was scared the police would come and get her and put her in a camp for illegals. And that was that. I don't know how many of these girls I've had since then, seven or eight at least.'

'And now you have to go, I think you said, Mrs Jones,' said Wexford, looking at his watch.

'Yes, I must. Imagine, I've got a date with a man! Who knows what will come of it? I'm really excited.'

'I'll see myself out,' said Wexford. As he left he heard her screaming to Raisa to be sure and put the burglar alarm on and lock the front door on all three locks before she left.

It was twelve noon. He needed a little more time before speaking to David Goldberg, time to think. Slowly he walked up into Alma Square, admired some Japanese maple trees, their lacy leaves scarlet, looked at a towering Magnolia grandiflora and turned back towards Orcadia Place. A car was now parked outside Orcadia Cottage and a van had drawn up behind it. The van had a long scratch, deep, wavy and snake-like, along its nearside above the rear wheel. Wexford stood under a laburnum hung with black bean pods and watched. It shouldn't have been a surprise to see John Scott-McGregor get out of the driver's seat of the white van, walk round it and open the back. That was what he did, moved client's property from one place to another. No doubt the neighbours round here all used his services. Scott-McGregor lifted a box full of books out of the van and on to a trolley and pushed it up the path. The front door was opened to him by Anne Rokeby, still in her outdoor clothes, as her husband came up the path from their car, carrying armfuls of clothes on hangers. More boxes and a large plastic bag full of something was fetched from the van and the front door closed.

The Rokebys had come home.

23

First impressions are sometimes deceptive. Wexford admitted this cliché to himself when he had been inside the house in Melina Place for no more than five minutes. David Goldberg might be reclusive, but he was far from the zombie-like paranoid creature Wexford had set him down as when he had questioned the man before. True, the television was on and it was ten o'clock in the morning, but it was showing a DVD of *Shadowlands*, one of Wexford's favourite films. You are always inclined to warm to someone who turns out to share your own tastes.

'In some people's eyes,' said Goldberg in his harsh, gravelly voice, 'watching TV in the daytime is the Eighth Deadly Sin.'

'Not mine,' said Wexford. 'I must tell you, Mr Goldberg, that I've no right to question you. I'm not a policeman, not any more. And I must also tell you that if you tell *me* anything that helps in this case I shall be obliged to pass it on to Detective Superintendent Ede.'

'OK. But I haven't got anything to tell you.' David Goldberg picked up the remote and pressed the key that put the DVD on 'pause'. 'I told you before I know nothing about that manhole case. All I know is what I read in the papers.' He spread out his hands and shrugged. 'I don't have drinks and snacks and things between meals, so I hope you don't want anything.'

'I don't want anything.'

The room they were in was small but very light because the rear wall was almost entirely of glass with a glass door set in it on the right-hand side. Outside was a small garden, neat as a pin, beds full of michaelmas daisies and asters surrounding a tiny lawn with a statue of a girl standing on a plinth and holding up a pitcher.

'Yes, in case you're going to ask, I do it myself. I may be disabled but that doesn't stop me weeding and planting. I use my hands.'

'It's lovely.'

'What do you want to ask me about?'

'A young woman from the Ukraine called Vladlena.'

Goldberg wasn't as surprised as Wexford expected. He nodded reflectively. 'Yes. Vladlena. No doubt you've been talking to that nosy old termagant Mrs Jones. Mildred. I call her Mildreadful.'

Wexford smiled. 'I'd better tell you that I'm not here to get Vladlena into any sort of trouble. If she's still here. If she hasn't gone back to wherever she came from. I have nothing to do with Immigration. I'm not even a policeman any more. Nothing you say will do her any harm.'

'OK. Right. Vladlena — it's a great name, isn't it? — she came to the door one morning and when I opened it she said she'd run away from a house in Orcadia Mews because she'd burnt a shirt. So I let her in and sat her down. It's not the sort of thing I usually do, but it wasn't a usual situation, was it? She'd burnt a shirt and she was afraid of the police. That's what she said.

Oh, and old Mrs Mildreadful was on her trail.'

This time Wexford did laugh. 'What did you do?'

'Well, basically I gave her a job. My cleaner had just left. I liked the look of Vladlena. I told her I'd want her to shop for me and do a few other jobs I can't do and she was happy with that. She was thrilled, poor child. I told her she wouldn't have to iron my shirts. Nothing gets ironed in this house.

'I explained to her that I don't go out. That means that anything I want from out there.' — he waved a vague hand — 'I'd have to ask her to do for me. I suppose I should explain to you.' The harsh voice deepened. 'A long time ago, twenty years ago and a bit more, I was attacked in the street. For being gay — what a word for me! Four thugs set about me. My left leg was broken in three places and my head was bashed in. That left me with epilepsy.'

'I'm sorry,' Wexford said.

'You actually look as if you are. I live on incapacity benefit and what I earn from the odd bit of journalism. I got compensation, which enabled me to buy this house. But I don't go out at all. Into the street, that is. Not ever. I'm scared, you see. I am simply terrified to go out. I watch DVDs, I write a column called Gaiety and I tend my garden.'

'I see why you needed Vladlena.'

'Yes. Well, she was great. She even cooked for me and that was a change from living on ready meals, I can tell you. I knew she hadn't a right to be here, she hadn't any sort of passport. I knew all that but I liked her, she suited me. I'll tell you something I've never told anyone. Well, I never see anyone to tell. I thought, I'll see if she'll marry me. I'm gay, of course, if I'm anything any more. It'll just be to get her citizenship, she won't even have to live here if she doesn't want to. I thought of all that and then Mildreadful accosted her in the street.'

'I gather she was still harping on about the shirt.'

'It was all of a year later. She told her she'd have to pay for a new shirt or the police would get her. Vladlena just ran away again. She came into the house with the shopping and said she was going away, she was going to hide. You can imagine I told her she wasn't in any danger. It was all nonsense on old Mildreadful's part, but she wasn't having any. I should have told her then, I should have said I'd marry her and then she could have stayed, but I didn't. I wasn't sure, you see. When it came to it I suppose I got cold feet. I didn't really think she'd go. But she did. She left and I never saw her again.'

'You didn't try to find her?'

'Yes, of course I did. I had her address. She had a room in the house of an old Russian woman in Kilburn. I had Vladlena's mobile number. Everyone has mobiles these days, don't they? Everyone but me. I haven't got one. I phoned, but her phone was never answered. I didn't go up there. I told you, I don't go out. It must sound wimpish but I can't go out, I just can't. I'm like someone with agoraphobia only I'm not agoraphobic.'

'So that was the end?'

Goldberg sounded irritable. 'No, it wasn't. I asked a friend of mine to help. I do have friends, a few. Sophie, she's called. I've known her since she was a child and I was young — and able-bodied.' He made a rueful face. 'I asked her if she'd go up there and inquire for Vladlena.'

Wexford remembered or made a wild guess that turned out not to be wild at all. 'Not Sophie Baird who lives in Hall Road?'

'That's the one. Do you know her?'

'I don't exactly know her, Mr Goldberg. I talked to her and her partner in connection with this case.'

'Yes, the partner. The arch homophobe. We don't exactly get on. In fact, we've met just the once and that was enough.'

'She said nothing to me about Vladlena.'

'Could you call me David, please? 'Mr Goldberg' sounds like a big fat banker, very rich and living in The Bishop's Avenue.'

Laughing again, Wexford said he could, making a mental note to find out what and where The Bishop's Avenue was. 'And did Ms Baird have any luck?'

'She went to the Kilburn address and saw Vladlena. But Vladlena wouldn't talk to her. Not then. She seemed to be terrified to say anything while she was indoors. I mean inside a house. She and Sophie arranged to meet in a café in Kilburn next day, but when Sophie went there she had disappeared. Mrs Kataev said the same thing. She'd disappeared.'

'When was this?'

'Let me think. Two years ago or a bit more. It was summer. I remember Vladlena had a big thick coat, very shabby, and she wore it every day through the winter and spring. She wasn't wearing it. When she came into the house that day with the shopping after old Mrs MD had accosted her she was wearing a dress, a cotton dress. Her arms were bare.'

Wexford thanked David Goldberg, took Mrs Kataev's address and phone number from him and said he might want to see him again, but gave him no explanation for his questions and none was asked for. Leaving, he noticed that while Goldberg seemed happy to open the front door he stood back from it, a full yard from the daylight and the fresh air.

John Scott-McGregor, on the other hand, marched out of his house in Hall Road, forcing Wexford to take a step backwards.

'You again,' are not pleasant words to be greeted with, but Wexford was used to worse.

'I was hoping to have a word with Ms Baird.'

'You hope in vain. She's not here. She's at work.'

Wexford didn't pursue it. Instead he walked back across Hamilton Terrace and Abercorn Place to the Edgware Road. There he got on the Number 16 bus for Kilburn and Brondesbury Villas where Mrs Kataev lived. The street surprised him. Kilburn High Road might be run down in some parts and blatantly gaudy in others, but Brondesbury Villas was staid and dignified. Two words seldom heard these days came to mind, 'select' and 'respectable'. And

Irina Kataev herself seemed both those things, a thin, upright, elderly woman who spoke precise English with a slight and attractive accent. The hallway of her house and the living room into which she took him, were hygienically clean and airy. Mrs Kataev herself wore a black dress with a red cardigan over it.

'I wish I could help you,' she said. 'I have worried about her. She gave me no notice that she would be leaving. One day she came home as usual from Mr Goldberg and went up to her room. She was in her room alone all evening. She was a quiet girl. She kept herself to herself, as I believe you say. Next day she was in her room all day. I think now that she was afraid to go out — like that poor Mr Goldberg.'

'When did she go?'

'I heard her on her phone many times. I listened because I was worried about her. She was only just nineteen, you know. Next day, very early in the morning — it must have been early because it was before I got up at six — she left and had with her the one suitcase she came with. She owed me some rent and she left the correct sum for me in an envelope.'

'How long had she lived with you, Mrs Kataev?'

'For about two years. Before that she had had a room in a flat in Kensal, very dirty and nasty, she said. She came here from the Ukraine in two thousand and six and all this you are asking about is two years ago and more.'

'*How* did she come from the Ukraine to this country?'

'Like they all do. In a minibus. She and her sister who was with her, they had to pay quite a lot of money to come. She told me there was some sea on the way, the last part — she meant the Channel — and when they were in England they were taken from the minibus and were put into a trailer. She and her sister had been told by one of the other girls that they were not to be trained as models like they expected, but to become servants to rich people. They would be paid, but for a while everything they earned would be to pay the people who had brought them here. She thought she had already paid them, so she ran away. She ran away that night, but her sister was afraid to go with her. For my part, I think they were to be something else to rich men. You understand me?'

Wexford nodded. 'When she ran away, where did she go?'

'She had a cousin here, in London. She is married to an Englishman who found her through a — I don't know how to say it — an agency? For dating? For looking for wives?'

'I understand.'

'Vladlena had no money. She hitch-hiked to London and she walked, she slept on the street, she begged. At last she found this woman, but she would let her stay only two nights. Her husband was not a nice man. He was old, forty years older than Vladlena's cousin and this woman worked for him like a servant. It was not a happy situation. But the cousin helped her find a room and told her how she could be a cleaner.'

Such stories were not uncommon. Wexford

found himself wishing that David Goldberg had obeyed his instinct, taken the plunge and offered to marry Vladlena. But he hadn't and now it was too late. Should he advise Mrs Kataev to report Vladlena as a missing person? Probably not. Vladlena herself would be too frightened of the authorities to answer such a call.

'Do you know the cousin's name and address?'

'I don't,' said Irina Kataev. 'Even if I did it would be no use. Vladlena wouldn't go back there. The husband, the old man, made a — I don't know how to say it . . . '

'An unwelcome advance to her?'

'That is it exactly. An unwelcome advance.'

'Can you remember her sister's name?'

'Vladlena called her Alyona.'

'Would you spell that, please?'

'A-L-Y-O-N-A.'

He walked back up the High Road, looking for a street which would cut through to West Hampstead. Someone had told him that in days gone by Irish immigrants had settled in Kilburn and in the name 'Biddy Mulligan's' on a pub there was evidence of that, but now it seemed that people from the Middle East and Asia had overtaken them. Women in burkas and some in the all-obscuring *niqab* from which only the wearer's eyes were visible, shopped alongside an indigenous population almost universally in anoraks, hoods and padded coats. A small establishment — that was the appropriate word for it, he thought — advertised beauty treatments and various types of massage, hair extensions, waxing and nail enhancement. Its name, Doll-up, though quite possibly referring to a woman's preparing herself to go out on a date, had a less innocent ring to it, implying that whatever blameless activities went on at street level, the true purpose of the place was concentrated upstairs. The poster filling most of its window showed a very beautiful young woman of South-east Asian origin, wearing a white overall which left most of her long bare brown legs uncovered, administering a 'Taiwanese' massage to an ancient wrinkled man of about ninety. Shoppers passed it by indifferently without so much as a glance.

Wexford thought of the story of Tithonus, the shepherd boy whom Eos, goddess of the dawn fell in love with. She asked the gods to make him immortal and her wish was granted, but she failed to ask them to give him eternal youth. Tithonus grew old while she remained ever-young, he grew bent and wrinkled, shrivelled like the man in the poster. At last Eos took pity on him and turned him into the cicada he now so closely resembled. No reinvigorating massages in those days, Wexford reflected as he turned into Iverson Road.

At police headquarters Tom Ede suggested to him that they have lunch together. Not in the canteen, if Wexford didn't mind, but in a small French restaurant in West End Lane. It was the first invitation as such Wexford had received from Tom and he felt gratified.

'It won't turn out to be La Punaise, will it?' he said, but Tom had forgotten all about the

246

disguised pin number.

Lunch, though French, was to be abstemious. Tom didn't drink and though he offered Wexford a glass of wine, he made it plain that to see a companion drinking alcohol while he had to abstain put him under too much of a strain. 'I wasn't exactly an alcoholic,' Tom said, 'but I was heading that way. The quack said my liver wasn't all it ought to be so I took the plunge and gave up altogether. I had my faith, of course, and that helped. It always does.'

Calling a doctor a quack came high on Wexford's list of undesirable expressions, but he only smiled and said of course he wouldn't have any wine. Tom's faith? Like most people Wexford was made slightly embarrassed by mention of God or religion, a prejudice he struggled vainly against. Fortunately the subject was changed by his telling Tom about Mildred Jones and Vladlena and David Goldberg and Mrs Kataev. Tom nodded reflectively while pursing his lips and pushing them forward in a way which might equally mean disbelief or acceptance.

'What evidence have you got that this Vlad — whatever is the girl in the patio tomb?'

Wexford drank some water that tasted even more insipid than usual. 'She's the right sort of age. She worked in the area in two places. She must have known it well. It's possible that at some point between two and three years ago she found out what was in the tomb — that is that three bodies were in there.'

'So blackmail, you mean?'

'I suppose I do.' Now it was so clearly

247

expressed Wexford found he disliked the idea. He had come — surely unwisely — to have tender feelings for Vladlena. But the poor girl — might not anyone in her unfortunate position have recourse to obtaining money by threats, if she could?

'So you're saying we should try and find her?'

'I think Lucy or Miles should come along with me or I go along with them to talk to Sophie Baird. She's the woman who tried to find her for David Goldberg.'

Tom nodded without much enthusiasm. Suddenly Wexford thought of all the pleasant and rewarding lunches he had enjoyed with Mike Burden in the past. 'Better be Lucy, I suppose,' Tom said. 'A woman to talk to a woman.' Perhaps because they were in a French restaurant, he followed up his last statement with, '*Cherchez la femme.*'

★ ★ ★

Sheila and her girls were with Dora when Wexford walked in. 'Where's The Bishop's Avenue?'

'It's a street of big houses, the kind the media call 'mansions',' said Sheila. 'It's Highgate and it turns out of the Hampstead Road. You've walked from the Spaniards Inn to Highgate, Pop. You must have passed it.'

Amy wanted to know what a bishop was and Wexford set about explaining to her. She said she would like to be one when she grew up, and was told that wouldn't be possible as things were at present but that would certainly have changed by the time she was an adult.

'I am going to be a banker,' said Anoushka, which silenced everyone for a moment.

'I find all this quite heartening,' said Wexford. 'It's so different from what I read in the papers about girls wanting to be models and marry footballers.'

They had been gone five minutes and Dora was talking of going to the cinema when his phone rang. It was Sophie Baird.

'I was about to call you, Ms Baird,' he said. 'I was hoping to come along with DC Blanch and talk to you.'

She was silent. He thought the connection had broken.

'Ms Baird?'

Her sigh preceded a breathy, 'I've just split up from John. He's gone. I didn't think he would, I thought he'd try to throw me out, though the house is mine. But I told him and he just went. I should have done it years ago.' She gave a sudden hysterical laugh. 'I'm sorry. It's just that I'm high on adrenalin. I shouldn't be telling you all this. I hardly know you.'

'It will be quite safe with me,' said Wexford.

'I know that. Somehow I know. David called me. David Goldberg.'

'Yes.'

'He said he'd told you about me and Vladlena. There's a lot he doesn't know about what she told me. There was no point in telling him. I tried to tell John, but he just said not to get mixed up with filthy illegals. Those were his words, 'filthy illegals'. I should have left him then or got him to leave me.' She drew a deep breath. 'I want to tell *you*.'

'So when shall DC Blanch and I come?'

'I don't want her, whoever she is. I mean, she may be very nice, but I don't want to tell anyone but you. I think you'll understand. But not today, not this evening. I've called a locksmith to get the locks changed in case John tries to come back. He says he'll never darken these doors again, if you've ever heard such crap, but he may if he changes his mind. So I'll get the locks changed and then I'm going to cook David's dinner and stay the night with him. He's the only person I really want to see right now.'

'Tomorrow, then, Ms Baird?'

'I'm taking the rest of the week off work. I've got holiday owing to me. Would you like to come along around ten?'

He said he would, flattered by her trust in him, intrigued by her hints that what she had to tell him might be a breakthrough. She had been with Scott-McGregor for years, yet she had apparently shaken him off in a couple of hours, turned him out and sighed with relief. Of course, the euphoria would pass and soon and regret and recriminations set in. For the first time he put his fear — or was it hope? — that the young woman's body in the tomb might be Vladlena's. No, it was fear. He already felt too much pity for her, fugitive that she had been, to hope for such an end.

They would definitely go to the cinema, he told Dora. Was it *Revolutionary Road* she wanted to

see or *Bright Star*? She wasn't sure, she would
tell him when he came back from wherever he
was going. Mapesbury Road, Cricklewood, to
take another look at the clothes the young woman's corpse had worn.

Tom was out. Miles Crowhurst showed him
once more the pathetic collection. Whore's
garments, he thought, and immediately casti-
gated himself for his harshness. Many perfectly
decent girls — 'good girls', as they were once
called — wore tight T-shirts, biker's jackets, tight
mini-skirts, hold-up fishnet stockings and knee-
high boots. But wore them without underwear?

He said to Miles, 'Where are her bra and
knickers?'

'She wasn't wearing any, sir.'

'You're young,' he said. 'You're a heterosexual
male. I don't know about these things any more
but you do. Would a normal, ordinary girl go
about without underwear?'

'Not in my experience,' said Miles.

Wexford had seen those clothes before, seen
them when he saw the men's clothes and the *La
Punaise* note and the jewellery from Teddy
Brex's pockets, but this point about the lack of
underwear hadn't struck him. It hadn't struck
Tom either. Would Sophie Baird be able to
resolve several puzzles tomorrow morning?

24

Bright Star made him want to go and see Keats's house. It was no distance away. Grove End Road first, though, and what he learnt there might make him put everything else off till a later date. He was setting off when Sophie Baird phoned. Would he meet her at David Goldberg's house instead? Wexford said he would. She volunteered answers to questions he hadn't asked.

'I'd feel better away from this house. Just for a while. It's my house and John's gone, but somehow I feel he's still here and listening to what I say.'

'That's quite all right with me, Ms Baird.'

'David's a good friend. I don't know what I'd do without David.'

Wexford took the 13 bus down the Finchley Road. Sitting on the top at the front, he thought about the short conversation he had just had. Sophie Baird's tone had given a weight to what she had said which wasn't in her actual words. Had she made significant discoveries and was it only now that she meant to share them with David Goldberg?

He walked to Goldberg's house by way of Orcadia Place. The fat young woman with the baby in a pushchair was once more outside Orcadia Cottage, staring up at an upstairs window where she had perhaps just seen the silhouetted head of Martin or Anne Rokeby.

Wexford nodded to her and she smiled. He thought how when his father was a young man most men wore hats and raised them to women they knew or even women they just knew by sight. Would he like a return to that custom? Not really.

Sophie Baird came to David Goldberg's door when Wexford rang the bell. She looked, he thought, quite different from when he had last seen her, younger, healthier, the transformation he had noticed when she smiled, now there all the time. It was a fine day and the French windows to the garden were open. Goldberg was sitting by them, but when Wexford came in he got up and closed them, saying, 'It's too late in the year for all this fresh air.'

Sophie brought in coffee and fruit juice and water, plates of cake and plates of biscuits. 'I wasn't expecting a party,' Wexford said.

'I just felt like doing it,' she said. 'A little celebration. I keep saying to myself, 'Thank God I never married John.' He wanted it. But even when we were at our best some warning voice inside me said, 'Don't do it.''

David Goldberg's eyebrows went up and he smiled a little. Sophie sat next to him and took hold of his hand. A classic case, Wexford thought, of a woman whose best friend is a gay man. 'Ms Baird,' he began, 'I hope you're going to tell me what you know of the whereabouts of Vladlena.'

She looked at him. It was the first time she had looked him in the eye. Their eyes met and then she turned hers away. 'I've told David everything I know,' she said. 'I mean, just before you came I told him. I lied to him before. It was wrong, I know that. I didn't know he'd considered marrying her. I'd have told him everything if I'd known. But I told John, you see.'

'And that was a mistake?'

'If ever there was an understatement . . . He went mad. He shouted at me that I was aiding and abetting an illegal immigrant. I could go to prison. Is that true?'

'Of course not,' Wexford said.

'I believed him. He frightened me, he was always frightening me. He was jealous of David, and tried to stop me seeing him. Oh, I mustn't go on. It's all over now. The upshot was that I didn't tell David, but I have now and now I'll tell you.'

She had met Vladlena in the café as arranged. It must have been a curious meeting, Wexford thought, with one woman neurotically fearful that her partner was lurking somewhere and able to hear all she said, while the other (with rather more reason) feared that representatives from the UK Border Agency were sitting disguised at the next table. Vladlena had found a room in Willesden and a job in a hand car wash. She was due to start next day.

'I asked her if Mrs Kataev knew she was going and she said no, she didn't want to tell her. She meant just to disappear. She was good, she said, at disappearing. And then she said that the man who had driven her and her sister and the others across Europe, she'd seen him again. I don't know who he was. She said he came up to her in the street and offered to buy her a drink. He'd been watching her, he said, when she was working for old Mildreadful and David. She knew he wasn't immigration or the police, so she went with him. They went into a pub in Kilburn High Road.

'Vladlena's English was quite good. It had to be because she never encountered anyone who spoke her own language except the cousin who was — well, off-limits for various reasons. So she understood what this man said to her. He asked her if she was a virgin.'

'*What?*' said Wexford.

'Yes. You did hear what I said.' Sophie squeezed David Goldberg's hand and dropped it. 'He asked her if she was a virgin and she asked him why did he want to know. 'I can get a thousand pounds for you if you are,' he said.'

Though he had presumably heard it before, Goldberg made a face and a sound of disgust.

'I'm sorry, David. It's hateful, I know. You're like me. You thought it was only old lechers in Victorian times who thought like that. But it's not. It happens today. There are people who think having a virgin is a cure for AIDS. Vladlena didn't think that. It sounded as if she didn't think much about it, only about the money. If she had a thousand pounds she could buy herself a passport, she said. I told her that this man might get a thousand pounds from someone, but what made her think she would see even half of it?'

'What did she say?'

'That I shouldn't worry because he'd told her that would be her share. The people who — well, organised it would get much more. Anyway, she might not do it through him. He'd given her the idea.'

'I take it,' Wexford said slowly. 'that those girls and Vladlena herself had been destined for — what was it? Some sort of massage parlour that's really a brothel? At best, a call-girl agency?'

'I didn't ask,' said Sophie Baird. 'It sounds ridiculous, but I was so shocked. And John, when I told him, he was horrified. He said he'd never heard of such a thing, but he must have heard of trafficked women. It's always in the papers, that stuff. She told me the name of the driver — well, she told me his first name — it was Gregory or something close to that. Whether she went to him or not I don't know. She wouldn't give me his address. Well, I didn't ask for it. I'd arranged to meet her again, but I didn't keep the appointment. John frightened me, he was so angry. He hit me and he'd never done that before.'

⋆ ⋆ ⋆

Tom listened to Wexford's account of his interview with Sophie Baird with attention which was almost enthusiasm.

'Yes, but it's all rather vague,' Wexford said. 'A driver of a minibus trafficking girls is called Gregory, but with no surname. Vladlena has a cousin whose name is unknown. Vladlena's own surname is unknown.'

'That's a rather defeatist attitude, isn't it?'

'Maybe. I didn't mean I was giving up. Sophie Baird was in a — well, a heightened emotional state. She may remember more when I talk to her again.'

'Better go with Lucy this time. As I said before, a woman to talk to a woman. That's best. I'm not saying you haven't done well, Reg, but you're very hot on all this psychology and knowing human nature and all that, but I don't think you're allowing for the fact that this Sophie Baird may have been jealous of Vladlena. Much younger than her, wasn't she? A pretty blonde and alone with this Goldberg day after day. It may be best to go back to Mrs Jones, see if she can put a different complexion on things. You and Lucy go back to Mrs Jones. Talk to the other neighbours, those Milsoms, for instance. They may have talked to her. Even the Rokebys. You didn't think of them, did you? But they're back living in Orcadia Cottage now.'

In his own kind of phraseology, Tom had got hold of the wrong end of the stick. Wexford was sure all these people would be useless, especially Mildred Jones who would have made a point of knowing nothing of her cleaner's background. It might be that even now the burnt shirt still rankled with her.

'Remember I like the idea of this Vladlena,' were Tom's parting words. 'Tongue-twister of a name, isn't it? I like it. She could be our girl in the patio-tomb. It's more than likely.'

'I'd like to bring Sophie Baird here to look at those clothes.'

'Good idea. You do that small thing. Must go,

I've a busy afternoon. And then the Harvest Supper at my church.'

Sophie Baird couldn't be reached until the following day. He tried her at home in Hall Road, on a mobile that seemed permanently switched off and finally got her on David Goldberg's landline. No, she wasn't living there; she hadn't moved in. She was going back home that day. Would she come with him to the Met Headquarters in Mapesbury Road, Cricklewood? They would send a car for her.

'Can I ask what for?'

'I want to show you some clothes that may have belonged to Vladlena.'

'Belonged to a girl whose body has been found' was what he should have said. But so far he hadn't told Sophie why he was so interested in Vladlena and she hadn't asked. Lucy went in the car to fetch Sophie Baird. Wexford was waiting for her when she arrived and showed her the clothes. Sophie herself was dressed much as she usually was in a tweed skirt and jumper with cream-coloured jacket and brown leather court shoes. The garments which had been on the young woman's body in the vault had become pathetic in Wexford's eyes; they so objectified their wearer and almost certainly had been worn not because she liked them or chose to wear them but as the uniform of her trade. Sophie Baird's reaction was very different. She recoiled, she blushed. Wexford had been about to ask her not to touch anything, but any caution of that kind was unnecessary. She actually stepped back from the table on which the boots, the jacket and the fishnet tights lay.

'I never saw Vladlena wear anything like that,' she said in a shaky voice. 'How did you — the police — get hold of these?' A possible solution occurred to her and she shuddered. 'Were they — were they on a dead body?'

'I'm afraid so.'

'The three times I saw Vladlena she was wearing a summer dress — well, a cotton dress, quite faded and shabby, and once a thick winter coat over it. Her shoes looked very worn and she also wore flip-flops.'

'But if she was going to do what she suggested to you she would do for the sake of a thousand pounds, she might have worn clothes such as these?'

'I suppose she might have,' said Sophie Baird.

'One more question before I take you in to see Detective Superintendent Ede. Would Vladlena have worn underwear?'

'Well — I don't understand. What do you mean, worn underwear? Of course she would. Everyone does.'

'So you believe she would have?'

'I assume she would. I don't know, though. I really don't know.'

Tom Ede asked her if Vladlena had any jewellery. Sophie Baird said she couldn't remember; perhaps a ring. The necklaces and rings and bracelets they had concluded had all belonged to Harriet Merton, were shown to her but she had scarcely glanced at them when she shook her head impatiently.

'You don't understand. She was *poor*. She was

much poorer than the poor in this country are. She had nothing. She earned enough to pay her rent to Mrs Kataev and buy food and that was all.'

'You mentioned the possibility of a ring,' Tom said.

'Yes, but I'm not sure I'm not imagining it. I seem to remember something silver she wore, a ring, a pendant. I *seem* to, but that's all I can say.'

Getting ready to drive himself and Dora back to Kingsmarkham for the weekend, Wexford asked himself what steps Vladlena would have taken to carry out her plan. The driver called Grigor or Gregory seemed the most likely for her to have contacted. But where was he to be found? If the transaction had reached a stage of Vladlena prostituting herself, where would she have done it? Not in a room at Irina Kataev's. In a hotel room booked for her? He didn't think so. More likely in a brothel disguised as something else. He had little experience of such places. So far as he knew there had never been in Kingsmarkham what used to be called a disorderly house.

★　★　★

But there he was wrong, as Mike Burden told him on the Saturday evening. The drinks they enjoyed together after work in the old days had come to an end when Wexford retired and Burden was promoted but had been replaced by meeting — often in a new and previously unvisited pub — every weekend Wexford returned home. It was becoming a tradition with a ritualistic quality to it. Many pubs had closed in the surrounding villages, largely due to would-be visitors intimidated by the drink-driving laws, but in Kingsmarkham itself the Olive and Dove still ruled supreme and the Dragon did a brisk trade. This evening they were to meet in the Mermaid, a small snug pub in a narrow lane off York Street.

But before that Wexford and Dora had spent half a day, a night and more than half the next day in their own house. Both their grandsons were at home and Robin had brought a fellow-student home with him. When he was young, though he had not attended one himself, Wexford said universities used to discourage if not expressly forbid undergraduates to go home for the weekend. All that had changed. Ben was there, too, his school having closed for half-term. With a fairly good grace, Sylvia gave up the bedroom she shared with her daughter to her parents, but made them feel guilty by whining miserably about her and Mary having to share a single bed put up in the dining room.

'How to make one feel one should have booked a room in a hotel,' said Dora.

'Why did we come, anyway?'

'We'd forgotten — if we ever knew — how many people there would be here.'

Matters weren't helped by an encounter Wexford had on his way to the Mermaid. He was halfway down York Street when a man and a woman came out of one of the houses and the man unlocked a car parked at the kerb with a remote. Wexford recognised them at once as the Wardles, parents of the dead Jason. And they knew him. They looked, stared and ostentatiously turned their heads away.

'I wonder,' he said when he saw Burden, 'what third thing is going to happen to make me feel guilty.'

'You don't believe in that stuff about things coming in threes, do you?'

'I didn't last week, but all this makes me nervous.'

Burden fetched Wexford a glass of claret and himself a Chardonnay. Nuts, once an enemy yet desired, had become no more or less than a pleasant adjunct to their drinks.

'You've lost a lot of weight. You look quite different.'

'That may be no bad thing. What were you going to tell me about brothels?'

'We had one here,' said Burden. 'A couple of months ago.'

'What, you mean a massage place or beauty and tanning and waxing, do you?'

'This was in a flat over a shop in the High Street. It was a clothes shop, highly respectable and selling dresses and suits for sizes 16 to 28.'

'If I'd been a transvestite they'd just about have suited me in days gone by.'

Burden laughed. 'A lot of men had been seen coming to the door at the right side of the shops in the evenings. I sent DC Thompson in there, posing as a punter. The girls he had to choose from were presented to him, but he obeyed my prudish instructions, said no thanks politely and walked out. We raided the place on the following evening.' He took a swig of his Chardonnay. 'It was quite exciting.'

'I can't remember the rule. It has to be more than one girl to constitute a brothel, doesn't it?'

'That's right. I wasn't there but Thompson told me one of the men fell on his knees and swore on his mother's head that if it didn't come out that he was there he would never do it again.'

'When I was a young DC in Brighton about a hundred years ago we used to come across them. Brothels, I mean. I suppose if I got someone to find 'brothels' on the Internet I'd just get quantities of porn.'

'That's an understatement,' said Burden. 'Come to me instead. What is it you want to know?'

Wexford told him about Vladlena and the sale she had proposed to make. 'Where would she go? Who would she have asked? There's a perfectly respectable-looking massage parlour in Kilburn High Road near the Tricycle Theatre — sorry, you don't know where that is — but it did occur to me she might have tried there. I shall have to find how long it's been there, and you know how these outfits come and go. The girl in the vault has been dead at least two years.'

'You know, Reg,' Burden said, passing the nuts it was no longer necessary to avoid, 'as you've rightly just pointed out to me, I don't know London well, but I've enough knowledge of the way these things work to say that this girl is most likely to have tried Soho. If those places don't outright advertise prostitutes everyone knows prostitution is what they offer.'

'You mean she'd just call at some lap-dancing club or place where there are strippers.'

'She might if she was desperate enough to get what was to her a large sum of money,' said Burden.

But it was more than two years ago, Wexford reminded himself. Had she complied and been killed because of what she had done and what she might tell? It seemed a possibility.

25

It was Monday morning and Wexford and Lucy Blanch were on their way to see Mildred Jones. Neither of them looked forward to the visit. The day began badly with Martin Rokeby emerging from his front door and shouting at Lucy not to park the car in front of his house. She moved it a few feet, explaining that they had calls to make in the neighbourhood and there was nowhere else to put it. Rokeby began on a long peevish complaint, the gist of which was that the police had been investigating this case for months and still had got nowhere.

They walked round the corner and into Orcadia Mews. Wexford was glad to be back in London for no better reason than that his stay in Kingsmarkham had been horrible. Returning from his evening out with Burden, he was told by Dora, whispering, that another child had joined the household, a schoolfellow of Mary's. The previous week Sylvia had promised this little boy's mother to have her son for the night while the parents celebrated a wedding anniversary. Ben would have to share his room with this child, had at first refused outright, then agreed with an ill grace and after putting up a lot of conditions.

'You and Dad might have given me a little more notice you were coming,' Sylvia had said, causing Dora to explode.

'This is *our house*, Sylvia! How dare you tell me we should have given you notice to come to our own house!'

'I wish we didn't have to be here,' said Sylvia. 'I'm not getting any pleasure out of it. Thank God I'm back at work.'

Wexford had not even attempted to bring about a truce but had gone straight to bed. Guilty now because he and Dora were occupying the largest of the four bedrooms, he lay awake for a long time, to be awakened almost at once by shouts and running feet in the passage outside. The little boy guest had been sick. He needed comforting and cleaning up and his bed sheets changed. In the morning Sylvia refused her father's offer to take all of them out for lunch, so he and Dora were on their way back to London by eleven.

Mildred Jones had had her once-pink front door repainted. Now it was lime green. Although Lucy had phoned her to arrange their visit, Mrs Jones behaved as if their appearance on her doorstep was the first she had heard of it. 'I've told you everything I know,' were her opening words, without even the preamble of a 'Good morning' in reply to Lucy's polite greeting.

Assessing this woman's character, Wexford had noted how dramatically she was changed by her view of the day ahead of her. When about to lunch with a man, she was ebullient, confident and assertive, but with a blank or tedious day in prospect she became petulant and sullen. Today was evidently going to be blank or tedious. Her mood seemed also to affect the way she dressed, to the extent that she wore unflattering clothes on bad days and attractive ones when things looked to be going well.

'I can't offer you anything to drink,' she said as she led them into the living room. 'Raisa's too busy.'

This attitude, that any domestic task must be performed by the cleaner and never by the employer, brought a humourless smile to Wexford's lips, a reaction he was later to regret.

'Something amuses you?'

He took it to be a rhetorical question and said nothing. Lucy said they would like to talk about Vladlena. Was she aware that Vladlena had a sister who had come to this country with her in a minibus driven across Europe?

'She'd be another illegal immigrant? Because if so, I don't want to talk about her or any of them. I told you before' — she glowered at Wexford — 'I've been frightened out of my wits I'd be in trouble with the immigration.'

'We're not concerned with immigration, Mrs Jones . . . ' Wexford began and Lucy added what he hadn't felt it was incumbent on him to say, 'We're concerned with the identity of the young woman whose body was with the others underneath Orcadia Cottage.'

Without exciting plans for her day, Mildred Jones was wearing no make-up to cover her sudden pallor. Her face turned a yellowish white. 'You mean you think that girl in the hole, the cellar, was Vladlena?'

'We only want to eliminate her from our enquiries,' Wexford said.

'That's what you all say. I'd like a pound for the number of times I've heard that on TV. What a ghastly idea.'

How much he would have liked to say that — considering her attitude towards her former cleaner — he would have expected her to be pleased at the prospect. But he had wanted to say that sort of thing when he was a young policeman decades ago. Now he was old there was all the more reason to restrain himself. Instead, politely, he asked Mrs Jones how Vladlena had usually been dressed.

Dress was a subject, he could tell, which greatly interested her. 'She wasn't what you'd call elegant.' She laughed, and paused to let her wit be appreciated. 'She wore this one cotton frock day in and day out. I asked her about it and she said it was all she had, so I took pity on her and gave her a couple of cast-offs of my own. She was practically anorexic, so of course she had to take them in a bit before she could wear them.'

'Did you ever see her in a miniskirt and wearing a leather jacket?'

She looked at Wexford as if he had asked something obscene. 'Why do you want to know?'

'Just answer the question, please, Mrs Jones.'

'A leather jacket, yes. A miniskirt, no.'

As she spoke, a diffident Raisa put her head round the door. 'You like coffee, madam?'

'No, I wouldn't. When I want you I'll call you.' Mildred Jones turned back to Lucy. 'I saw her wearing a black leather jacket and a long floral skirt, not a very attractive combination in my opinion.'

'Where was that?' Wexford asked. 'When she was shopping for Mr Goldberg?'

'Of course not. Whatever put that idea into your head? It wasn't round here at all. It was in Oxford Street. I'd been in Selfridges and when I came out I found the police had closed the street to traffic. Some silly woman had run across in front of a bus and got knocked down. So, of course, everyone had to suffer and while I was walking all the way to Marble Arch to get a taxi — carrying heavy bags I may add — I saw her coming out of that cheap store, Primark. She was doing all right, carrying bags of stuff she'd bought.'

This meant little to Wexford, but he could see that Lucy's reaction was very different. 'Are you sure, Mrs Jones? The closing of Oxford Street for a street accident was only about a year ago.'

'I know *that*.' Mildred Jones eyed Lucy indignantly. 'I hope you're not calling me a liar.'

'You're telling us you saw Vladlena a year ago?' said Wexford.

'For God's sake. How many times do I have to tell you?'

'Once more, please, to be sure.'

'*I saw her a year ago.*'

He and Lucy were silent until they had rounded the corner into Orcadia Place. They looked at each other and laughed and Wexford said, 'Maybe we should be thankful for small mercies. I'm glad to know she's alive and apparently quite prosperous, aren't you?'

'Yes, of course I am. I'm glad she's not the girl in the patio-tomb, but someone was and it did look as if it was her.'

'I'd like to think she was out of it, clear of it. But I don't think she can be. She may know all sorts of things we don't dream of. She can't be the girl in the vault, but she may know who the girl in the vault was. Besides, I confess I'm curious.'

'So am I,' said Lucy. 'I'd like to know what happened to her, how she got from being a homeless, poverty-stricken sort of — well, waif — to owning a leather jacket and shopping in Primark. Shopping at all, come to that.'

Wexford said nothing. He thought of what Vladlena had told Sophie Baird she would do to get money. He must really be getting old. He was certainly getting soft if the means she had spoken off could revolt him so deeply — yes, even shock him. He who had believed nothing could shock him any more.

★　★　★

He was curious and Lucy was curious, but did their curiosity justify trying to find Vladlena? It was too late. All that was of importance to them was that she was not the girl in the vault. She had a sister somewhere in this country, a cousin somewhere in London. David Goldberg knew nothing of her whereabouts and nor did Sophie Baird. What of those others living in the immediate neighbourhood? The Milsoms? The Rokebys themselves? Then there was Mildred Jones's ex-husband Colin Jones. He had known Vladlena, even if she had never attracted him.

Wexford thought it was possible that in the two years or so that Vladlena had worked for Mildred Jones and then for David Goldberg she had occasionally talked to the neighbours and perhaps mentioned her relatives. Put like that he could see it was a long shot. But then there was the driver, the man who suggested she sell her virginity. Who was he? Was there any point in asking those people he listed?

Sophie said Vladlena and the driver had met in a pub in Kilburn. His mind went back to Kilburn High Road and the massage parlour. Could he have told her that if she agreed to his proposition, the transaction could take place in one of the upper floors of Doll-up?

But Vladlena was alive or had been a year ago. Whatever might be the truth of all this, whatever any of these people might have to say, the young woman's body in the tomb could not be Vladlena's.

* * *

It could come to be a matter for the Vice Squad, Wexford thought, but first a preliminary reconnaissance was called for. Tom agreed to a search for Colin Jones being made online and WPC Debach was given this task. Wexford himself set off for what called itself a 'beauty centre'. He had come prepared with a story to gain himself entry to the two upper floors if admission to them was refused, and he glanced up at the top windows before going in. All four were masked in opaque blinds.

271

A receptionist asked if she could help him. Wexford had already noted the array of treatments on offer, from chiropody to full-body exfoliation. One specially caught his eye and he asked if he could book a Brazilian massage. Certainly, but their masseur was fully booked until the following Monday.

'Masseur?'

The look he got was unfriendly. 'Do you have a problem with that?'

'I expected a masseuse.'

'Really? I wonder if Doll-up is quite the location you are looking for?'

Location! He put his head on one side, said in a lower voice, 'What goes on upstairs?'

'I have no idea,' she said stiffly. 'The premises have nothing to do with us. They are quite separate and are, I understand, to let.'

'Do you know who the agent is?'

'No, I do not. If that's all, Mr Er — ? I am rather busy this morning.'

He walked down a narrow side street from which he could see the backs of a row of buildings of which Doll-up was the nearest. From here it looked even smaller than from the High Road. The building was just one room wide and if there were more than three rooms, however subdivided they might be, on the ground floor that was all there were. Back in the High Street he noticed a shabby door in the wall next to the 'beauty centre'. There was no nameplate, no bell, no knocker, only a letter box. He flapped the lid of the box without much hope of anyone answering and no one did answer, but a window above was flung open and an elderly man put his head out.

'Go away! How many times do I have to tell you randy bastards this is not a knocking shop?'

Wexford started laughing. How he wished he could tell this irate chap that he was a policeman. 'I'm sorry,' he said. 'I understand your place is to let.'

'I'll come down.'

He was a short spare man with a lot of hair on his face and none on his head, dressed in a black sweatshirt and jeans. 'I've told them again and again what'll happen if they give the place a bloody stupid name like that. But do they take any notice? Do they hell. That's why I'm moving out. For ten years I lived here in peace and quiet and then they came along and buggered it up.'

'So you wouldn't recommend me to take it?'

'No, I wouldn't, but I can give you the name of the agents if you like.'

* * *

Tom was amused. 'Well-spotted, Reg,' he said. 'Not your fault it was a wild goose chase. Should I send Miles along to the agents so he can give that flat the once over?'

'If you feel it's worth it, but I'm sure it's perfectly innocent.'

'Rita Debach has run Colin Jones to earth.'

She had found him in Kendal Avenue, SW12, and a phone number for him. Finding someone was easy these days, Wexford thought, even when his was a name shared by hundreds. You might

273

know where he lived, but after that he was lost to you if he failed to come to his door or answer his phone. Messages were left for him to contact the police, but for what? What help could he be, a man who was once married to Mildred Jones, who had lived in the house where Vladlena worked and who had once recommended to Martin Rokeby a contractor he had already found? When I think of him, Wexford reflected, it's always as the man whose shirt Vladlena burned . . .

Two days ahead, the weekend would not be spent in Kingsmarkham. Relations between Wexford and Dora and their elder daughter were too strained for that. Sylvia had phoned, but there had been a coolness on both sides. Her reason for calling — that she had found a house, though not yet sold her own — led her to say that she would speed things up as much as she could because she knew 'only too well' that she and her children weren't welcome in her parents' house.

So those parents stayed in London, walked on the Heath, bought books in Hatchards and socks for Wexford in Marks & Spencer's and on the Saturday night went to the theatre to see Sheila play Mrs Alving in Ibsen's *Ghosts*. On the Monday morning, when he called the number of the house in Kendal Avenue, a woman answered.

She was Mrs Jones, she said. Her husband was away on business but would be back on Wednesday. She would tell him the police wanted to talk to him. Her tone was that of a woman speaking of a promise rather than a threat and she sounded quite unfazed.

The threat came from the first Mrs Jones. And if it wasn't aimed at him, it concerned him. Tom told him as soon as he walked into the glass-walled office.

26

'She contacted the IPCC,' said Tom. 'Mildred Jones, I mean.'

For a moment Wexford had to think what the initials stood for. Of course, he knew perfectly well, but for a moment the meaning had eluded him.

'The Independent Police Complaints Commission? What on earth is that about?'

'Well, it's about you.' Tom laughed to soften the blow. 'Lucy's in trouble for taking you along to interview her.'

'Old Mildreadful is what Goldberg calls her.'

'Yes, but for goodness sake, she doesn't know *that?*'

'Of course not, Tom. What's her specific grievance?'

'It's all rubbish, but she alleges you 'laughed scornfully' when she 'declined to provide you with refreshment'. That you asked her to answer a question in the manner you would talk to someone who was under arrest, and that Lucy allowed you to conduct the interview as if you were the police officer and she, I quote, had 'just come along for the ride'.'

'I see.'

'The thing is that Lucy will have to be investigated and two officers appointed to do that. There'll be no investigation of you, of course. In the eyes of the IPCC the onus will all be on Lucy and you don't exist.'

'Thanks very much,' said Wexford. 'Taking me on as your aide wasn't such a good idea after all, was it?' Tom made no reply. 'I shall quietly disappear.'

'No, *I* was wrong,' Tom said in the quiet and just way he had and was what had made Wexford like him. 'I shouldn't have insisted you accompany an officer, but have left you to your own devices. I'm going to leave you to them now and ask no questions.'

'Fair enough.' As he said it Wexford was aware that it was an expression he hadn't heard for years and he repeated it with emphasis. 'Fair enough.'

★ ★ ★

He was left with nothing to do until Wednesday, unless he made tasks for himself. Any task connected with this case would now require careful thought. He must explain to those he interviewed that they were under no obligation to speak to him. They could show him the door and probably would. He must become a private detective without any sort of licence to practise, not even the fame which attached to a Hercule Poirot or Peter Wimsey, their names on everyone's lips, their exploits chronicled. His role was more that of the private eye who — no longer even able to occupy himself spying on adulterers — was reduced to searching for missing persons. He wondered how on earth he was going to introduce himself to Colin Jones.

As it happened, other people intervened to help fill those two days. Perhaps it was true that he couldn't keep away from Orcadia Place for long, though avoiding the Mews was essential. But he had paused outside Orcadia Cottage to look at its front garden and think about the builders and architects who had dismissed creating an underground room as an impossibility — Kevin Oswin and Trevor the heavy smoker, Mr Keyworth the reluctant fiancé, Owen Clary and Rod Horndon — when Martin Rokeby came out of the house and spoke to him. Recalling their last encounter, Wexford, to say the least, was surprised.

'Are you too busy to come in for a cup of tea?'

'I'm not busy at all.'

Life would be simple if all the people involved in this case came so willingly to him. He followed Rokeby inside.

'Anne's out shopping. I feel I owe you an apology. I've been bloody these past few months and not just to the police. The thing was I felt the end of the world had come, that I owned a house I couldn't live in, that I'd lost my children, that I was doomed for ever to be famous — well, infamous — as the man who lived in 'that house with the bodies in the coal hole', and everyone thinking I'd put them there.'

'But you're better now?'

'It's strange how things change. We know they do, but when we want that to happen we're convinced that this time they won't. Milk? Sugar?'

'A drop of milk but no sugar, thanks.'

'The mob are no longer hanging about outside, I'm back in my house and it feels just like it used to. My wife's not going to leave me and my kids are coming home again. Remarkable really, isn't it? You won't believe this, but I'm going to have that underground room made after all and incorporate the coal hole. It'll feel quite different when there's a real room there. Apparently, there's a staircase inside, and I'm going to have a door put in down at the end of the passage. Anne's quite excited about it. I've applied for planning permission and I think I'll get it.'

'I daresay you won't be using Subearth or Underland, though.'

'It's funny you should say that because I've got Chilvers Clary the architects making a — well, I suppose you'd call it a design. It'll take in the whole area under the patio and the actual manhole will go. The only access will be from inside. I don't have a problem with natural light, I can take it or leave it, but Owen Clary says he could put in a sort of shaft up to the patio with a window in the top. Sorry, I'm boring you.'

'Not at all,' said Wexford.

'I'm so keen on this I get a bit carried away. Another cup?'

'Thanks, but I must go in a minute. There's just one thing I'd like to ask you. There are bolts on that door of yours into the mews. Have you ever bolted that door?'

'Only when we were away on holiday.'

'So when you were in Australia it was bolted and when you were in Florence this year it was bolted.' Wexford looked at him and Rokeby nodded. 'You must have gone away at other times in the past four years?'

'Oh, yes. It's best for me to think of it by the year. We were away twice in 2007, that was Spain and Vienna, and then in 2008 to Thailand, Vietnam and China, Spain again in 2009 and Italy that year as well.'

'That would have been a long trip in 2008. How long were you were away on the China holiday?'

'Well, if it's of any interest, we were away for a few days visiting Anne's mother in Wales at the end of May,' said Rokeby. 'And a few days after we got back we went off on our long trip. The door was bolted — oh, it must have been from the end of May until halfway through July. The door was bolted all that time.'

Wexford felt a tingle of excitement which was to become a surge of adrenalin when Rokeby said, 'And as a matter of fact we left it bolted for a couple of weeks after that. We forgot about it until the window cleaner was due and he couldn't get in. He was hammering on that door till we unbolted it.'

Wexford decided that to walk all the way home was carrying fitness to extraordinary lengths. The 13 bus would take him part of the way. He was in Pattison Road, heading for the Heath, when a young woman he recognised came out of one of the houses and unlocked a car with a DOCTOR ON CALL sticker on its windscreen.

'Good afternoon, Dr Hill.'

She, too, had a good memory. 'It's Mr

Wexford, isn't it? Are you still at work on the Orcadia Cottage case?'

Wexford said cryptically, 'Let's say work on it is still being done.' Oh, the uses of the passive voice! 'You are a long way from your Hornsey practice.'

'I've been visiting a private patient.' She opened the car door. 'I'm glad I've seen you. There's something I should have told you, I don't know why I didn't when I looked at that jewellery that was in the — the tomb.'

'What would that be then, Dr Hill?'

'I said I thought all of it had belonged to the poor woman who lived there. Was she called Mrs Merton? Well, I've thought about it since and there was one thing — item — I don't think could have been hers. It wasn't her kind of thing at all. A plain silver cross on a chain. I think that must have belonged to someone else. I should have got in touch and told you.'

'You've told me now,' said Wexford, 'and that's what matters.'

★   ★   ★

It was a cold day with a sharp wind, heralding autumn. The leaves were still green, though tired-looking. The beginning of a shower brought rain dashing against his face as he walked from Clapham North Station along the street where Colin Jones lived.

His home was one of a long terrace. It would have been considered small in the mid-nineteenth century when it was built, a white

281

two-floor house with a basement. Wexford wondered if he was underestimating when he calculated its value as something over a million. We expect unpleasant people to have or have had unpleasant spouses, and Wexford was anticipating someone rude and brusque. But the man who opened the door seemed affable enough.

'Good morning. I believe you want a chat about the goings-on in Orcadia Place. Come in. Bitterly cold, isn't it?'

He was as tall as Wexford, younger than Mildred by perhaps five or six years. He had a fine head of greying fair hair and a ruddy face with eyes of that attractive greenish-blue that is almost turquoise. This was the man whose shirt Vladlena had burned, but today he was wearing along with his black jeans a sweatshirt of such a dark brown that no burn mark would have showed. The interior of his house was as unlike his former wife's as was possible, its decoration minimalist, the colours predominantly white, black and beige, the only ornament in this living room a large black and red jar full of dried grasses and beech leaves.

'Can I offer you anything? I suppose it's too early for a drink.'

'Too early for me, thanks, Mr Jones.'

'And I'd better not. If my wife catches me at the Scotch before midday I shall get a lecture. She worries about my health, poor love. What did you want to talk to me about?'

'I believe you recommended a company called Subearth to Mr Rokeby when he was thinking of having an underground room built.'

282

'No, it was an oufit called Underland. And he had already been on to them and made an appointment. We got chatting over the garden wall — literally over the garden wall — and when he mentioned Underland I said I'd used them and they were OK. They went bust soon after.' Colin Jones laughed. 'I wasn't to know that, though. The chap who came had an architect with him, but I don't know anything about them. Sorry I can't be of more help. You know, I think I will have that Scotch. Just a small one.'

He left the room and Wexford could hear him talking to someone and just catch the tone of a woman's soft voice. The glass in his hand with, as he had said, a very small quantity of neat whisky in it, Jones came back, preceded by a slender young woman with long fair hair, wearing jeans and a pale grey sweater against which hung a silver cross on a chain. She too was carrying a drink, but hers looked like water.

'Let me get you something,' she said to Wexford. 'You don't have to have the — what do they call it? — the hard stuff. Have some sparkling water like me, why not?'

Jones laughed. 'Let me introduce my wife Vladlena.'

27

It was on the tip of his tongue to respond by telling her they had been searching for her high and low, but he restrained himself, and said instead, 'How do you do, Mrs Jones?'

'Please, call me Lena.'

It was Colin Jones who began to explain. 'I expect you know Lena used to work for my first wife, then luckily for her for a very nice guy called Goldberg. Do you know him?'

'I've met him and he is very nice.' Wexford turned to look at Vladlena. 'And another friend of yours, Ms Sophie Baird.'

She put a glass of sparkling water with ice and a slice of lemon on the table beside him. 'Some people have been very kind to me.'

'But not old Mildred, eh?' Colin Jones gave a hearty laugh and as he did Vladlena's face lit up, so that she was suddenly beautiful. 'The old bitch. I don't know how I stuck her so long. Well, I was telling you. Mildred really scared Lena and she ran away yet again. She'd saved up quite a bit of her wages from David and she got herself a room in a grotty little street round the back of Lisson Grove.'

'It was a nice little room, Colin,' Lena protested.

'If you say so.' Colin Jones's smile seemed to signify that whatever his wife said would be fine with him. 'Anyway, Lena was walking along the

Marylebone Road and I was coming from Baker Street Station. We met, we recognised each other and — well, the rest is history.'

'He buy me a cup of coffee and we talk and . . .'

'And from that moment we've not really been apart, have we, Lena? We got married a month later.'

Their eyes met and the naked love in each face, enraptured with the other, aroused in Wexford a sudden shaft of envy. It died as soon as it began. After all, he had known that and often knew it still. Whatever people say — however they knock it and rush to say it can't last — there is nothing so good as being in love. Perhaps it was partly this which made him very careful what he said and asked. He would do nothing to spoil it. He was, after all, no longer a policeman. And this, which he sometimes cursed, could be an enormous advantage, for because of it he was not obliged, as he would once have been, to communicate what he knew to the UK Border Agency.

But still, the less he knew about the circumstances of these two the better. In some ways it wasn't his business. Could they help him in finding the identity of the young woman in the vault? That was his only concern.

'I don't want to enquire too much into your circumstances,' he said carefully. 'I am no longer a policeman. I'm nothing. An ordinary pensioner, if you like.'

Colin Jones interrupted him. 'Look, I really do need a real drink.' He looked at Vladlena. 'May I have a drink, darling?'

'Of course.' It surprised Wexford that she agreed so readily.

'And I'm fetching one for our guest, no matter what he says.'

The moment he had gone she was writing something on a card she took from her jeans pocket. It was quickly handed to Wexford and he read it seconds before her husband came back. *Meet me in Sainsbury's 12.45.*

Wexford was unused to whisky these days, but he obediently took a small swig, taken aback a little by the way it went straight to his head. He held Vladlena's card clutched in his trouser pocket. They talked of innocuous things, the cold weather, unseasonable for early autumn, the pleasantness of being so near Clapham Common, the excellent local shopping, at mention of which Vladlena caught Wexford's eye. And then they talked of something important, the child she expected to be born in April.

It was ten minutes to midday when he left. Walking in the Balham direction, he enquired for Sainsbury's and was told it was no more than a hundred yards away. Why had she arranged to meet him without her husband's knowledge? Not because she intends to deceive him in any serious way, he thought. He couldn't be wrong about those two. Most likely she wanted not to involve Colin in any further trouble that might result from her revelations.

He went into a café and asked for a black coffee. The whisky was zinging around not at all unpleasantly in his head. That must be quietened. He tried to remember the residential requirements for naturalisation. You had to be a resident of the United Kingdom for three years, to have been present three years before your application, have not spent more than something over two hundred days out of the UK — he couldn't recall how many more — and here came the crunch, *have not been in breach of the immigration rules at any stage* during the three-year period. You might say Vladlena had been in breach of those rules every day during that period. Well, that was that then. But they wouldn't be found out through him. He wasn't a policeman, he thought, and almost laughed out loud. Would the baby make any difference? He seemed to remember that a child's mother's nationality established its nationality, but perhaps not if she was married to a British citizen? Whatever happened, the marriage couldn't be undone. He paid for his coffee, left and set off for Sainsbury's.

★ ★ ★

It was a very large store, but he spotted her from quite a way off, drifting slowly with an empty trolley along an aisle between cereals and breads. She had on a black leather jacket and he wondered if that was the one Mildred had seen her wearing when she identified her in Oxford Street. She smiled at him and slightly raised one hand.

'I'm deceiving my husband,' Vladlena began, 'but not to hurt him. It's to save him knowing what I meant to do. I never did do it, but I meant to.'

'I think I know what you're talking about,' Wexford said. 'Sophie Baird told me.'

She nodded. 'Yes, but I never did do it. I had gone from Mrs Kataev and I had that room I told you about. I had the money I save, but it was nearly gone and I thought I have to do what Gregory ask me.'

'You had a phone number for him?'

'I call him and he say to me to come to a house. He will meet me at this house. It is in West Hampstead. You understand?'

The massage parlour, Wexford thought. The place ridiculously called Elfland, up the road from Chilvers Clary. 'The Finchley Road?'

'Oh, no. This place was in a house near West Hampstead Station. I come in the Tube from Baker Street to West Hampstead and the house is just down the street.' Vladlena hesitated, looked away and up at the packets of various types of muesli on a top shelf. 'I never told my husband. I never did do it, but he must not think I even *think* to do it.'

'Lena,' he said. 'I doubt if I shall ever see your husband again. If I do I shall tell him nothing of what you tell me.'

She smiled, showing beautiful white teeth. 'You look at my teeth. My husband pay for dentist, he is so good to me. My sister and me, our teeth were bad and hurt a lot when we come here.'

'Your sister' — he had to think — 'Alyona?'

She seemed surprised. 'You know about her?'

'Only what Irina Kataev told me. That the last you saw of her was in a trailer at Dover — what? Three years ago? Four?'

'I see her again maybe two years ago. A bit more than that, in the summer.' The smile had entirely died and her face sank into sadness. 'I see her when I go to that house. I tell you. I stand outside for a bit because I am — scared. I am a bit scared. And I look up at the windows and I think which one is the one I must go to? And then I see her. I see Alyona.'

'At the window of a house in West Hampstead?'

Vladlena nodded. 'Let us move a little.' She pushed the trolley down the aisle, turned to the left and right again along coffees, teas and sugars.

'I am always a bit scared of people watch me.'

'What happened when you saw your sister?'

'First I think I must go up there and find her and then I think what *this place must be*. Sophie and David tell me where they would take Alyona and take me if I let them. Gregory tell me also. So I look at her and I make signs to her. Like this.' Vladlena beckoned with her right hand, then with both hands in a gesture that seemed to indicate imploring. 'I do this and I make with my mouth like this but make no sound.' In dumb show she mouthed, 'Come to me, come to me.'

Speaking aloud to Wexford, she said, 'I do not ring the bell, I do not go in. I find a seat nearby and I sit and wait for Alyona to come. I sit for a long, long time. I wait. I look up at the window again, but she is gone. I stay down there until ten

289

at night, until eleven, and I watch. Men come and ring the bell and some person lets them in, so I know for sure what the place is. And then a man comes along and talks to me, asks me you know what, and I say no and another comes and then I am scared and I go back in the train to my room.'

'Did you ever go back?'

'Yes, I did. I look again up at the window and I wait, but I never see Alyona again. One day I ring the bell, because I think maybe she will come to the door. But it is a man come and say what do I want, and I am too afraid to say and I go away. You understand I am scared to ask for Alyona and I am scared to go to police, always scared of that.'

'You never saw her again?'

'No, never. I worry, I think about her all the time, but I know it is no use, I can do nothing. And one day I am walking back from Baker Street Station to Lisson Grove and I meet Colin and he is so kind to me and — well, you know what happens then.'

Wexford said, 'Would you take me to this house? I mean where you last saw your sister.'

She began pushing her trolley in the direction of the checkouts. 'I don't want Colin to know. He could ask why I went there and then he would know what I meant to do.' She was silent for a moment as she began unloading items from her trolley on to the belt. 'Tomorrow he will be at work all day.' She turned to look Wexford straight in the eye. 'I love my husband,' she said. 'He has been like an angel to me. But if it is that

290

we find what happen to Alyona . . . '

'That's what I hope too.' Wexford sighed inwardly. 'I will pick you up at nine tomorrow — is that all right?' She nodded, but a little reluctantly. 'Till then,' he said and left her.

The silver cross that hung against her grey sweater . . . He half-wished he hadn't noticed it. He half-wished he was less observant, had a poorer memory. But at any rate he wouldn't have to take her to a place that would frighten her, where she might in fact refuse to go — a police station. She need not look at those demeaning garments, the stuff of pornography. Even a DNA comparison was hardly necessary, though he knew it would have to take place, for as soon as he had seen that silver cross he had known the girl in the vault was her sister Alyona.

28

Donaldson had driven him everywhere he needed to go. Occasionally he had driven himself. What he had never needed to do was walk or take public transport. No wonder he had gained so much weight, so that even the relentless cutting out of cashew nuts and other delights had made little difference. Now, therefore, he was confronted with a choice he had never before encountered. Should he pick up Vladlena in his own car after a doubtless dreadful battle through south London traffic or go to Clapham on the Northern Line, of which he had no experience but of which he had heard hair-raising tales? All tube users had their individual horrific Northern Line anecdotes. One of Tom's digressions had concerned his being stuck in a train between Mornington Crescent and Camden Town for three-quarters of an hour, surrounded by panicking passengers.

Perhaps it was this story which prompted his decision to go by car. That and because he was a man and choosing a car was what men almost always did. Women might not or might choose a taxi if they could afford it. Could that be another of Wexford's laws, must be the seventeenth or eighteenth by now? One of the difficulties was that he had not much idea of when he should start out, but he was ready to leave at a few minutes after seven-thirty when the landline phone rang. It was Sylvia to say she had had an offer on her house.

'Your mother is still asleep.'

'Yes, maybe, but she'll want to know about this, Dad. I promise you she will. Couldn't you wake her up?'

'I could, but I'm not going to. You can phone again in an hour. Congratulations, though. I'm very pleased for you.' Not as pleased as I am that my own house will soon be my own again, he thought.

It took him less than the hour and a half he had allowed. He parked on the other side of the road outside her house like the driver of a hire car who makes a point of arriving early. But he was on a yellow line and had to move off when a traffic warden bore down on the car. Round the block then, hooted at by other impatient drivers, back to his chosen spot to see the warden or the back of him just turning the corner into the main road. He parked again, realising that eluding traffic wardens, defying parking rules, was something that had never happened to him before. Donaldson had had to handle these stings and arrows of fortune, or his sergeant had if she was driving him.

He had forgotten all about Colin Jones and it gave him a small shock to see Vladlena's husband come out of their house at ten to nine, carrying a briefcase and turn in the direction of Clapham North Station. If he had rung their bell when he first arrived . . . But he hadn't and all was well.

She spotted the car and came out just as he

293

was preparing to cross the road. The first thing he noticed about her was that silver cross. It seemed to flash as it caught the morning sun. She had dressed up in a skirt suit and striped blouse, as if she were going to some significant engagement instead of helping him locate a brothel.

'It is not good to deceive my husband,' she said as she got into the car. 'But whatever happen I will tell him of it after. I am not doing anything wrong, am I?'

'Certainly not,' said Wexford. 'Rather the reverse. You are doing a good thing.'

Another long drive. 'This house,' he began, 'is it old — say a hundred years old — or newly built?' As he asked he realised she would hardly know. 'Like that' — he pointed out of the window — 'or like that?'

She selected a late Victorian house that was detached, a fairly big house that had been converted into the offices of a dental practice. 'Like that. A bit like that. There is more than one.'

'More than one of what?'

'More than one house like that. All together but not joined up. It is down a turning. The next one, now you turn left.'

So the house was not in West End Lane, a hilly winding street, but in a side turning. He turned left into Churchlands Road. All the way along here stood detached and semi-detached Victorian and Edwardian houses, not the ice-cream beauties he so much admired, but solid brick buildings, many of them divided into flats. He had to drive on past the house Vladlena pointed out as he searched for somewhere to leave the car. Every possible space was filled, and passing West Hampstead Station he began to realise how much wiser he would have been to have come by tube. Down this side turning, up that one, back into West End Lane, he understood at last what he must do. You're no longer a policeman — it was becoming a mantra — he told himself, parking the car on a yellow line. It went terribly against the grain but it was hardly a crime . . .

He and Vladlena walked back down the hill and into Churchlands Road. She was silent. He saw that she had clenched her hands — to keep them from trembling? There were three houses, not identical but differing only in that one had a pillared portico, another a bay window in the ground floor, the third a garage on its left-hand side, Numbers 6, 8 and 10.

'That one,' Vladlena said. 'The middle one. Number 8. It is the window above the front door I see Alyona.' She had turned pale, every vestige of colour gone from her face. 'A blind is down now, but then the blind is up and I am seeing her face.'

'Here, take my arm,' he said. 'We'll find somewhere you can have coffee.'

She leant on him and he cursed himself for bringing her. She could have described the place to him, had indeed described it quite adequately. In the tiny café a latte brought the colour back into her face.

'I am sorry. I am a fool.'

'No. You won't have to go there again. I am

going to get you a taxi to take you home.' Book it on the account Dora had opened in a fit of profligacy. He called her first, because he had forgotten the reference number.

Vladlena said, 'I can go in the Tube.'

'No, you can't. I wouldn't dream of it.' The number turned out to be the day, month and year of Dora's birth. 'They'll be here within fifteen minutes and they'll take you home.'

'I sat on a seat opposite those houses. You can just see it from here. People came out of the station and down the street and passed me and a man tried to — well, you know about that. I don't know if Alyona could see me. Someone pull down the blind at the window. I should stay, but when another man come up to me I was afraid and I went away. I tell you I go back next day and the next, but I think they take her away and hide her somewhere.'

Wexford saw her into the cab. He gave a thought to his car, parked illegally, a sitting target for the first traffic warden to pass along the street, but it was a fleeting thought, soon gone. Without Vladlena he felt free and strong. Whatever awaited him, he at least wouldn't have her to protect. A postman, pushing his scarlet trolley, was advancing very slowly up the hill on the opposite side. He went through the gate into the narrow front garden of Number 10, pulled the red elastic band off the handful of post he was carrying, dropped the band on to the paving and pushed an envelope through the letter box. Only it didn't go through but stuck there halfway. The postman apparently had nothing for

Number 8, but a small package for Number 6. This package also stuck halfway through the letterbox.

Wexford crossed the road. There was only one bell on Number 8. It appeared to be an entryphone, but when he pressed the bell the door made the groaning sound of unlocking and he easily pushed it open. Inside was a hallway, exactly the sort of thing you might expect in a doctor's premises in Harley Street. No red plush and gilding, no chandelier, but white walls, dark green carpet and a long polished table on which lay a single copy of *Country Life* and another of *Vogue*. Stairs, carpeted in dark green, and a lift. He was deciding what to do next, to climb the stairs or ascend — to what? — in the lift, when a small, rotund man came out from a door marked PRIVATE, followed by a very thin woman in a black dress.

Wexford knew him at once as Trevor Oswin, but the man seemed not to recognise him. Even from two yards' distance, Trevor reeked of tobacco smoke. 'It's a bit early, sir,' he said. 'I don't know if any of the young ladies is free. Had you anyone special in mind?'

'Alyona,' Wexford said.

'Sorry about that, but it must be quite a while since your last visit. Alyona left us a long time ago.'

'I can see if Tanya is free,' said the woman.

'Thanks, but I'll come back later.'

Had Trevor known who he was? Wexford thought not as he made his way back into West End Lane. The package stuck in the letterbox of the house next door with the bay window, Number 6, indicated that no one was at home, as did the letter in a similar position in the letterbox of Number 10. The latter was very well kept, its yellow brickwork recently repointed, its window frames glossy white and its front door, through whose polished brass mouth the letter protruded like a tongue, painted a soft jade green.

Just because this place was next door to a brothel, there was no reason to suppose any connection between them. The house looked about as unlike what used to be called a house of ill fame as could be imagined. It, too, had just been painted, it, too, had a polished brass letterbox and a front door, though not green, a recently applied dark blue. But that was the connection, Wexford thought. Not necessarily but the chances were that Number 8 and Number 10 had the same owner. Now he could see by the number of bells by the front door, that the house on the other side, Number 6 with the pillared portico, was let off into single-room apartments, probably bedsits. The tenants, even if they knew, would be unlikely to object to being neighbours to a brothel. He went through the gate of Number 10 and at the front door, looked to his right and to his left. There was no one about, no one passing up the hill on this side and only a man pulling a suitcase on wheels on the other, intent on nothing but getting to the tube station.

Wexford tried to pull the envelope out. It stuck on something and tore. But not enough to obscure the name and address printed on it. Mr

D. Keyworth, he read. Slowly he pushed the letter back into the letterbox. This time it passed through and he heard a light flop as it fell on to the mat.

★ ★ ★

Afterwards, when it was all over, he thought that he had done a few things wrong. He had put himself — ridiculously — in danger. He should have gone straight to Tom, asked for Lucy or Miles to come with him to Hendon (or for permission to accompany Lucy or Miles), but he was afraid of the humiliation of a refusal. Uppermost in his mind was old Mildreadful's complaint about Lucy, and indirectly about him, to the IPCC.

So he went alone to see Louise Fortescue. First to fetch his car. By some miracle no parking ticket was attached to his windscreen. Nor had worse happened and the horrible yellow metal Denver Boot of the clampers disabled it. Up the Hendon Way and on to the Watford Way. Parking restrictions outside K, K and L Ltd, Below Surface Home Extensions, but the kind easily complied with. You could leave your car for an hour in the little lay-by outside the shops. It was nearly three months since he had seen Louise Fortescue, but he could recognise a changed woman. Her black trouser suit had been replaced by a pencil skirt, a tight white sweater and high-heeled shoes, but what he principally noticed was the engagement ring on the third finger of her left hand.

'I was a bit of a misery when you were last here,' she said.

'Life treating you better, is it?'

'Oh, yes. I'm getting married on Saturday.'

Wexford congratulated her. He explained that he was no longer a policeman and that she had no need to answer his questions unless she wanted to.

'If it's about Damian Keyworth,' she said, 'I only went on working for him because I needed the job. This is my last week here and I can't wait to shake the dust of this place off my feet. Not that he's often here. Could you tell me what he's done?'

'I don't know, Ms Fortescue. Something serious, I think, but I can't tell you any more than that at this stage.'

'All right. It doesn't matter. I don't see him from one week's end to the next, thank God.' She took a deep breath. 'Look, sit down, why don't you? I'm going to.'

'You said you moved in with Mr Keyworth, but after a week you broke off your engagement and left. Would you mind telling me about that?'

There were just two chairs in the tiny room. Louise Fortescue sat behind the desk and as she began to talk he noticed how her colour heightened. 'I wouldn't mind at all. I'd be glad to. I've nothing to hide. It was so — well, it was outrageous. We were getting on very well, or it seemed like that to me. I'd been living there and I'd taken two days off to settle in. It was a Friday and he'd just got home from work. It was maybe six in the evening. Someone rang the front

300

doorbell and knocked as well and rang again as if they were desperate. I went to the door to answer it and Damian came behind me. There was a girl there, a very young girl, blonde, pretty, I suppose, wearing awful clothes — well, I won't say what she was like, a very short miniskirt and a leather jacket and — well, you can imagine.'

'Mr Keyworth saw her?'

'Oh, yes. And he knew her all right. It was easy to see what had been going on. He didn't say a word to me. He took her into the lounge and I went upstairs and left them to it. It was getting dark, but not so dark I couldn't see the two of them leave the house and get into his car. A long time later he came back alone and tried to explain to me. He said she'd been his girlfriend and still was, but he meant to break with her and should have done before I came to live there. I still loved him, but that was more than I could stand and I packed my bags and phoned for a taxi and left. He really tried to make things all right between us, he went on and on, and when he saw it was no use he begged me not to stop working for him. So in the end I said I'd stay — I mean, I needed the job — but everything was over between us. Actually, we hardly ever meet these days. I've been running the business, such as it is, and I talk to him on the phone. That's about it.'

'Mr Keyworth hasn't much work then?'

'Virtually nothing. I don't know why he keeps it going unless it's a front for something else he's up to. So far as I know — and I would know — he's got no replacement for me.' She gave a satisfied nod. 'Oh, there's one other thing,' she said. 'I don't know if it's important, maybe it's nothing. But that day, it was August first, there was a girl hanging about outside the house next door and she'd been there the day before too. There's a seat on the pavement opposite and she sat down on that. I watched her, wondering what was going on. She'd gone before that girl came to the door. I don't suppose it was important, was it?'

'It may have been,' said Wexford. 'Thank you very much, Ms Fortescue.' He glanced at the ring. 'I hope you'll be very happy.'

29

It was a foolhardy thing to do, to go back there. He had simply made several assumptions: that Tom Ede would prefer him to keep out of the way while the investigation went on into Mildred Jones's complaint; that the men running the brothel in the house with the bay window were not dangerous; that Louise Fortescue would not tell Damian Keyworth about their interview. But why would she not? In a phone conversation, no doubt, she might have told him out of revenge. Wexford could almost hear her — 'I don't know what you've been up to but you'd better watch it. The police are interested in your activities, whatever they are.'

Before he left he talked to Dora about the offer made to Sylvia. She had almost decided to accept it, even though it was less than she had asked for.

'I told her that was certain these days,' Dora said. 'And she's inclined to accept it. I did wonder if I should have advised her not to and then she would have been bound to jump at it.'

Wexford laughed, but he was thinking about the offers of money that were made to youngish well-off middle-class women with British passports and the offers of money that were made to young poor women from the Caucasus with no passports, and the difference between them. 'I think my business here will soon be over,' he said. 'While Sylvia's moving out and in to her new place shall we go somewhere nice on holiday? Somewhere warm? Think about it.'

He turned his thoughts to those holidays the Rokebys had taken. The Thailand-Vietnam-China one was the significant trip, he thought. That was when the door in the rear wall had been bolted for six weeks and then for two weeks more until the window cleaner came and couldn't get in. This was in the summer of 2008. While the Rokebys were visiting her mother in Wales, Alyona's body was put into the vault. Intending to do what Teddy Brex had failed to do or been prevented from doing, the perpetrator had come back, bringing with him the materials for paving over the manhole. But by then the door had been shut and bolted.

Probably he had returned. Maybe several times. But for eight weeks the door had been bolted and once the Rokebys were back and it was open, carrying out construction work even by night on someone else's property was impossible.

★   ★   ★

It was Sunday evening and the weather had turned cold. St Luke's Little Summer when summer seemed to return and which fell on St Luke's Day, 16 October, and the days before and beyond, was past and a damp chill was in the air. Blue skies were coated in layers of cloud. Wexford put on the dark brown padded jacket which he admitted was warm, however much he disliked it, decided he had walked enough and took the car, anticipating no parking problems at the weekend when restrictions came off. But it was not as easy as he had thought. Although not much past eight and still British summertime, it was very dark. He was wary about parking on West End Lane itself and began the slog of driving from side street to side street to find a space. Winding hilly streets with shops along some of them, a yellow brick chapel lit-up and labelled The United Free Church, a petrol station, a café with deserted tables outside, every parking space taken. At last he found one, a very long way down a very long street that wound downhill towards Kilburn.

Though Wexford felt that he knew Damian Keyworth thoroughly, could have made a character sketch of him, the two of them had never met. Once he knew that Wexford was no longer a policeman, but had only the rather dubious status of an 'expert adviser', he might well shut the door in his face. On the other hand, he would know his caller had a strong connection with the police, could bring the police to his door at any time — could he? — and would likely know about the visit to the house next door and the encounter with Trevor Oswin.

As he almost reached the turn into West End Lane he realised that no one knew he was here. More than that, no one except Vladlena knew the nature of the house with the pillars. And would Vladlena ever disclose it? He should have told Tom and, hesitating no longer, he pulled out his phone and called Tom's number. Almost at once he was put on to Tom's voicemail. At least he could leave a message. As for Dora, she was too accustomed to being a chief detective inspector's wife to ask him where he was going or what he was doing. When he came to think of it, as he thought of it, now, his job had been a real adulterer's charter, one which he may have considered once or twice of using to his own advantage, yet never had.

When he had passed Keyworth's house in his quest to find a parking place, no lights had been on. Now the ground floor was brightly lit and a table lamp could be seen in a front bedroom. He rang the bell. In making his character sketch of Keyworth, he had drawn no picture of him. And yet he was surprised that the man was solidly built, broad-shouldered, rubicund and with a lot of fair hair.

'What can I do for you?'

Wexford asked if he could talk to him. He had decided to be truthful, more or less, and said that, though no longer a policeman, he had a police connection. He was looking for a missing woman, the sister of Mrs Colin Jones, of Clapham. Even as he spoke he could tell that Keyworth knew. He knew Wexford had been to the house next door, he knew he had talked to Louise Fortescue both the day before and three months before.

'You had better come in.'

Keyworth took Wexford into a hallway and then into what Louise had called the lounge, both rooms furnished in a so-called 'French'

306

style with ornate chairs and pie-crust tables, the walls silk-panelled in crimson and every surface having a gilded rim. It was far more like Wexford's idea of a brothel than the real brothel next door.

'Sit.'

As if I were a dog, thought Wexford. Keyworth was one of those who think saying 'Sit' instead of 'Sit down' and 'Come' instead of 'Come in' is a sign of a masterful personality, of a man who is a leader of men. Instead of an exploiter of women and a trafficker of children.

'What do you want to know that you don't know already?'

In for a penny, in for a pound. It was an expression of his father's, applicable here. 'Alyona Krasnikova, why was she killed?'

If it was a shock tactic, it succeeded. 'I don't know what you're talking about. You can't expect me to admit to that. It's preposterous. What do you take me for? I'm a chartered surveyor.'

'You're a ponce,' said Wexford, but to himself.

'That place next door, I know what it is, but it's quiet, it's well run. Mr and Mrs Oswin run it very discreetly.' Keyworth, who had been standing over Wexford, suddenly sat down. 'Brothels — actually it's time they had a new name, something more contemporary — brothels, as I say, are becoming respectable. Men of all classes use them, don't think twice about it. The sooner the police realise that the better.' Wexford listened patiently. 'Anyway, it's nothing to do with me. If that girl came here to me — it was years ago, years — it was because I'd once been

307

to her for sex. There, I'm being very frank.'

'I know why she came, Mr Keyworth. She didn't know you. If she had she'd have avoided you like the plague. She wouldn't have gone into the lion's den. She hoped you'd give her refuge.'

Keyworth swivelled round in his chair so that he was facing a white and gold desk. He pulled open a drawer, said, 'I'd like to give you something for your trouble. You're not police. I doubt if the police take much notice of you. I don't suppose you get much of a pension, do you?'

Wexford said nothing. The man was too ridiculous to make him angry. He was simply interested to know what he was going to be offered. A cheque was passed across the desk, held out to Wexford. The sum was ten thousand pounds. He looked at it, at its pale blue surface, patterned like wallpaper, the writing an incomprehensible scrawl, except for the figures which were clear enough. He handed it back, said, 'Use it to buy passports for those poor girls.' And he an ex-policeman! Whatever next?

He went back the way he had come and let himself out of the front door, crossed the road and sat down on the seat where Vladlena had sat, wondering why it was there and who had put it there. Perhaps it was only to offer rest to those commuters exhausted after their struggles with Transport for London and before they began the walk home. While he was inside Keyworth's house someone had parked a white van on a yellow line outside. Why should that alert him to something unsuspected? One unmarked white van was much like another and there must be thousands in London. It was time he went home himself. After he had watched an elderly man, eminently respectable to look at, lock his car, approach the brothel house and press the bell to be immediately admitted, he got up. His car was further away than he remembered. He passed the car the punter (if that was the word) had just left parked on a double yellow line, passed the white van, pausing for a moment to take in the snake-shaped scratch on its rear nearside, and walked along the silent street. Houses were brightly lit, but most behind hedges or tall shrubs and trees. Street lamps laid a skin of yellow light on the damp stone surfaces.

He heard footsteps behind him and stepped closer to the hedge to let whoever it was pass him, a young woman sprinting along in five-inch heels. At the bottom of this gradual incline he could see his car, always a comforting sight, signifying rest, safety, a refuge, the means of getting wherever you wanted to go in privacy. How awkward it must have been when you relied on a horse, a carriage or a cart. No protection from the weather, no means of safeguarding that transport unless you had a servant to leave with the horse and that would have its own problems. He was thinking along these lines, trying to put himself in the shoes of the poor man who must have relied on what his father had called 'Shanks's Pony', when he saw someone move off from where he had been standing under the overhanging branches of a tree and walk round the corner. Sheltering from the rain? It hadn't rained for hours. Never mind. He was gone.

Wexford unlocked the car with his remote and walked round to the offside front. His hand was on the driver's door when a powerful whiff of tobacco smoke struck him. He spun round and took the knife in his shoulder instead of his back. It felt like a blow, not a cutting sensation but a blow, as if he had been struck with a heavy implement. This is what it must have been like for Sylvia, he thought, when she was stabbed as I've been stabbed. For that's what it is, the man under the tree — the one that seemed to go away — has stabbed me. He kicked out and hit softness, fatness, his legs weakened and gave way and his last thought before he lapsed into unconsciousness was, how much they must care: ten thousand pounds or this. Then it was darkness and the damp hard ground underneath him.

30

An attempt had been made to blow him up, a woman had tried to run him over and there had been other efforts to cause him grievous bodily harm, but until now he had never been the victim of a stabbing, Britain's murder method of choice. It might have been much worse and would have been if he hadn't swung round in the nick of time. There is nothing vital to be damaged in one's shoulder. Apparently, the knife was very long. If he had taken its blade in his back, between his ribs, it might have pierced a lung or his heart. And his rescue was as much due to Tom as his own nose for the smell of tobacco.

After Dora, Tom was his first visitor. He brought neither flowers nor grapes, an omission for which Wexford was thankful.

'Tell me something. How did you get to me so fast? Ten minutes at the most from when I left that message.'

'I was just round the corner,' Tom said. 'I was in church.'

Wexford recalled that frustrating drive past the shops and the garage and the little chapel. 'The United Free Church?'

'That's it. I'm always there on Sunday evenings.' Tom spoke simply and he smiled. 'My phone pinged in the middle of a hymn and I nearly didn't pick up the message. But it made me uneasy, I don't know why. You weren't uneasy.' He laughed. 'Everyone was staring at me — and not in a friendly way.'

'And I fetched you out of Evensong.'

'The better the day, the better the deed,' said Tom.

He told Wexford that Number 8 Churchlands Road had been raided and Trevor Oswin, his wife and Damian Keyworth arrested and charged with brothel-keeping, trafficking and false imprisonment. Oswin would also be charged with the murder of Alyona Krasnikova when a case had been prepared against him.

'I think we can make it stick. He's scared stiff and I hope we'll get a confession out of him.'

Sylvia came next. She kissed him, smiled ruefully at the dressing on his shoulder and said, 'Snap!'

'Yes. But it might have been worse — for both of us.'

'We're moving tomorrow. You'll have your house back. You can go home.'

'When they let me.' Home is Kingsmarkham, he thought. Not the coachhouse, lovely though being there has been and will be again. One day.

'I was very — well, ungracious, Dad. When you let us all move into your house. Ungracious and ungrateful. Thank you, though. I don't know what we'd have done without it.'

The worst thing about being wounded at his age, he thought, maybe at any age, is that you feel so tired. He realised that most of the time he never felt tired, but he did now, overwhelmed by exhaustion. He loved seeing Dora because all he had to do when she was there was have his hand held and not talk, close his eyes and drift off to sleep, wake again and be glad she was still there. But he would talk when Burden came. He would tell him the whole thing, how he had worked it out. Then he wouldn't be tired.

'They want to keep you in another couple of days,' said Dora.

'I know. They're afraid of infection.'

'Mike says he'll come tomorrow.'

It might be hurtful to show too much enthusiasm. 'That's nice of him,' he said in a lacklustre tone. 'Fine if he's not too busy.'

She raised her eyebrows. 'Why do I detect an undercurrent of madly longing to see him?'

He laughed, but said no more. Next day, when Burden arrived, Wexford was in the bathroom and as he returned to the ward, the young nurse with whom he was a favourite whispered, 'Your son is here.'

'I knew I'd aged,' he said to Burden, 'but not that much. Or maybe it's that you look remarkably young today.'

'I haven't brought you anything. Can one man give another one flowers? It seems a bit funny.'

'I don't want flowers or anything else for that matter. They'll bring us tea in a minute. Do you feel up to hearing about the Vault?'

'It feels a bit weird hearing it in a hospital. We ought to be in the Olive.' Burden drank some of his tea. 'And this ought to be wine.'

'They do let me have the occasional glass of red, but it has to be at the appropriate time. Well, the Vault. This is how it was . . . '

313

Two days later he was sent home. Hospitals avoid keeping their patients in over a weekend. He was driven home to Kingsmarkham by Dora and by dint of exercising an iron self-control, did no back-seat (or passenger-seat) driving. Each time he felt like saying she was going too fast or braking needlessly he examined his reactions and asked himself if, a man being at the wheel, he would have criticised *his* driving. He decided he would not. Well, he might if the man was his grandson Robin, but that would be on account of Robin's youth. And Dora was his wife. Maybe all the more reason for not finding fault with her. Suppose it was one of his daughters? Yes, he might well criticise them. A good rule would be never to back-seat drive. No one ever took any notice, anyway.

Thus the drive passed in pleasant and perhaps valuable speculation and when they got to Kingsmarkham Dora asked him if he was feeling all right. 'Fine. Why do you ask?'

'Oh, no reason. I just wondered why you never asked me if I was keeping my eyes on the road or if I'd like you to drive.'

'No doubt I was asleep.'

He hadn't been, but once in the house he went to bed and slept for three hours. The phone woke him and he reached for it. Burden was adamant that there could be no visiting the Olive and Dove, but he would come round if that was all right.

'Don't do anything silly.' Dora didn't speculate

what the nature of the silly thing might be. Something to do with food or drink, no doubt. 'I shall go and see Sylvia's new house.'

Burden was early. He must really want to hear the rest of it, Wexford thought, and thought simultaneously that once, not long ago, such an idea wouldn't have entered his head. A sudden soreness in his shoulder brought him back to the matter in hand. The story of the girl, its beginning and its ending.

'For a while,' he began as Burden was pouring the wine, 'I thought she must be a cleaner employed by a certain Mrs Jones.'

'Why do you say 'a certain'?'

'Because she's near to being that 'worst enemy' you were talking about earlier. She's the one who complained to the Police Complaints Authority — not about me, of course, but about poor Lucy Blanch, the DS. You've no idea how often in the past months I've had to stop myself short and remember I'm no longer a policeman.'

Burden listened in near-silence while told of the quest for Vladlena and later of the escape of Alyona and her attempt to throw herself on the mercy of Damian Keyworth. 'Trevor Oswin had known Keyworth slightly for years. His brother Kevin had done a building job for him and Trevor had done the driving of the van. Apparently, Kevin Oswin's sight is too bad for him to drive. They weren't exactly on social terms then, but it was about this time that Keyworth lost his driving licence through being startlingly over the limit. Trevor started driving for him and they got to know each other better.

Keyworth wanted to move and Trevor told him the house next door to his in Churchlands Road was for sale. Keyworth bought it and when he seemed to find money no object Trevor invited him to invest in the company he and his wife were running next door and come in to it with them. It seems Keyworth didn't turn a hair when he found out the nature of the firm. They called it a model agency, but Keyworth knew very well what it was.

'Keyworth, of course, had no mercy. The night Alyona came to his house, by making some sort of promise to her, presumably, he got her into one of Oswin's cars — he had no car of his own — and drove away. He must have known by this time that either he or Trevor Oswin had to kill her. If she were left free she might tell the police, having a fair idea that trafficking was a serious offence in this country, but even if she dared not do that, she would tell someone. She would tell someone that she had been a sex slave — horrible term but apt — and that there were others like her at the house in Churchlands Road.

'Another serious consequence for Keyworth was that his fiancée Louise Fortescue, who was living there with him, saw the girl and drew the obvious conclusions. Once he had handed Alyona over to Trevor Oswin or, more likely, called Oswin and asked him to drive to an appointed place and meet him and the girl, he would have no more part in it, but have returned to Churchlands Road where he found Louise packing. What reasons he gave to justify himself I don't know, but she left and that was the end of their engagement.'

'He could hardly have said, 'No, she wasn't my girlfriend,'' said Burden. ''She was just a trafficked immigrant I forced into prostitution with my mate next door.''

'Right. I believe Alyona was handed over into the tender care of Trevor Oswin, my assailant. He killed her, possibly by strangling, possibly by bludgeoning her. Her skull was fractured, as was Harriet Merton's.'

'And put her body into that vault in Orcadia Place? Was that really the safest place from his point of view he could have put it?'

'I think so, Mike. It was either that or driving her to open country or woodland and leaving the body there to be found quite quickly. Subearth Structures, represented by Trevor's brother Kevin, were the last firm to go round there and look at the place after Rokeby had decided he wanted an underground room. As you will remember, Trevor also went and while Kevin was in the house with Rokeby, Trevor went down into the vault. He saw the bodies and he must have understood that no one else had seen them. By that I mean none of the other plumbers, builders, assessors, what you will, had seen them. Because if they had it's inconceivable they wouldn't have reported what they had found and it would have been all over the media.

'Therefore, it was a safe hiding place and a burial chamber in which to bury poor Alyona's body. So, with the body in his car, he parked in the mews after dark and tried the door in the wall. As usual it wasn't locked. The body was dragged into the paved yard, the pot removed, the manhole cover lifted and the body dropped into the vault.

'Now, Trevor had decided on what Teddy Brex had ten years before decided on, to return there one night soon and pave over the manhole opening and those bodies would never be found. It would be a simple task for him. He had himself once been in the building trade. But when he went back the door into the mews was locked and bolted, as it always was when the Rokebys were away on a long holiday. Trevor had to take the risk of the bodies being found one day, as they were, two years later.'

Burden re-filled their glasses, saying that meant he would have to walk home, but never mind. The wine, its quality somehow more apparent the second time round than the first, had been brought by Burden. It brought Wexford a heady feeling of pleasure and a kind of small triumph. He was considering the last phase of his narrative when his friend said, 'What about the driver? You never mentioned him again. Has he been arrested?'

'Oh, yes. Tom Ede told me all about that. Goldberg — you remember him? — he had a friend called Sophie Baird. It's one of those close 'best friends' situations you often get between a woman and a gay man. She was living with her partner also in St John's Wood in a house that happened fortunately to belong to her. She works as a PA to some company chairman and her partner runs or ran a removal business. That among other things, one of which is driving trafficked women here from Eastern Europe.

'I had no idea. But when she and I were talking about those two girls and she told me about the towering rage he had got into when she talked about her befriending an illegal immigrant, that he had struck her and ultimately walked out on her, I started to wonder. Those seemed extreme steps and then his name came back to me. John, she called him, always referred to him as John, but his surname was Scott-McGregor. It wasn't very far from that to come to Gregor or Gregory. I suppose I knew when I saw an unmarked white van outside that place in Churchlands Road. One of those, you might say, is very like another but this one had a distinguishing mark. A snake-shaped scratch on the bodywork above the offside rear wheel.'

★ ★ ★

Wexford and Dora had been on two long holidays, one to Charleston and Savannah in the United States, the other to Turkey to Ephesus and the site of Troy. They were still commuting between London and Kingsmarkham, but having not enough to do was beginning to make him fidgety when an envelope arrived addressed to 'Mr Wexford', forwarded by Tom Ede and postmarked Kiev.

The printed card inside told him that Colin and Vladlena Jones announced the birth of their son Igor on 10 April 2011. The address looked like a private house, it looked as if they were living there. Wexford thought he would write back and find out, but he was sure he need worry about Vladlena and her possible fate no longer.